BEYOND THE CALL OF DUTY: THE
COMPLETE TALES OF KOROPOK, VOLUME I

BEYOND THE CALL OF DUTY:
THE COMPLETE TALES OF
KOROPOK
VOLUME 1

SIDNEY
HERSCHEL
SMALL

ILLUSTRATIONS BY
HAMILTON GREENE
AND
FRANK KRAMER

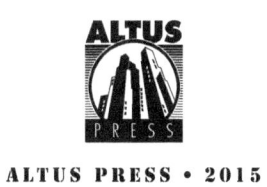

ALTUS PRESS • 2015

EDITED AND DESIGNED BY

Matthew Moring

PUBLISHING HISTORY

"Beyond the Call of Duty" originally appeared in the February 1944 issue of *Adventure* magazine. Copyright 1944 by Popular Publications, Inc. Copyright renewed 1971 and assigned to Adventure Pulp LLC. All Rights Reserved.

"The War-Fan" originally appeared in the May 1944 issue of *Adventure* magazine. Copyright 1944 by Popular Publications, Inc. Copyright renewed 1971 and assigned to Adventure Pulp LLC. All Rights Reserved.

"Flight Without Wings" originally appeared in the August 1944 issue of *Adventure* magazine. Copyright 1944 by Popular Publications, Inc. Copyright renewed 1971 and assigned to Adventure Pulp LLC. All Rights Reserved.

"Belt of Steel" originally appeared in the December 1944 issue of *Adventure* magazine. Copyright 1944 by Popular Publications, Inc. Copyright renewed 1971 and assigned to Adventure Pulp LLC. All Rights Reserved.

"Lost Face" originally appeared in the March 1945 issue of *Adventure* magazine. Copyright 1945 by Popular Publications, Inc. Copyright renewed 1972 and assigned to Adventure Pulp LLC. All Rights Reserved.

"The Last Banzai" originally appeared in the July 1945 issue of *Adventure* magazine. Copyright 1945 by Popular Publications, Inc. Copyright renewed 1972 and assigned to Adventure Pulp LLC. All Rights Reserved.

THANKS TO

Doug Ellis, Everard P. Digges LaTouche, Rob Preston, and Gerd Pircher

TABLE OF CONTENTS

BEYOND THE CALL OF DUTY

TOKYO SHIVERED under a bitter wind. All afternoon black clouds were flattened against the city by the fury in the sky; night brought higher wind, more numbing cold. Thick wet snow, by nine o'clock, began to swirl down into the gloom of the streets. It froze where it fell.

The wind had started in the north, from Kamchatka and across Chishima Strait and over the Kurile Islands. There it had ripped snow from the rocky flanks and cones of the volcanic peaks which guard the northernmost Japanese naval base of Paramushiru, hurling snow and rocks down into the base itself. The storm hampered labor battalions which were feverishly repairing some of the damage caused by American Liberators. And the wind howled across the graves of Japanese soldiers who could no longer do anything at all.

Outside the fortified area of Paramushiru the storm had raged above another burial place, also freshly dug. A hundred Ainu, whose ancestors long ago had been driven to the rocky northern islands by the Japanese, had been dragged out of the caves and mountain huts in which they lived, and shot. They had witnessed the Japanese loss of face when bombs had fallen. Their wives and daughters had followed them down; and while the old women buried the men, the younger women were taken to barracks. The storm covered their screams.

Officially, as all Tokyo knew, including the two policemen who leaned against the wind as they patrolled, the Ainu might

*Davies heard from the outcast
Ainu what happened to American
prisoners in Japan....*

have been guilty of signalling to the feared and hated *Amerika-
jin* flyers. If the peaceful Ainu had not actually signaled to the
great bombers, perhaps they would have liked to have done so,
which was sufficient reason for punishment.

It was even whispered that one of the Ainu was suspected
of being a spy, although this was instantly denied. Such a
thought was ridiculous. There was not one single person within
the empire who could in any way direct an attack on Japan's
sacred soil, nor assist the enemy. The Japanese authorities,
knowing so well all of the things which they had planned to
have done in America, had prepared against counter-action in
Japan with great thoroughness.

Even so, as a new and additional precaution, a dozen Ainu
men in each of the squalid pariah villages, where these *eta*
performed such work as the Japanese considered degrading,
had already been killed as a warning, and fifty young Koreans

*They knew, for the were
the grave-diggers.*

had also been executed as an example. The authorities did not intend to neglect the slightest detail which would protect Japan.

This was what one of the patrolling officers said to his mate as they reached the corner and turned into the dark east-west street which was partially shielded from the icy lash of the wind.

"*A iu fuzetsu wa ate ni naranai,*" he said. "Likewise, I have heard that their knives are to be taken from the Ainu dogs. That is an excellent decree. It is very wise. I shall feel safer on nights like this."

His companion jeered, "Do you believe that those cowardly pariahs would attack anyone? Oh, what nonsense, Kawase!"

"If it is nonsense," protested Kawase, "why have the officials given the order? Answer that question, if you please."

The other said, as the pair paused now that they were out of the worst of the wind, "The answer is simple. The Ainu cannot make a living without their knives. The pariah dogs who repaired our *geta* can no longer do such work. Naturally, they will starve, thus saving us the trouble of exterminating them."

Kawase, the stockier of the two, demanded, "And what will we do when our clogs are old and must be repaired?"

"You are not patriotic! Our clogs cannot wear out. It is not permitted. They must last until we have won the war."

Although Kawase nodded, he had to protect his reputation for being obedient to decrees, as well as his courage. So he said hastily, "The pariahs are allowed to slaughter food animals for us. If they have no knives, how can they perform this necessary function, Ichida?"

The thin policeman thought of a pan of sizzling horseflesh. "Again," he said, "you fail in patriotism. You think of meat! The only animals which may be killed are for our brave soldiers. Not many Ainu dogs are needed for that task. The rest can starve." Because he was hungry, he added savagely, "And the *Amerika-jin* had better not accuse us of murdering them, either! Oh, how I would like to get the neck of an American between my fingers!"

"An *Amerika-jin*," snorted Kawase. It was he who could now jeer at the other. "Ho! What chance do you think there is of one being here? None!"

"*Sore wa kodomo demo wakaru*," agreed Ichida. "Even a child understands that. Of course it is impossible."

THE PAIR stood against the side of a dark house. When the wind diminished a moment, they could hear inside the chop-chop-chop of *nanakusa-no-kayu* being prepared, and both swallowed, because a bowl of the thick rice gruel in which seven varieties of pungent greens were mixed would have tasted very good. They could also hear, before the wind whipped up again, the song being sung as the savory greens were beaten to a pulp on the chopping-block.

Few crimes were ever committed in this district, in which clerks and artisans lived. The street, after several twists and turns, ended at the bay, where river boats and small coastal steamers docked, although any traffic of importance went along a broader thoroughfare to the west. The worst thing which ever happened on this beat was the homeward return of a drunken clerk and the reception which his wife might give him.

The two officers had nothing to fear nor guard against except the rounds made by their sergeant; and certainly he would prefer to remain in the station on this bitter winter night. Both were cold. Both were hungry. Both told themselves that these were honorable feelings, because by being cold and hungry they were assisting fighting men to be warm and well fed.

"We have only three more hours of duty," said Ichida. "At least we are better off than the thousands of starving *Amerika-jin* soldiers whom our clever generals have trapped on Attu and Kiska. And we are certainly happier than the flyers our brave aviators shot down at Paramushiru. Oh, how I wish I had been there when they crashed to earth! I would know what to do with such arrogant and insulting men! I pray that perhaps some day I may be fortunate to get my hands on an American flyer. Then I will—"

He stopped. A new sound, weird and penetrating even in the storm, moaned down the dreary snow-covered street.

"*Na-be-yaaaa-ki-udooon! Na-be-yaaaa-ki-udoooon!*"

The dimmest of lights appeared at the cityward intersection, light from a long square paper lantern. The snow, where the flickering yellowness made a feeble glow in the gloom, reflected the dull color.

"*Na-be-yaaaa-ki-udoooon!*"

The melancholy cry of the hot-dough vendor, the sight of the hawker's lantern, and the condition of Ichida's own belly, made the thin policeman lick his lips and swallow painfully. When the cry was repeated again and doors began to open, Ichida demanded of his companion, "Have you any money?"

"No," admitted Kawase.

"Not even four *sen?* Enough for one bowl? We could divide it."

Kawase said hungrily, "I gave my wife my last weekly money to buy hot roasted sweet potatoes for us when I return to our room. A hot potato is—"

"Do not mention food," growled Ichida. "I am indeed empty. If it were not a violation of regulations, I would order the vendor to trust me. It is possible," he mourned, as the lantern became stationary when customers from houses came up to buy the little cylinders of hot dough, "that there may be fish and vegetables cooked with the *udon.*"

"Yes," agreed Kawase sadly.

The lantern now hung from the hawker's staff, which had been thrust into the earth. The vendor himself was kneeling in the snow, crouched before a small iron cooking apparatus. He was kindling the charcoal fire by fanning the coals with a round-fan; the little pots of *udon* would soon begin to steam.

The charcoal fire gleamed on the dark, gaunt face of the man crouching over it and the startled policemen saw that it was the bearded face of an Ainu.

"It tastes best when eaten directly from the pot," said Ichida. "Putting *udon* into a bowl spoils the flavor."

Soon the fragrance of food was blown along the street, and the nostrils of the policemen began to twitch. Because purchasers were standing around the vendor, all that the hungry pair could see of him was his shabby blue jacket and the discolored and tattered blue cotton drawers which covered his legs. But when a heavy gust of wind whipped at the women's *kimonos* as they waited, and they moved to better cover themselves, the officers had their first real look at the stocky man who was crouched before the cooking-fire.

The charcoal was glowing well. It gleamed on a dark face, and seemed to strike sparks from dark eyes. The face was gaunt, what could be seen of it; but, as the startled officers saw, it was bearded.

An Ainu! A pariah.

Ichida said, under his breath, "I must be so hungry that I see something which is not there! Why, this is not possible!" He closed his eyes, while his companion stared dumbly at the

vendor; but when he opened them again he still saw the bearded, gaunt face with light gleaming on it.

"Stop!" he shouted. "This is not permitted!"

H E   WA S   running toward the light, the waiting matrons, the vendor who was now ladling out steaming *udon* and sauce into a bowl which one of the women was holding. Kawase was at Ichida's heels. Ichida snatched the half-filled bowl from the woman and slapped her twice, hard.

"You should not buy food from an Ainu," he cried furiously. "For all you know, the *udon* has been poisoned with bear-gall. You will sicken. You will be unable to bear children. You will be unable to work. How can you be so lacking in patriotism?"

"*Kekko desu,* officer-*san,*" a grandmother pleaded. "Please forgive her, and all of us. The pariah has been in this street twice before. He has a police-signed permit to sell the *udon.* It is good *udon,* officer-*san.* We have all eaten of it and not been made ill. It—"

Ichida turned on her. "How could he have been in the streets without our having seen him? *Bakana koto wo itteru.* You are talking nonsense."

His mate, Kawase, suggested mildly, "It is a large district which we patrol, Ichida. Surely that is why we have not encountered him before."

Ichida, nodding briefly, jerked off a glove, thrust his fingers into the bowl which he held, and shovelled dripping *udon* into his mouth. "Let me see this permit," he demanded of the bearded vendor, speaking with full mouth. "Come, pariah dog! Hurry!" He swallowed and filled his mouth again. "I have no time to waste. Show me! Or do you only understand dog language?"

The stocky, bearded man, crouched on the snow, bowed submissively as he placed his ladle down. If it hissed on the snow, the wind covered so small a sound.

The man opened the Ainu bag-purse which was fastened to

the bearskin girdle about his middle, and took out a folded piece of paper.

"*Taihen ni o mat'se mosh'ta,*" he said in Japanese, but with the Ainu accent strong in his quiet voice. "Forgive my slowness."

Because Ichida had rammed more *udon* into his mouth, it was Kawase who asked, "Have your dog-parents given you a name, Ainu?"

"*Wat'kush' wa Koropok to mosh'masu*" the swarthy vendor replied. "My name is Koropok. My father's name was—"

"It is doubtful if you had a father," Ichida broke in.

The women laughed at such a humorous comment. Ichida, pleased that his wit was recognized, drained off the liquid in the bowl noisily. Then he grabbed the permit from the crouching vendor and held it so that the brightly glowing charcoal cast a flickering light upon it. He examined it carefully.

Wind almost ripped the paper from the Japanese' greasy fingers as he read. "I do not see how you obtained this permission to sell *udon,*" he grumbled. "However, it appears to be in order."

The man who called himself Koropok said nothing.

He had been given the permit because for months he had repaired *geta* for the family and relatives of a minor police official named Kodzuke Yotsuye, and had never received any payment. He had refused payment the first time, pleading that the honor of cutting down a great personage's clogs so that an honorable male-child of the official could wear them was sufficient reward. After that, payment was never mentioned. But when knives were taken from the pariahs, Yotsuye realized that the pariah would need the money, which the official feared had mounted to an inconvenient sum; and while Koropok would be thrown out of a police station if he went to complain, the circumstance would be a blot on Yotsuye's record. He did not want his superiors to hear of his debt, so he had figured out a solution.

Since an old *udon*-vendor had died, Kodzuke Yotsuye had

arranged for the pariah to take over the meager equipment, the little bag of flour, the charcoal and fan. It was to be used only until a Japanese *udon*-vendor could be found, Yotsuye said to his superior; surely it was wise not to deprive war workers of their favorite cheap nightly food. The higher official had agreed, after insisting on half of the profit which Yotsuye was to receive, which was to be half of whatever the pariah might earn. In addition, both Japanese agreed that if they were called upon to explain the issuing of the permit they would deny having done so. They would insist that in some way the Ainu dog had found a paper bearing their signatures, and had forged their names.

All three involved in the arrangement were satisfied. Kodzuke Yotsuye was relieved of what might have been an embarrassing little debt. The higher official was pleased to receive a few extra coins in these days of terrible taxes. And the fellow who was called Koropok, the Ainu, the despised pariah, could continue to earn enough to keep him alive on the streets of Tokyo.

It did not occur to Kodzuke Yotsuye that the gaunt, bearded man in tattered, insufficient clothing might actually have singled him out as one who had a poorly paid police assignment. Nor did it occur to the Japanese that the pariah might know what the assignment was.

ON THE icy street, the officer Ichida shoved the empty bowl at the silent man on the snow. "Fill it," he said. When this was done, he explained to Kawase and the others, "I do this at great personal risk, and for your benefit. If the *udon* has been poisoned, to kill your husbands and sons who make the implements of war which are defeating the cowardly and unspeakable *Amerika-jin,* it is I who will die, and not they. I hope you appreciate this fact."

The vendor said humbly, as he fished around in one of the steaming pots, "Oh, such courage!" and Ichida lapped up the praise along with the hot food. "Please," the bearded man asked, as he began to fill the women's bowls without objection from the officers, "is it true that the people whom you call *Amerika-jin* are now being captured in large numbers, officer-*san?*"

"This very night," said Ichida importantly, feeling very fine now that his belly was full, "there will be many—"

The Japanese broke off in the middle of the word. Japanese police were trained to ask questions, and not answer them. He stared at the vendor, and then he snapped, "How dare you ask a question of me, dog?"

Ichida's hand went from the butt of his holstered gun to the handle of the club at his belt. The man in blue bowed his head to accept the expected blow.

The officer used neither of the weapons. His eyes lit until they had a gleam like the charcoal. He reached down, tore the iron ladle from Koropok's hand, and thrust it into the glowing coals; he withdrew it quickly, and with almost the same motion pressed it against the cheek of the kneeling man.

The heated metal made no sound when it touched skin, nor did the man himself. There was the wind, and the banging of a loose door, and the indrawn breath of a bystander, and Ichida's own ejaculation of rage. There was a little hiss, also, as sweat from the pariah's forehead dripped down to the iron.

Koropok's eyes did not shut, but his teeth ground together. Sweat beaded his forehead and, in the vermilion glow of the charcoal fire, glistened in his shaggy hair and beard. Once it looked as if he might reel from his knees and fall forward to the snow; but he did not. If the physical agony was tearing at him, it showed only in the throbbing of his veins, which the audience could not see.

"He is an animal," Ichida yelled. "He has no feelings."

Kawase mumbled, "If he makes complaint to our superiors—"

"I will say that he was drunk and fell against his stove, and you will be witness to it." Ichida threw the ladle down to the snow. "Let me tell you this," said the policeman, lifting his voice, "if he were an *Amerika-jin* soldier, he would have screamed and begged for mercy. Oh, how I would enjoy marking one of those fiends who dare to think of attacking our sacred Nippon!"

The eyes of the pariah flickered, but he said nothing. He reached out, a bit slowly, for the ladle; he did not touch his cheek with the other hand, but began fanning the coals again.

"This is amusing," grunted Ichida, obviously casting about for some other way to degrade the pariah and show his own importance. "Why not—"

Kawase pleaded, "We must make our rounds."

"Do not remind me of my duty," said Ichida. He was frowning, being disappointed because the Ainu had not grovelled; he said to the man on the snow, as Koropok prepared to fill the bowls of the chilled women, "Cause me trouble again, and you will be accorded the treatment given an *Amerika-jin* flyer."

"Oh, please, no," whimpered the man in tattered blue. "Oh, no, lord. I could not stand such terrible things. I would die!"

"So do they," Ichida snarled.

"*G'men nag'ra,*" apologized the kneeling man abjectly, in his Ainu accent. "I am sorry to have troubled you, lord."

He was not sorry at all, not even at the cost of his seared cheek, which, as the officers trotted off along the street, was beginning to blister. He was not in the least sorry that he had asked a question which had brought him agony, because, as he had hoped, the pompous Japanese policeman had been unable to resist indicating to the audience that he, a great man, knew the answer. Ichida had said enough for the vendor of *udon* to guess the rest.

And this was why he was peddling hot dough cooked with sauce, since clogs could not be repaired without a knife, on the wind-swept streets of Tokyo on this bitter winter night. This was why he was in Japan.

He said to himself, as the wind roared with renewed force, keeping the coals glowing even without being fanned, *You damned fool! He wanted you to beg for mercy. Why didn't you do it, you stiff-necked idiot? You're as bad as he. You had to show what a tough guy you are. If something like this happens again, get some sense into this dumb dome of yours.* But he kept ladling out *udon.*

LIEUTENANT LLEWELYN DAVIES, AC, was, to the Japanese, an Ainu named Koropok. A stocky, bearded, dark man, like his Welch ancestors, he was amazingly similar in appearance to the Ainu of north Japan.

He had been set ashore there in dense fog, and had made his way in Ainu dress to a mountain settlement, to be accepted by the peaceful kindly people. The locality was far from the one in which he had lived with his doctor father, and where he had played with the Ainu children almost as one of them. His disguise, when he left the village for the coast again, had fooled the Japanese authorities, despite their boast that not one single American was in the empire, except in prison camps or in graves. He had finally reached Tokyo.

Twice already he had brought misery to the Japanese. Each time he did it, he knew, brought detection and death that much nearer. Therefore each succeeding operation must be as damaging to the shrewd enemy as possible. Whatever he did must badly cripple the Japanese war effort. He had directed American bombers in dropping their explosives on an arsenal which looked like houses; he had destroyed the entire quantity of a strange oil crushed from fireflies which was used in the building of Japanese warplanes.

Now, he wanted to do that which would hurt the Japanese for a third time. If only he could know the targets which his old companions would seek out in Tokyo! That was what he decided to try and find out.

Davies, disguised as Koropok, had figured out several ways to cause the Nips such grief as the thin policeman, Ichida, had never dreamed of. Each meant risk. Of course, everything he did meant risk; this was why Davies told himself that every objective had to be the most important he could find, because it was apt to be his last one. What would the gang want knocked out?

As the rickisha *dashed by Davies saw that it
contained a Jap army officer, well bundled in furs.*

He knew Tokyo. First as a *getad*-mener, now as a vendor of
cheap food, he had ranged the streets, showing his permit
whenever demanded, insulted a thousand times a day, and as
often by night. He slept when and where he could. He did not
always eat; sometimes what few coins he had earned were taken
from him by *bukuchi-uchi*, ruffians and thieves, after they had
thrown him, unresisting, to the street. He became gaunt, but
there burned a steady fire in him, far more bitter and painful
than that now on his cheek; he knew what had happened to
his fellow-soldiers who had bombed Tokyo's military objectives.

The wind shrilled like the rasping of metal on metal as
"Koropok" filled the last of the bowls. After the women hastened
back to their houses with the steaming food for their men, the
pariah picked up his cooking apparatus and began walking
again, his lantern yellowing the snow.

He cried mournfully, *"Na-be-yaaa-ki-udoooon!"* but few
people, sheltered from the storm, could hear him. Everyone
who did not have to be out was huddled indoors, trying to keep
warm. The wind was rising.

Wind and snow slashed at the great blister on his cheek and
broke it. Before long the wound became raw and ugly, sending
a growing pain into his head. He kept on shouting his wares,

in case the same officers, or others, might chance to see him, but he no longer paused to give householders an opportunity to come out and buy from him. He kept walking more and more quickly, burdened as he was with lantern, staff, stove, pots, and bag of dough, always making his way toward the arm of the bay and the usually deserted dock where prisoners were landed under a heavy guard from coastal ships.

This was the sort of knowledge which Davies picked up, a bit here, a bit there, on the Tokyo streets. The sort of thing he had to know in order to be able to accomplish the sabotage work he was doing single-handed.

I can do this once, Lew thought. *Just once. It's what I've got to do. I must feel that every time I try to raise hell with the Nips it will be my last shot at them. It's got to count. Then, if I get away with it, and live, I can begin worrying about the next time.*

The prisoners wouldn't be fellows who might have been knocked down at Paramushiru, because there hadn't been time for them to have reached Tokyo; but Davies fervently hoped that someone from Air Forces would be in the group of prisoners. Men from that branch of the service would know which objectives the command most wished eliminated. Given such information, Davies intended to do whatever he could about it. He had prepared himself well. If he failed, it would be while attempting something worth doing.

I can raise hell with one of their war plants, Lew thought, as he neared an alley not far from the muddy waters of the bay, *but it must be the right one. It can't be done twice.*

He had catalogued the plants in Tokyo, but there was no way of knowing exactly what was manufactured inside, not even for a person who listened to workers, half drunk, in the *muryo shukuhakujo,* the inns to which they went when they had no *sen* left to sleep in the cheapest of pay-inns.

He did know that the Japanese had stepped up production now that it was becoming obvious that the supposedly soft and cowardly Americans were beginning to attack.

It was his duty to do something about it.

One man.

But first he must contact one of the prisoners who could tell him which plants were considered by G-2 to be important military objectives.

DAVIES SAW the feeble flicker of a lantern when he reached the next narrow intersection. From the manner in which it was bobbing up and down, it was fastened to a *rickisha.* He blew out his own candle hastily and backed against the black wall of a warehouse. He could not hear the cart's approach; but when the old man who was pulling it came into view at the corner, Davies saw that he was exerting himself to the limit. Truly hurrying. In the cart itself was an army officer, well bundled in furs.

When the *rickisha's* lantern vanished, and the snow slammed down with renewed force, Davies looked about him. Prisoners were certainly being landed. No paunched Nip officer would venture out on a night like this except for a reason; and what better reason could he have, since he was going toward the isolated landing dock, than the arrival of a contingent of prisoners? Therefore the blurted, boastful words of Ichida seemed verified.

Lew had overheard what happened to prisoners who were brought to Japan. Every low eating-stall buzzed with the stories. He had heard more of them from the Ainu in the pariah village on the city's outskirts, and these simple and unhappy people were incapable of elaboration. They knew, firsthand. For they were the attendants at executions, and the carriers of dead bodies, and the diggers of graves. Some of them were herded to the dock when a prison ship arrived; and what they told "Koropok" had convinced him of the practicability of his plan.

The time had come to put it to the test.

He looked about for a place to hide his stove, lantern and pots, and found one in an empty stand where, when excursionists had flocked to the pier before the war, boiled clam-bellies from the bay had been sold. The moment he had concealed that with which he earned food for himself, he hurried bay ward.

Davies forgot the throbbing pain of his raw wound. He thought, *I want to see my own kind again,* and this made him shake a little, because he had been so utterly alone.

Then, as the deserted street made a right-angled turn, and he could see the shielded lights of the dock and hear the whine of the wind in the wires, he muttered, "What's the matter with you? Are you going to start feeling sorry for yourself?" He lowered his head, crept along the edge of a warehouse and, alert and on edge, peered to see what he hoped was somewhere on the dock.

At first all Lew saw was the few lights and the yellow pools beneath, where groups of Japanese soldiers were huddled together. The dock was completely open to the storm. Next Davies made out a crude wooden windbreak, erected to protect officials and officers. He saw, or thought he saw, a winking light down the bay, which might be the prison ship.

Not until he edged closer was he able to make out the miserable, half-frozen Ainu, with two Japanese soldiers guarding them. Every so often, the Ainu were pushed out of the circle into which, for the warmth of bodies pressed together, they instinctively formed. The soldiers enjoyed the suffering of the true natives of Japan, and forced them to feel the full brunt of the storm. Nor did the sorrowful, bearded men protest. The Ainu knew better.

When the ship landed, as Davies knew, the Ainu would carry off the bodies of those prisoners who had died during the voyage.

The winking of the light, sometimes curtained and invisible when the snow fell more heavily, was becoming brighter. Davies crept as close to the Ainu who stood nearest shore as he believed wise.

When the ship's siren hooted, Lew's heart began to beat faster.

*It was not easy for Lew to stand like a cowed
pariah while the American prisoners marched
proudly off the ship, showing no signs of fear.*

Would he recognize anyone? And, now that the time was
approaching, would what he had planned really work? A
hundred doubts assailed him, he who had been so sure before.
If I muff it, thought Lew, *I'll never have another chance.*

He hoped, but without fear, that if things went wrong he
would be shot, and shot dead, on the dock. That would be better
than… than what happened to Americans. And the rage of the
Japanese, if they penetrated his disguise, was a terrible thing to
contemplate.

The ordinarily placid bay and the river mouth were roiled
and muddy. Waves were shouldering at the end of the dock
and, when the coaster inched near, tried to pound the shallow-
draft vessel against the piles.

Davies, crouched in darkness, did not move. His eyes were
on the two soldiers guarding the huddled Ainu.

A rope was thrown, and a second. The soldiers, all except the
two guards, came to attention. The officers strutted forward.

When the gangplank was rolled up and the highest officer
on shipboard appeared and began to walk down, the guards

also came to attention, facing the ship. At that exact instant, Davies raced to the dock and stopped only when he was standing between two of the Ainu, an inconspicuous member of their ragged group. None of the soldiers had seen him.

He looked like them: dark, bearded, swarthy. One of them. A pariah.

One of the men was repeating, "*Tokap rere ko tu*," as protection against the demons which brought storms, and the rest dutifully mouthed the words along with him. One said, "Koropok." That was all.

Davies knew that he had nothing to fear from them. They would say nothing of his joining them, unless the Japanese asked. Lew did not believe that the guards knew whether there were sixteen Ainu, or twenty, or thirty. And unless something happened to draw attention to the fact that there was an additional pariah in the group, nobody else would care either.

This was not guesswork. He had found out, from the Ainu themselves, how the Japanese did their checking. It was done on arrival at the pier, and only then. So he, as like them as one man can be to others, should be as safe as his dangerous undertaking would allow him to be.

Whatever he did, up to the time of attempted accomplishment, had to have the best possible chance of success. That was why he was in Tokyo.

THE OFFICER from the ship, followed by others, were shaking hands and bowing on the dock. Lew could imagine the congratulations which were being made, and the pseudo-modest replies, though he would not hear them.

An infantry officer gave a command and the soldiers formed quickly for the march to whichever station would start the prisoners on their railroad journey to camp. At least, Lew thought, they aren't going to the coal mines or they wouldn't have been shipped to Tokyo.

He watched the squad which formed near the Ainu, which would lead the way; two lines formed behind, six feet apart. There would be a rear guard at the end.

Here they come, his lips formed. *Here they come.*

It was not easy for Davies to stand like a cowed pariah, because the Americans came down the gangplank with the pride of men who had fought well and whose hearts were strong.

My gang, thought Lew. *My gang. Guys with guts.*

The unwounded officers and men came first, to be marched between the lines of untidy Japanese infantrymen. All bars and stripes had been torn off. Not an American wore a coat. But they stood so straight and tall and defiant that a Japanese official, infuriated by their attitude, shouted a command and the Jap soldiers dutifully began to sing one of their war-songs.

There were few unwounded Americans. Before these had been marched to where the first squad waited, to head the procession to the railway station, the walking wounded, bandaged, limping, the one helping the other, started down the gangplank. And they, too, showed not the least sign of fear.

My gang, thought Lew again. He couldn't let them down. They, he felt, had done much; he had done so little, compared to them.

It was not easy to discern the faces of the prisoners in the dim, snow-obscured light. Davies saw no man who was familiar to him. But if only some one of them was on his toes! *Just one, please,* Lew prayed. *Just one. I need one fellow who'll use his bean. That's all.*

The head of the American column had stopped. It was less than ten feet from the guarded group of Ainu, and the two assigned soldiers were staring at the prisoners, who showed their lack of fear in eyes and carriage and who looked straight ahead.

"They are large and strong," one of the Japanese soldiers whispered. "It is not surprising that my three brothers are dead."

His mate said curtly, "Animals are large. Animals are strong. They are animals. They are *keto-jin,* hairy ones, like the pariahs. Spit at them."

This was the time. Now. He dare not wait any longer.

"G-2," Davies cried clearly, almost as an echo to the Japanese' words. "Give me an objective." He ran this together like one word. Then, finding it hard to control his voice, he repeated, "G-2! G-2!"

Would it work? Oh, would it work? There were no officers, who might have known what G-2 meant, anywhere near. Would it work?

The curtly-speaking Japanese shouted, "Which of you Ainu dogs has been kicking? Who barked, *'Ke-ru'* like the dog he truly is?"

G-2. Ke-ru. The sounds, in the storm, were almost exact. But if one meant Intelligence, the other meant that the person who had uttered it was protesting at having been kicked. The words that Davies had slurred together in between had been taken by the Japanese for Ainu dialect.

On shipboard, the sailors, not to be outdone by the Army ashore, were shrilling their own song:

> See! The sun flag! How it flutters
> Shining in the morning sunlight!
> See! Advance our battle-squadrons
> From Chishima....

Only it was the American Liberator squadron which had roared over Chishima, as Davies, waiting painfully, like ice now, knew.

Would it work? Would it work?

There was the singing of the seamen on the ship, and the whine of wind in the wires, and the grinding of the vessel's side against the dock.....

Prisoners on stretchers were being carried from the ship; soon the Ainu would shuffle up the gangplank, to return with the dead. There was little time left; and as the heartbreaking minutes passed, Davies saw that one of the prisoners spoke to another, who shook his head violently in dissent.

They think it's a slick Jap trick, Davies realized.

There was one more thing to try.

"Davies!" Lew called swiftly. Any fellow-soldier would know that no man assigned to Davies' duty would have revealed his name so that the Japanese could make use of it. Now... was there anyone among the Americans who had known him, or who knew the duty to which he had been assigned?

The guards, about to scream at their pariah charges for crying out a word which must be an Ainu-language protest against the previous kick, heard the abrupt order which meant they must bring the body-carriers to the ship.

"Beside a dump where they go with lanterns," Lew heard. "Luck, boy!"

An infantryman slapped the officer who had spoken. Hard. The wind whined like the twanging of a *samisen.* The pariahs, "Koropok" among them, were pushed along the dock toward the gangplank.

"BESIDE a dump where they go with lanterns." That's all he knows, thought Davies. *It's something he's heard. Where'll it be? What'll it be?* Well, he would find out. You bet he'd find out. Nothing would stop him. Nothing.

"Luck, boy!" was in his head as he accompanied the pariahs

along the dock and up the gangplank. He was struck with gun-butts when he moved too slowly, or for no reason at all. He was kicked when he stooped to lift one end of a coffin. "Luck, boy!" A Japanese officer slashed at him, as at the others, with a cane. But he was unchallenged as he bore his share of the load from the ship.

Who was in the coffin? Some poor devil who had died on shipboard.

Beside a dump where they go with lanterns, pondered Lew. *I've got to figure that out. And when I do,* he promised, thinking of the soldier whose body he was helping carry, *I'll square things for you, old man.*

A dump? A coal dump? Possibly one outside a mine where lanterns were used? No. The prisoner had called, "Beside a dump where lanterns are used," which must mean the lanterns were used at the "dump" itself.

The prisoners were being marched in one direction; the body-carriers and their two guards moved in another. The Ainu would carry the coffins all the way to the place of interment; that was the cheapest means of transportation. If they were paid, the infinitesimal amount would be flung at them.

The customary night-sounds of Tokyo in winter were almost all smothered by the wind as the cortege moved through the city as quickly as the guards could hurry the half-starved pariahs. "Koropok" carried the rear end of a coffin. To him, as he puzzled over the cryptic answer of the Americans, a few sounds managed to penetrate. The sad *"Ammaaa kamiii-shiiimo!"* and the peeping of the whistle of the blind masseuse who begged for customers. The rattle of a *rickisha.* The howls of a drunken colonel who had an opium concession in occupied China.

The snow was diminishing, but the cold grew. It was crisp underfoot now. The ground crackled when Davies' sandalled feet trod down.

Beside a dump where they go with lanterns. Beside a dump....

The man known as Koropok heard a different and not usual

sound, which broke into his thoughts. It was the ringing of small bells. Although the street on which the cortege moved was empty, he knew almost at once that the little bells were being carried by *kammairi,* white-robed worshippers running to the temples—to Funkagawa, Kotohira, Toyokawa-Inari—running, carrying their lanterns....

A dump... a place! Of course the prisoner wouldn't say what the place might be, so he'd used slang. A dump. Beside a dump where lanterns were used; beside a temple. That was it. The Japanese were great on having potential air targets near shrines or temples, believing that the stupid Americans would leave these unbombed. Why, one great ammunition dump was near a shrine....

Did the American at the dock mean an ammunition dump? Davies did not think so. Lanterns were kept far from explosives.

"Dump" had to be slang for the place beside the objective. The place had to be a war plant which Air Forces wanted to eliminate. Davies had been given information as to where it was: where Japanese went with lanterns.

It must be a famous temple, decided Lew, as the line of body-carriers reached a principal street. *Otherwise people at home wouldn't know about it. Which came first to my mind? Funkagawa. Of course. I'll check on it first. It's a cinch to do that. The* hadaka-mairi *will be tickled to buy that* udon.

He couldn't do it this night; he had to get back to the pariah village first. But tomorrow, when the naked worshippers ran with their lanterns and bells to the temple after dark, "Koropok" would be there also.

It didn't matter what sort of war factory would be beside the temple. The Nips constructed one just like another. No wonder the Chinese called them the small brown monkeys.

In the bag, thought Lew. *In the bag.*

It was then that he realized that two Japanese policemen, who had been standing out of sight on the main street, were staring at him. The shielded electric light was on his face, his

*As Davies shuffled along carrying one end
of a coffin, he pondered over the mysterious
words of the captured American officer.*

scarred face. Although Davies could not make out the officers clearly, and dared not look up and stare, he was suddenly afraid.

He had good cause. Ichida and Kawase, who had paused at the far end of their beat, had recognized him.

What would they do? Neither had moved as yet.

Don't let anything stop me now, Davies prayed. *I've prepared for this. I've got the stuff to do it. I've only been waiting for the right thing.*

He understood the policemen's uncertainty. If they attempted to arrest him, the military guards would refuse to recognize their authority. Neither of the two guards would take up the end of the coffin which the supposed pariah was carrying, under any circumstances. Nor could the policemen follow the cortege and, after the burial, take the "Ainu" back with them; they dared not leave their beat. Yet Ichida would not give up easily. His monkey-curiosity had been aroused; the *udon* vendor "Koropok," he must feel, was certainly making trouble for him, and Ichida had warned him against just that.

Then both of the policemen were walking over to the guard at the rear of the somber procession.

He's thought of something, Davies knew. *What? I must be ready for it.* He had no notion as to what it might be, but his heart was pounding.

T H E S O L D I E R to whom Ichida was speaking shouted the order for the carriers to stop; the guard ahead came running back. Police and guards conferred; Lew could hear nothing of what they said.

As the cold increased, the wind was fading. While Davies waited, he guessed that it was continuing south. Formosa. Manila. How long it was since he had left! The islands beyond. What was happening there… and what was happening here, behind him? And what could he do about it?

All four uniformed men walked up toward him. Ichida's gun was out. To Davies' surprise, he, an Ainu, was not greeted with the usual blows. As a matter of fact the guards stood a distance away from him.

Ichida's left hand held an electric torch. The Japanese turned it full on the vendor's face. Davies blinked under the beam.

"You see?" said Ichida.

Both soldiers shuddered.

"*Raibyo-yami*," Ichida said. "A leper. Examine his face."

Wind and cold had ripped at the raw, burned skin of Davies' cheek until it might well have been caused by what the wily policeman claimed.

Davies' heart missed several beats.

One of the guards muttered, "*We* did not touch him. Another dog shall take his end of the coffin. We ourselves will take turns at the coffin which that other dog was previously carrying. *Ai!* What a terrible thing!"

Ichida purred, "Be positive to have a policeman bring that Ainu who takes his place to a station. The second Ainu also will be unclean, since his hands will be on the coffin where the first dog touched it."

"We will see to it," both guards promised.

Ichida, blown up with the importance of having given orders to soldiers, said sharply, "Do not forget!"

"Oh, no!"

"Good." Ichida snarled at Davies, "Put down that coffin. Come with us." And the Japanese licked his thin lips as he gave the command.

Davies thought, *I've got no choice;* but he had more in mind than Ichida could have believed possible for any pariah to be thinking. Lew lowered the coffin as gently as he could, and stepped out of line.

Ichida was on his left, Kawase on his right. The thin officer began to whistle an obscene Yoshiwara song....

The Japanese was in high good humor. He had apprehended an Ainu who should have been selling *udon;* he would be praised and possibly rewarded and promoted for his alertness. He would also be permitted a hand in whatever was done to the pariah before the Ainu "Koropok" was imprisoned... which would be plenty.

Davies knew that the two guards would say nothing of what had happened unless questioned by their superiors, which could happen only if Ichida turned in a report stating the actual occurrence. This wasn't going to happen, Davies found out soon, because Ichida slapped him again and again, squarely on the wound, proving that the leprosy tale was pure invention designed to get "Koropok" away from the soldiers. Ichida's story would be that the Ainu had been roaming the streets in a suspicious manner and without his apparatus. The nervous Japanese authorities, already keyed up by the action of the military in killing Ainu after the raid on Paramushiru, would do the rest.

"*Fugo-jiru no,*" whistled Ichida, strutting along. Sheer exuberance compelled him to trip his prisoner. He kicked the *keto-jin,* the hairy one, several times before ordering him to stand up.

"If he were an *Amerika-jin,*" Ichida confided to Kawase, "I would kick him to death. It would be very pleasant."

Davies shambled along between the policemen. He knew the way to the station, knew the streets, knew that his captors would cut across the black, shrub-filled park with its shrine....

He weighed the future.

First of all, he must go back and get his cooking things. It was far too late to do anything tonight. He would sleep a little after he had returned to the pariah village; he would do his checking on temples during the day, as he peddled, and by tomorrow night he would be ready. He had prepared for tomorrow night. He had done everything possible; but nothing he had done, or would do, seemed half as courageous to him as the manner in which the American prisoners had marched off, heads high, lips firm.

Of course, if he had been caught earlier it would have been different. For example, when he had paid a true Ainu, several times, to handle prisoners' bodies at the camp hospital, just so he could learn where emergency anesthetics were kept; he had managed that well. He grinned a little now as, head down, he entered the park between the officers. If he had been caught stealing the little can of ether, he would have been killed on the spot, although he was positive that no one who had a hand in his death would have had the slightest idea why he wanted the liquid.

After he was dead, the Japanese would have said, "An Ainu will steal anything which he thinks will make him drunk. It is regrettable that we killed him so rapidly. We should have poured the ether down his throat."

Davies had hidden the little can in the pariah village.

THE PARK, where the only light, shielded from the sky, glowed dimly under the shrine's lacquered eaves, was black as a pit until Ichida flashed his electric torch. The broad main path was empty. There were no sacred nightly processions now; fear of American bombing had put an end to such earlier jubilation. No longer did scarlet-robed Shinto priests, faces painted, lips reddened, eyes darkened with kohl, walk in boastful glory at

Quickly picking up Ishida's gun, Davies shot
the unconscious Kawase in the neck.

the head of thousands of Nipponese. Nor did victory-mad raw recruits, after an evening with girls in the Yoshiwara, sleep off their drunkenness in the bushes.

Ichida's beam of light pried inquiringly from side to side and ahead, at rock gardens and rock-bordered pools where ugly giant whiskered carp lay motionless on the bottom. Ice was forming on the water's edge.

Shambling along like the animal which the Japanese believed an Ainu to be, Lew waited patiently until the shrine was passed.

Then, coldly and with the precision of a machine, he swung his right fist against Ichida's jaw. Everything he had went into the punch. He whirled as Ichida went down; he had both arms around Kawase before the policeman could so much as reach for his gun, and flung him to the ground.

Davies' throttling hands were like steel clamps on the Japanese' throat, and they tightened until the officer went limp.

Without haste, cold as the night, Davies covered the butt of Kawase's gun with the tattered cloth of his own Ainu jacket. He placed the muzzle against Ichida's jaw, where he had struck him, and pulled the trigger.

The sound of the discharge was enormous. Sacred crows, worshipped as messengers of the sun-goddess, flapped up from their nightly perches around the shrine, invisible evil shapes in the black night.

Davies now took Ichida's gun, handled it in the same manner, and shot the unconscious Kawase in the neck. He did this so swiftly that the sound of the second discharge hammered into the echo of the first.

The raucous cries of the crows grew louder.

Davies placed each gun-butt back in the hand of the policeman to whom it had belonged.

He was grinning grimly as he thought, *A cute little variation of Nip suicide. Two persons believe that they have been disgraced. They make a suicide pact: You kill me and I'll kill you.* Which was how the authorities would figure it.

Without hurrying, Davies began retracing his steps, one hand brushing against the bushes to his left to make sure that he wouldn't pass the stone lantern which marked the side path. Thanks to Ichida's beam of light, Lew had been able to mark the way he intended to leave the park.

Every pair of excited Japanese policemen within earshot were already converging on the park, but Davies was unworried. In true and nervous Japanese fashion, they would warn him of their approach by their flashlights.

By morning the account of the "suicide-deaths" would be on every lip. Gossip would ultimately concentrate on one story, which would run like wildfire through Tokyo. Davies did not believe that the two soldiers assigned to guard the Ainu body-carriers would speak of their particular belief to anyone. Firstly, to do so would be to invite trouble, because they themselves had not noticed the "leper." Secondly, before they had marched a hundred feet both of them would resent having been ordered about by a member of the police. Thirdly, they would solemnly tell themselves that they had better obey the Japanese army regulation: "Let your officers do all talking and thinking for you."

Their guess would be that in some way the policemen had

touched or been touched by the supposed leper. Whereupon the policemen had, by pact, each killed the other rather than suffer a terrible living death. As to the unfortunate pariah who had taken "Koropok's" place at the end of the coffin, it was a certainty he was dead by now, and probably had been tumbled into one of the graves already prepared for the Americans who had died on shipboard.

The guards would report that the pariah had "resisted."

Once, twice, three times Lew slipped between bushes and lay on the freezing ground until Japanese police, always paired, converged on the shrine above which the crows flapped and cawed. At last he cleared the park, found a narrow street and, now hiding behind a bamboo fence, now dodging into a doorway, finally was able to reclaim his cooking apparatus, staff and lantern.

It was not long before he had the charcoal glowing, before the weird cry of "*Na-be-yaaas-ki-udooon!*" wailed in the streets again. But it was after four in the morning before he reached the silent pariah village.

No amount of will power could keep his teeth from chattering after he crept into the ragged newspaper-stuffed quilts in the hut where he lived with six other Ainu. *I'll never get warm enough to sleep,* thought Lew. *And I've got to sleep. I have a day ahead of me.*

Lord, but it was cold!

He wished he dared making positive that the little can of ether was safe, but if he did so, some hungry Ainu might observe him, to see if "Koropok" might have a hidden handful of mouldy millet or a fat brown bottle of *sake.* So Davies tried to roll himself tighter in his quilts.

Sleep refused to come. Doubts, induced by his very physical ill-being, began to assail him. Would what he had planned so long and held in reserve until the proper time, really work? It was based on solid engineering talk which had come out of a bull-session in the States, when he had been at an airplane plant. It had seemed such a beautifully simple method of raising hell with production that he had remembered it....

Get to sleep, he told himself.

But sleep did not come easily for the gaunt man who had been playing the part of a pariah. He thought of home. Sleep came hard.

"KOROPOK" WAS kicked out of his quilts at eight in the morning by the police. It was more than routine inspection. However, to Davies' initial satisfaction, it did not concern itself with the deaths of two policemen, nor with the wound on his cheek, but only with the insolence of an Ainu body-carrier. Because of it, as a lesson to the Ainu here, five men were to be "tried."

Davies knew all about such trials. He cursed himself for having returned to the village and slept, instead of securing his little can of ether and departing immediately.

The pariahs, men and women alike, were arranged in lines between which Japanese officials strode, selecting the strongest-appearing of the Ainu to take for a torture-trial and death. Davies was in the third line. Would he be picked? He wouldn't mind dying, after he'd made his attempt. That would be O.K. But to be knocked on the head like an ox....

That's how it should be, Lew decided. *If I let 'em know who I am and what I have been doing, just for the pleasure of sounding off and getting shot instead of being tortured, I'll make it that much tougher for some other fellow who might follow me. If I go, it'll have to be as Koropok.*

He appeared as cowed as the others.

Then, eyes on the earth as the officials approached, he heard, "This one is young." A hand pulled him out of line. "Your name, Ainu?"

Davies mumbled, "Koropok."

I could kill one Nip with his own gun, thought Lew. *Maybe two. Why not? I'll be a dead duck anyhow.*

He kept his eyes on the frozen earth, but his muscles tightened.

"He looks simple," Davies heard a different voice say. He let his shoulders droop more abjectly. "Surely we can do better?"

"They are all simple," the first voice remarked. After laughter, he continued, "Suit yourself, Kodzuke-*san*. Let us find another one."

Kodzuke Yotsuye. The minor official who had signed his permit, whose *geta* he had mended without pay.

Shot with luck, realized Davies. *He sees a chance to milk me dryer.*

When five pariahs were driven off to "trial," sad old Ainu elders began whittling five sticks. These would be thrust into the ground, and would represent the spirits of dead men. The Ainu knew what would happen.

Davies waited until the settlement went back to shiver in the hovels; then he took the river-path, dug up his ether can, placed it in the charm-bag fastened to his skin belt, and started for the city proper.

His cooking apparatus was slung over his shoulder. The pots banged against his thighs. Lieutenant Llewelyn Davies.

Checking on the shrine which the American prisoner must have meant was easier than Davies had anticipated. His first feeling was correct; it was Funkagawa. He really knew this before he reached it, because there were food stands in the district where war workers could eat, far more than were needed by the residents, who depended on vendors anyhow.

Funkagawa. To the shrine, at night, during *Kanchu,* the season of the midst of cold, came hundreds of worshippers, all carrying lanterns. There were other spots to which the Japanese came, but here, if one prayed, was assured protection against fire; and what greater thing was there to fear now that American warplanes were being awaited in terror? This was the place.

Davies did not need to go near the food stands to learn what was being manufactured in the underground plant. Aircraft.

Heedless of the clawing nails of the pimply-
faced hakoya, *Davies grasped him by*
the throat and throttled him.

His eyes told him what was taken to the factory, and what was trucked away. What he did pick up from a boastful charcoal stallkeeper was that a new warplane was being made, and one which would keep up the nightly bombings which were taking place in America as everyone knew. Yes, great destruction was being caused in America.

The plant itself was well concealed. One entrance was set between houses at the edge of the shrine courtyard; another appeared only as a tree-bordered path. How Intelligence had learned of the plant was not Davies' worry; what concerned him was the location of the intake for the air compressor which created the pressure for riveting. Whether the air lines inside were overhead or under the floor would make no difference. The intake, once Davies determined the outer limitations of the underground plant, was easily found.

It was unguarded; the Japanese knew that no man could crawl through such a small opening. But, at night, when no one could see him....

He shuffled off, not returning toward the shrine until eight.

The cold caused every split place on bamboo fences to crackle; it was truly *Kanchu,* the midst of cold. Everywhere, as Davies shambled in the direction of the shrine and the warplane plant hidden near it, there was the sound of hundreds of little bells carried by the *kammairi,* the worshippers.

Each carried a long paper lantern with his name painted on it. Everyone was clad in white, heads bound about by white handkerchiefs, feet covered with white *tabi,* socks. And, as in ancient times, the worshippers ran, the sooner to reach the shrine, the better to keep warm.

Davies was shoved this way and that and cursed for being in the way, as the *kammairi,* the women with hair unbound, raced toward the shrine.

They're all intent on purification and prayers, thought Lew. *It couldn't be better. It ought to be in the bag.*

BLACK NIGHT and ghostly runners with their bells and lanterns. Pinpoints of pale yellow light where stallkeepers served those *kammairi* who had completed a long prayer to the temple-god to protect them from the great and terrible American warplanes. The crowded doorway to a teahouse inside of which *amazake,* a beverage made of fermented yeast, was boiled in great pots to warm the chilled Japanese. And now and again a hurrying truck, taking parts of planes from the underground factory to an assembly plant.

And the cold. Always the cold.

Davies, moving with the throng, knew where he was going, exactly how to get there, and what to do. If he was cursed for blocking the way of the *kammairi* who ran so much more rapidly than he shambled, he did not mind. If he was spat upon, he wiped away the spittle as humbly as any pariah.

To the left of the shrine was the hall of purification, to which the worshippers first went; and as Davis shuffled past it he could see naked brown bodies of men and women ladling warmed water over themselves just as he ladled hot *udon* out of his pots. After purification, they would bow down at the shrine. In such manner they were made sufficiently pure to address the gods.

He passed the shrine itself, now walking near a row of food stands. Which jealous proprietor first screamed at him, he never knew. But in no time at all a hostile crowd gathered about him, and his little sack of dough was pulled away from him.

What he heard next, as the Japanese jeered at him, turned him doubly cold. An old Japanese, in white like the others, was speaking.

"When I was young," stated the wrinkled old man, "such a thing as this would not have been tolerated! *Ai!* When I was young, things were different. No pariah dog would have been permitted to walk here—"

"Nor take money away from honest stallkeepers," yelled the Japanese who had called the crowd's attention to the "Ainu."

"And we," the ancient announced, "would have worshipped properly! In those days we were not called *kammairi*. No. We were known as *hadakamairi*, naked worshippers, and that is what we were. We ran honorably naked to the shrine, which is now forbidden by the authorities. We did not shrink from the cold winds—"

"Force the Ainu to become a dog-*hadakamairi*," shouted the stallkeeper, seeing a way to stop completely any coins going to the udon-vendor. "Oh, how enjoyable it would be to see him run!"

A burly, white-clad Japanese had Davies by the arm.

Voices pleaded, "Please, no. It is forbidden."

"Should pariah dogs wear clothing?" yelled the big Japanese, smelling excitement and fun. "Is not his own hair sufficient covering, even on a night of great cold? Surely not even the police would object to a dog being chased away from a sacred place, and this dog"—he hit Davies furiously on the ugly wound—"is a mangy one at that!"

The stallkeepers now all egged the tormentor on.

The "Ainu" was hurled to the ground. Hands ripped off his tattered jacket and trousers, his blackened socks. The skin girdle defied rough jerks; as the burly Japanese' hands went for the thong fastening, he saw the real despair on the face of the throng's prey. Connecting this truly enough with the girdle and the charm-bag which was tied to it, the big Japanese howled gleefully, "O dog of an Ainu, you can keep it if you lick my hand!"

On hands and knees, Davies did it.

Then he was kicked to his feet, spat at, slapped.

"Run, mangy dog! Run!"

The audience squealed with delight. Nothing like this had ever been seen before. Oh, how the dog ran! And he ran in circles, too, without sufficient intelligence to take the shortest route away from his tormentors. This way and that he ran, with the threats of the men and, worse poison, the shrill venom of the women, in his ears. The Japanese buzzed about him like wasps.

He appeared to be blundering aimlessly, but was not; he wanted the Japanese to have their fun here, and not harry him through the streets and far away from the shrine. Once he was chased off, he would never be allowed to return. Soon he began to gasp, and bets were made as to how long he could remain on his feet. At the end, as if completely exhausted, he stumbled and fell headlong against a stunted pine's rough trunk, at the edge of the courtyard.

While the mob goggled down at him, cold started to seep through his skin. But the Japanese finally left him, all except a penniless *hakoya,* a Yoshiwara attendant who, after the others had gone for hot *amazake* at the teahouse, knelt beside the motionless naked body.

DAVIES WAS rolled to his back by the pimply *hakoya.* The Japanese' eager fingers found the charm-bag, in which he hoped to find a few coins; and then, heedless of the *hakoya's* clawing nails, Davies throttled him.

Luck again. *But if I put on his clothes,* thought Lew, almost before the *hakoya* was dead, *I take a chance at being caught for wearing 'em.* If he were caught later, it wouldn't matter so much. Not after he'd done his job. *Come on, you bathing beauty,* Davies goaded himself. *Get going, Mr. Tokyo.*

He removed the *hakoya's* clothing, rolled it into a bundle. Then, ears alert for any returning Japanese, he crept off. Several times he flattened himself, with the clothing flung to one side where it couldn't be seen, until the Japanese who stopped and stared down continued on their way. Once he lay as if unconscious, but all he had seen was a stone lantern.

It seemed as if he could hear the tiny bells ringing all of the time. By now almost all feeling had gone from his feet. On hands and knees, shaking with cold, he examined the distance ahead which he must travel.

He had to make a dash for it. He had to take that chance in the black night. The cold was taking away control of his muscles.

There was no one to slap him on the back. No one to say, "Let's give 'em hell, boy." No one. Not even a fellow-prisoner. Not anyone.

But, as he knelt on the ground, fumbling to get the little can of ether out of the charm-bag, he felt like what he truly was. An American. A soldier. A duty had been assigned to him and, so help him God, he would carry out his orders.

He stood up and ran. He could only tell when his feet struck the ground by the pain which shot up his legs. But he ran.

The air intake for the underground plant's air lines… where? Oh, where? Here! Right here. Now, unscrew the can's cap. Stuck. Damn! Fingers don't want to hang on to the tin. Fingers no good. Damn fingers! Cap… ought to come off easily. Did when tried before. Maybe the cold….

It took Davies' teeth to grind the cap from the can.

He flung the contents through the wire-covered intake. For a fraction of time he heard only the ringing in his ears, part real, part imaginary, while the smell of ether further dizzied him. That moment of waiting was the longest Llewelyn Davies had ever experienced in his life.

Wouldn't it work? Were the States engineers all wrong? Wouldn't the piston of the compressor, squeezing down on ether instead of on air, blow the whole set of lines inside all to hell—and everything else with it?

Had he failed?

Then he heard a sobbing sound. Not loud. Like the exhaled breath of the pimply *hakoya*, just before he died. A sob. At the air intake.

It grew, clattered, became metallic; and then it screamed like tortured metal. Sounds like nothing Davies had ever heard before followed hard on the new shrill noise from below, from inside the plant where a secret Japanese warplane was being fabricated. It was metal crashing against metal as the air lines exploded. It was ruin. It was the most wonderful, beautiful sound Davies could imagine.

"What do you know?" said Lew Davies right out loud. "What do you know?"

If workmen were screaming in the underground plant, the noise of destruction kept their shouts from Davies. What they were shrieking was "Fire! Fire!" because flying pieces of metal, in addition to the havoc which Davies expected, had ripped down electric power lines also, and not all the earlier prayers at the shrine could stop the swift spreading of the flames.

Davies had forgotten how cold he was. Without knowing it, he stood straight as he listened to the magnificent sounds. He wished he dared wait until the Nips came swarming out of the plant, running as they must have run from American bombs at Paramushiru. It would have been swell to watch. But a fellow always had to have something keeping him from having fun.

He pulled on the Japanese attire, covering his skin belt and charm-bag with it. He must keep out of sight until he reached the pariah village.

Grinning, he waited a second longer, hearing the tumult, seeing the bobbing lanterns. He thought that he smelled smoke, and that he saw smoke swirl out of an entrance, but that was too much to hope for.

Then, with what he believed was strictly a G.I. stride, Lieutenant Davies marched off. Actually, he was limping, although he didn't know it.

Everything was fine. Everything. It was a little cold, but you had to expect such weather at this time of the year.

THE WAR-FAN

IF THE Japanese soldiers, sailors and civilians who walked on the dimmed-out Tokyo street had known that the despised Ainu pariah who shuffled cringingly along between pavement and car-tracks was an American, they would have smashed him down before the traffic-directing policeman at the near intersection could have turned and shouted approval. If they had also known that the stocky, dark, bearded man was an officer in Air Forces engaged in the performance of his duty, Lieutenant Llewelyn Davies would not have resembled anything human when the Japanese were finished with him.

A *rikisha*-man, approaching the shambling figure, obeyed the order of the half-drunken soldier in his cart and swerved so suddenly that he brought a shaft of the *rikisha* heavily against the ragged man's ribs.

Davies made no effort to maintain balance. He fell weakly, just as a pariah would have fallen, and sprawled into a puddle, sending water splashing out. Covering his head with his arms, he waited for the customary beating.

The soldier yelled, above the laughter of the onlookers, "*Teppo motaba uchikorosu no desu?* How dare you get in my way, Ainu dog?"

Davies cowered lower.

"*Abunai yo!*" he heard a different voice cry out, but not at him. The shriller voice added, "Take care, soldier! When I desire to bathe, I do it at the proper time and in the proper place!"

Tatsu broke in on Davies' story. "Please to
wait. The best is last," he said. "I will now
show you the exact dying of an Amerika-jin!"

"You sailors bathe in the ocean," the soldier retorted, "and I
have heard that the *Amerika*-jin select the time and place for
it."

By carefully looking over one arm during the silence following the interchange of insults, Lew saw that the seaman had
been well spattered by drops from the muddy puddle. A year
ago, the pair would have been apologizing and smiling and
bowing because of the incident; now, they snarled.

Davies knew why. Despite the most rigid censorship, the
Japanese army knew what had really taken place at the "victories" which the Japanese navy claimed; and the navy knew the
truth of army "advances to the true sphere of defense." Each
was beginning to blame the other for losses, and at last a little

trickle of truth was beginning to seep through to the civilians at home.

We must be really putting on the pressure, thought Lew. *We must be hitting them pretty hard, because we've got them squabbling.*

It was more than enough to make a fellow who had seen no Americans except prisoners feel pretty good, not only because it was more proof that matters were no longer going so well for the Japanese, but because it seemed proof to Davies, as he lay there on the street, that what he was planning made sense.

The argument had continued. As more sailors gathered around their mate who had been spattered, the offended seaman shouted, "Ho! What a brave soldier! One who has never so much as smelled blood! When you leave Japan," the seaman taunted, "you will not return until you are ashes. Soldiers who have been fighting never receive furloughs, lest their behavior at home be like their behavior abroad—"

"*Nanda ore ga yotteru mono ka!*" screamed the soldier. "Do you say that I am drunk? Do you insult the Army?"

Lew saw that other soldiers were coming out into the street, to stand interestedly beside the *rikisha.*

"You cannot be insulted," another sailor called out. "If the Navy were not always forced to carry you away from island after island—"

"*Sa!* If the Army could receive ammunition and reinforcements… if the Navy were not fearful of *Amerika-jin* submarines and aircraft—"

The seaman who had been spattered could stand no more. He had leaped out into the street, and at the same moment the soldier in the *rikisha* jumped down to meet him, slobbering in his rage.

THE POLICEMAN at the intersection, although unable to see exactly what might be taking place, began to blow his whistle frantically because of the stoppage of traffic. Amazingly, in Japan, no dutiful obedience followed the tooting.

While the horrified civilians, men and women alike, stared in silence, soldier and sailor met and sought for a maiming blow. Both, as they missed and grappled, were flung from their feet as their companions tore out and joined in the struggle. Davies was at the bottom of the pile of enraged men.

If these skunks knew who I am, he thought as he continued to protect his head with his arms, *they'd turn me into mementoes to be taken home to the children. See what papa has brought home! A nice* Amerika-jin *eyeball!*

He had known what would happen to him, were his disguise penetrated, even when he himself had suggested the assignment in Manila at the outbreak of hostilities. For two years now he had been "Koropok," the Ainu pariah. In appearance he was remarkably similar to the original inhabitants of Japan, who had been driven to the mountainous northern provinces by the conquering Japanese. He had lived there as a boy with his father, a doctor; he spoke the language of the Ainu and knew their customs. His disguise, even in a spy-fearful land, had thus far proven perfect; a slip, at any time, meant torture and death.

When he first reached Tokyo, working his way down from the north where he had been set ashore in fog, he repaired *geta*, clogs, until edged tools were taken from all non-Japanese by the nervous police. After that, Davies managed to exist by becoming a vendor of cheap food, which also had allowed him to get about the capital of the empire and discover the things he could do to cause trouble for the Nipponese.

He had marked the objective for a flight of American bombers. He had destroyed the Jap's supply of an oil used to give strength and resilience to military airframe construction. He had ruined an aircraft experimental plant as completely as bombs could have done. Now, because the worried Japanese were moving factories away from Tokyo as Allied bombers came nearer and nearer within range, Davies had been forced to figure out another means of causing them misery.

It was his wandering about the city, his being treated by the Japanese as if he were an animal and unable to understand what they might be saying, which had given him this new notion. And what was taking place above him, the antagonism which was developing between the branches of the Japanese war machine, seemed proof that his plan was based on something more than hope.

But what I'll do, and what I'll be, thought Lew, because he felt that he must hold down the immediate desire which surged through him and the best way to do it was to think about something else, *will make me lower than even the Nips could imagine for an American. Yes, I'll be something!*

Searching fingers stroked his neck, seeking a muscle to twist. Davies had to use force to get away from them.

It was then he realized that, buried as he was at the bottom of the heap, there was no way that the snarling, squirming mass of Japanese could know his neck for a pariah's neck at all. It had been a soldier who had sought for the maiming grasp;

Davies' bare neck would cause the soldier to believe the neck was that of a uniformed sailor. Neither soldiers nor sailors could see him; he was just another man mixed up in the ugly brawl.

What do you know? Lew grinned. *I've been waiting for a chance like this for two long years. Boy!*

He slipped his right arm away from his head, bringing it to his side. He had to wait an instant, he who had waited for two years, and it seemed a long time. Then, still grinning, but cold as ice down to his bare toes, he got his chance. Into the short blow he struck, Davies put all of the repressed thoughts and all the previously restrained strength of his hard, stocky body. His fist exploded against a brown Japanese nose, flattening it even more than it had been before; his fist came away warm and wet with blood.

His own blood tingled. It was a magnificent sensation.

That was for the men who bombed Tokyo and were murdered for carrying out their proper military orders. And now I'm going to give you a little something on account to pay you for the way prisoners are treated in Japan. See how you like this, you slime-blooded devils!

Lew arched his legs slightly, getting the toes of both feet pressed down to the street so he could get purchase. Someone was trying to gnaw at his shoulder, and he had to push up, squirm, and rub the Japanese sailor's bullet head off by shoving it against whoever was above. Another Japanese' fingers were slipping along Davies' left arm, striving for a maiming grip at the armpit; Lew had to maneuver the fellow away.

The smell of the Japanese, a combination of sweat, giant radish, and cheap perfume, was in Davies' nostrils. Their snarls and grunts and hisses and blasphemies were in his ears. But it was all very wonderful, because they were fighting one another. Nothing like this had ever happened before.

The man disguised as the pariah Koropok had to struggle and twist in order to get a little space for his right arm again.

Then Lew's lips formed, "Here's one for the prisoners."

This time his fist sunk deep into a belly, and Davies heard with pleasure the gasp of the Japanese who had received the short, fierce blow. What was even better, the Nipponese slumped, a dead weight, across the prone form of the American at the bottom of the heap of struggling bodies.

THE MAN who was knocked out must have been a soldier, for Davies' knuckles were smarting and probably cut from a belt buckle.

I'll bet I marked his belly more than his buckle has marked my hand, thought Lew with glowing satisfaction. *He won't enjoy his food tomorrow.*

Then he sobered. If either man whom he had struck recognized the dreaded *Amerika-jin* manner of fighting-with-fists, the cut knuckle would direct suspicion toward the pariah Koropok. And even if the suspicion could not be turned into satisfactory proof, he would be killed merely because the rival branches of the service would want a source for their rage. What he had been doing, he told himself, was a pleasure, and not duty at all. It was the freeing of his long bottled-up feeling, of his anger; and he had to quit it.

He did. He groveled down, pariah-fashion, merely protecting himself as best he could, while soldiers and sailors brawled and bit and scratched. But those two blood-bright blows had done a lot for him. He felt more like Llewelyn Davies, and less like Koropok the Ainu pariah, than at any time since he had assumed the disguise.

It was a good thing he felt so swell, he thought, as he ducked away from raking claws, because before very long, if his plan worked out as he intended, he would become the lowest form of life in Tokyo. He wondered, grinning a little as he lay at the bottom of the pile, what his fellow-officers or his old C.O. would say if they could have known what he wanted to become.

He intended to get himself engaged as a *hakoya,* a man who escorted geisha girls from their quarters to the restaurants where they entertained guests.

It would take some doing, but Davies believed it could be managed. Only the oldest men performed this duty now, and they were invariably being sworn at or discharged for their lack of agility. Their duties were of a nature which were not considered disgraceful in Japan, but which caused Americans to gag. However, in escorting the girls to the places where they were engaged, *hakoya* certainly saw men who at other times were surrounded by bodyguards.

This, of course, was well known; and on it Davies' plan was based. What he intended to do if he were able to get himself such a job was exceedingly simple. He believed that it would be effective, because he had listened to the way in which civilians were whispering to one another about this war which was now bringing Japan only the ashes of the dead.

He would say, in a food-stall or fried-fish shop, "General— oh, I dare not speak so important a name!—was entertained last night."

The Japanese, *rikisha-men* and clerks and laborers, would snarl at him for being an Ainu; but Davies knew their huge curiosity. After they had cursed him, they would press for details, the details of food and drink and entertainment by geisha which they themselves would have liked to experience.

"*Ma!*" Davies would say, enviously. "What beautiful girls were ordered for the party! What fine saki was enjoyed… Oh, so many bottles! How generous the general was! Observe what remains of the tip which was given me!"

The Japanese would probably take from the pariah whatever coins he displayed; the feel of money, wasted by being given to an Ainu, would put them in exactly the proper state of mind for the sort of thing which Davies would then say.

"The general is no longer a poor man. Not any more."

He would be questioned about that, too. He would say nothing until the Japanese threatened him.

Koropok would then whisper, "The general has the entire

opium concession for seven cities in China. That is why he is no longer poor."

Word of this would spread from listening clerk to receptive and hungry wife and friends... just as other rumors had reached Davies' ears when he had been repairing *geta* and selling cheap food.

How far would he dare go in putting thoughts in the Japanese' heads?

He had a chance to test this out now. He was certain that the policeman from the intersection must be dancing around at the edge of the milling mass of soldiers and sailors, and grabbing at any arms and legs which could be reached. No mere yelled order would stop the brawl.

Here goes, thought Lew.

Not in the guttural Ainu dialect at all, but in middle-province Japanese, Davies snarled, "*Maketa ni ch'gai wa nai!* The policeman is clubbing soldiers! He is clubbing sailors! He is attacking all of us! *Aita!*"

A muffled voice growled, "Is that true?" and, with the words, Davies felt the speaker attempting to pull himself away from the furious tangle.

"*Kore!*" some other Japanese crackled. "This cannot be permitted!"

The men around Davies and above him no longer sought to injure anyone within reach who, from the feel of the uniform could be determined to be in the opposite branch of the service. Even as the pile began to untangle, doing it badly because of the very haste, Lew could hear opinions regarding policemen who remained safely at home while sailors were being burned to death on ships bombed by the damnable *Amerika-jin* flying men or lost at sea because of the equally terrible *Amerika-jin* submarines... and while soldiers were now forced to face *Amerika-jin* land forces with choice of death by steel or starvation.

I'm on the beam, thought Lew quietly. *It works. And if it works*

here, it will work even better when I drop a little careful poison into
the ears of hungry clerks to take home for their wives to pass on.

In no other way at the moment, Davies was sure, could he
cause more trouble for Japan. Coming from a degraded *hakoya,*
a servant in the Yoshiwara, his stories would be believed as
things overheard when some important military official had
been in his cups, surrounded by geisha, boastful and flushed
with liquor.

THE WEIGHT above him was quickly becoming less.
When he was able to get to his knees, and then to his feet, the
policeman had already scampered off, probably chased by some
of the soldiers and sailors. It gave Lew satisfaction to see that
one of the Japanese was wiping blood from face and uniform,
while another was vomiting from the smash in the belly which
Davies had given him.

To have moved off, however inconspicuously, would have
meant that the pariah would be remembered as the cause of
the entire fight. So Lew remained motionless.

The street lights were dimmed, as were the lights of the shop
windows of the big stores. There were the usual portable stalls
on the pavement, for people too poor and timid to enter the
foreign-style buildings. But the street did not resemble Japan
before the attack on the United States. There were a few tinkles
of the alarm bells on *rikishas;* but the honking of automobiles,
the whistles of trains at the nearby station, the rumble of tram-
cars, were all gone. Only the beggars remained.

"Ladies and gentlemen of the east and west, something for
an old sick one who now has no sons!"

The old woman who shouted this, vying with other beggars,
had a shrill voice which rose above the others; Davies, standing
in the street, could see her and the infant balanced on her knee.

He saw her and, perhaps of all of the throng, he saw a small
man not in kimono, accompanied by a geisha, attempt to elude
the beggar's outstretched hand.

Davies had been stationed at Manila. The small man, with

a very dark and pockmarked face, was almost certainly a Filipino. One of the countless "commissioners" who, ordered to Tokyo, returned to attempt to bring the propaganda of "co-prosperity" to the men in the Commonwealth. Hated men.

Here was another and equally good opportunity to make absolutely certain that the Nipponese, alarmed at the way in which the war was beginning to go, were ready to listen to trouble-makers. As tools Davies still had several sailors, including the one whose nose he had bloodied so well, standing near, their backs to him. The crowd was moving off slowly.

Speaking so swiftly that he had finished before the sailors turned, Lew snapped, "That *kurombo,* that nigger, has slapped the beggar-woman!"

Actually, the dark, pockmarked Filipino quisling had done nothing of the sort; he had merely continued strutting along with the geisha following in his perfumed wake. But the sailors, with the poison in their ears, saw him, and the beggar with her scrawny grandchild, and the Japanese girl. They stared for a moment, and Davies had guessed well the feeling which rose in them.

They did not whisper together. One of them shouted, through lips purple with fury, "*Emo-kushi!* Pockface!" while some of the others repeated the epithet which Davies had put into their heads: "*Kurombo!*"

The sailors began to yell as they ran toward the cowering Filipino. How dare he strike an honorable beggar-grandmother and her grandchild? He was worse than an *Amerika-jin!* He was worse than a *Shina-jin!* He was filth!

A soldier who had joined them cried, "Look how he parades before us with a girl such as none of us can afford!" and this fanned the flames.

Davies, who had heard a little of what had happened when men of the type of the pockfaced Filipino had assisted the Japanese during the first attack on Manila, wished he might stay to watch. Instead, he worked his way, head low, through the crowd, and shuffled quietly in the direction of the railway station, beyond which was the district where he hoped to be engaged as a *hakoya*.

It seemed strange not to have the end of the brawl turned into a beating and harrying of a pariah. It also seemed very fine.

He couldn't whistle, because no Ainu ever whistled, but he hummed inaudibly as he shuffled along.

> "I reclined on a divan of lager-beer foam,
> With a pillow of froth for my head,
> While spray from a fountain of sparkling gin-fizz
> Descended like dew on my bed."

Where were the fellows with whom he had sung that song now? Dead? Prisoners? If not, where they were flying?

Lieutenant Davies had been in a fighter command. P-40's. What would it be like to fly a ship like the twin-tailed American fighters about which the Japanese were so dazedly moaning? What sort of ship was it, anyhow? Gossip, which a *geta*-mender or food-vendor was bound to hear, had it that the airplane which had two tails instead of one was like lightning in the sky, and that it was *seppuku,* hara-kiri for a Zero to attempt to meet it unless the odds were ten to one.

How long would it be before such fighters, escorting formations of bombers, would be over Tokyo?

Davies, passing the station and walking along the street near the small river called Sanjukken-bori—a dark street lined with fashionably-built houses with gates and ornamented doors—grinned wryly as he compared what he was about to attempt to do with what was being done by flyers, pilots, bombardiers. Yet if he were able to drop one small bomb of rumor so that it would explode and spread like fire, all of the degradation of his position as a *hakoya* would be worth while.

"Even so, it's a hell of a way to fight a war," Davies muttered. Then he added, "Will you quit feeling sorry for yourself, you lug?"

CHAPTER II

A DANGEROUS STORY

THERE WERE dimly-lit lamps on many of the gates. These places were *machiai*, waiting-houses. They were not restaurants, although food was served in the handsome private rooms; nor did geisha live there. Instead, Japanese girls were engaged to attend parties at the *machiai*, parties far more lively and informal than those given by wealthy Japanese in the regular eating establishments.

The geisha who came to the waiting-houses to entertain male guests arrived with empty hands, burdened only with their robes. Even the small weight of *samisen* and fan, according to Japanese belief, would have cheated the guests of a little of the girls' freshness and beauty. The carrying of instrument, silken bag and fan, was done by the *hakoya;* and it was the least indecent of his tasks.

The *hakoya* cleaned up after drunks. He accompanied his master when a new girl was being engaged—sometimes, if sufficiently intelligent, playing a part when her price was being argued with the father. He summoned *rikisha* and took the few miserable coins which were extracted from the puller. People scorned him, but if he kept his ears open he heard things told indiscreetly by drunken men. And even if he did not hear them, it would be believed that he did.

Between the *machiai* and the Yoshiwara were the usual stands put up after dusk. Many of them were crowded with uniformed men. Here *sushi* was being bought and eaten—pickled rice mixed with eggs, fish, and vegetables. And as Davies walked carefully past, he glanced enviously at the little square pieces of egg, the white slices of cuttlefish, the bits of lobster.

He was always hungry. For any food.

A steak, thought Lew, after he had passed the food-stands and headed toward the dark side-street by which the Yoshiwara

Speaking swiftly, Davies, cried, "The
kurombo *slapped the beggar-woman!"*

was approached. *A steak. Potatoes. Any kind of potatoes—mashed,
baked, French-fried. And coffee. And a real cigarette. Just one. Not,*
he thought soberly, *that I'll turn down whatever I get to eat, if I
catch on as* hakoya. *Anything, just so it's food.*

The corner was so dark that a decrepit *rikisha*-man said,
"*Danna, Oyasuku mairimasho,*" in an attempt to secure a fare,
before discovering that the person addressed was an Ainu
pariah. After that, he cursed so furiously that he was still
choking when Davies turned the corner.

Another *rikisha* approached Davies, drawn slowly and painfully by an ancient Japanese whose skinny, knobby legs were
trembling with fatigue. The former sturdy and insolent young
pullers were all in the army; only the ailing and aged remained
on the streets. And naturally, only similar old men were available
as *hakoya.* So Lew, who could guess easily enough how few
scruples were possessed by the type of men who managed the
places in the Yoshiwara for important families, was reasonably
sure that he, although believed to be an Ainu and a pariah, still
had an excellent chance of being engaged.

Aside from the lack of men, he would come cheap. In addition, he would be an innovation; he would be something which,
with laughter, a shrewd manager could capitalize on, using him
as a *taikomochi,* a jester, who could be made to prance about

idiotically for the guests' amusement. He would be the butt of every joke, the object of every possible cruelty from manager, other employees, and guests. He knew that. But it, too, was all right.

THERE WAS the customary entrance to the licensed quarter, through which every visitor and inmate must pass; and there was the customary unpleasant policeman at the broad, carved gate. Through it, as Davies came nearer, could be seen the rows of long houses, with soldiers and sailors and a few civilians examining the girls who sat behind the bamboo-barred show-windows nearest the entrance and trying to decide which girl's tobacco pipe to accept and smoke, which was the sign of selection.

Even before he snatched at Davies' permit, the officer demanded by what right a pariah and an Ainu came to this place of pleasure for men, and ordered him to leave immediately.

"You smell like a dead animal," the policeman shouted, knowing that one of the few occupations allowed pariahs was to work in Tokyo's slaughter-houses. "Go away. The odor about you will be bad for honorable business here."

Davies continued to hold out his permit apologetically.

"You stink," said the policeman. "You stink like an over-ripe dead cow, which is almost as bad as the odor of a dead *Ameri-ka-jin.*"

The man in the tattered jacket did not move.

Snatching the permit and reading it rapidly, the Japanese grunted, "Koropok! What sort of name is that? I do not like it. I do not like the way you stink. Go away. Or do you wish to be arrested?"

"*K'r'hodo os'rosh 'katta,*" mumbled Davies. "Please do not arrest me. I was told that guests within the gates might give me a coin after I related my story, and because I am very hungry I dared to come here—"

"What story can you know?" the policeman sneered.

Davies was prepared. He said, cringing, "I was engaged in

"Executions! What executions?" the startled
policeman demanded of the groveling Koropok.

cleaning a drain for a noble lord who allowed me to receive
four *sen* for the work. He did not wish to engage an Ainu,"
apologized Davies, "but the drain was clogged and he could
not find anyone else. When I had completed my permitted task,
the lord asked me if I had ever been an attendant at executions,
a task required of us. To this I said yes, because once I was
ordered to—"

"What do I care about your drains and executions?" shouted
the policeman. "I have more important things to do than listen
to your endless nonsense!" Then, blinking, he stared at the groveling Koropok. "Executions?" he asked. "What executions?
Come! Answer me!"

"Of *Amerika-jin* flyers," said Davies.

ACTUALLY, HE had not been present; but he had
heard sufficient from pariahs at the squalid settlement where
he kenneled with them to be able to tell the story. It was one
which Tokyo was avid to hear, since the executions of those
men in uniform were intended to frighten off future raids.

"You lie," the policeman accused. But he said it doubtfully.

"I was told," said Davies, "that I might be given a few mouth-
fuls of food in return for the story. And I am hungry." He
continued to help the policeman along with what Davies had

believed would occur to the Japanese. "I would not expect money. I would not expect payment. I—"

"Payment?" the policeman said. "Payment! Ho! I should hope not!"

The officer, as Davies knew, was well tipped by managers to direct custom to their places. Lew could see, now, how the policeman was weighing the value of the story as entertainment for which guests could be charged; and how the Japanese' cupidity was causing him to lick his lips.

He's figuring out who'll pay him the most, thought Davies.

He could hear a girl's voice, singing as she waited to be called to a *machiai,* coming from one of the side-streets beyond the gate, from a number-one or number-two place, where there was no show-window.

> Over the mountains, back to my home;
> What shall I bring as a present for baby?
> A kettle-drum and a penny whistle?
> A doll that jumps up
> When you push him down?
> Or a wheel that turns in the wind?

"What you suggest," the policeman said suddenly, "is without value. But perhaps it may amuse some important manager to listen to it, and then to kick you out. Therefore you are to go to Number Nineteen, Middle Street, informing the hostess at the guide-house that I, Officer Manabe, have ordered you to be taken to see Suriga-*san.* Now repeat the names for me, Ainu dog."

As Lew did so, in the guttural Ainu tone, he realized that the policeman had decided that Suriga, at Nineteen, would probably pay the most to secure a fool of an Ainu who could be put to use, not only for his story, but in other ways. Strong young men were no longer to be found.

He was told repeatedly how to find Number Nineteen, lest, he knew, he fall into the hands of someone else who would not tip the officer so well.

First, as Davies shuffled into the quarter, there were the show-windows, behind the lattices of which were girls in red and purple who joked and cajoled the sailors and soldiers. Rows of them. Next came long lines of wooden fences on which were framed photographs of the girls who waited in the houses behind the fences. Where the main street turned toward Middle Street and Number Nineteen, groups of uniformed men were gobbling crushed fish, *hampen,* served to them by girls in the stalls.

Number Nineteen, as Davies had hoped and expected, was imposing. The front was of carved and lacquered wood, the roof of tiles. It was the sort of opulent place from which a grafting policeman might properly anticipate excellent payment for any favor or touting; and it was exactly the sort of place where Davies wanted to be a *hakoya.* Geisha from here would certainly be of sufficient youth, beauty and training to be sent to *machiai* to entertain important men who would never visit the house itself. It was what Davies wanted. As the *hakoya* of such an establishment, he would be set.

He stopped before the *hikite-chaya,* the guide house, from which guests were taken deeper inside. Because a maid was peeping out, Davies became Koropok for her benefit; he would take a step or two toward the entrance, and then stop and back away as if fearful of entering. He looked up, and then glanced hastily back at his feet in their worn sandals of Ainu make.

The maid, he knew, would report his actions faithfully to the hostess, who, because she had not already come out to order him away, must be busy elsewhere.

It was a full five minutes before the guide-house door was flung open. An officer of Davies' own rank strutted out, followed by the hostess, the maid, the girl who had been assigned to him, and her own assistants. All were calling their thanks for the generous tips. The *taikomochi,* the malformed jester, shrilled in a cracked voice, when he saw the pariah, "Oh, another honorable guest to favor us with his presence! The fame of this place is surely becoming very great!"

While the smiling hostess cursed Davies out of the corner of her mouth, and the powdered girls wished that custom allowed them to take their grateful eyes from the departing figure of the guest, the Japanese lieutenant studied Davies with narrowed, glinting eyes. His judgy brown hand dropped automatically to his holster.

"Would you like to see how a dog is killed?" he asked his audience.

"Yes," urged the deformed *taikomochi* instantly.

The lieutenant said savagely, "It would show you how the *Amerika-jin* die. This dog also will beg for mercy. It is a great sight."

If you draw your gun, you'll shoot, thought Lew, *and my mission will end. But I'll get you first. You'd kill a pariah just to show off.*

"Why do you wait, honorable sir?" deviled the *taikomochi*.

Davies saw the twitching of the lieutenant-guest's fingers. He himself said, in the clipped Ainu dialect, "The honorable policeman named Manabe-*san* commanded me to come to the famous house of Suriga-*san*. Oh, do not kill me for having done as I was ordered! Oh, forgive me for having begged for my life! I—"

A short, fat Japanese was at the doorway; he must have heard his own name, for he demanded, "How does a pariah know my name? What is taking place?"

"The officer-*san*," sneered the *taikomochi*, "was about to shoot the pariah dog, but has changed his mind."

CHAPTER III

A CLEVER FOOL

DAVIES' BODY tensed; the Japanese lieutenant's gun was half out of its holster. Instinctively, Lew's lips tightened under his beard, and he began to sweat.

"Wait," snapped Suriga, the manager. "Where did you learn my name?" he demanded of the pariah. "And what do you want?"

"Manabe-*san*, the policeman, sent me," whined Koropok. "He—"

"It is I who am the jester," cackled the *taikomochi*, "but now I have a rival! Which girl will the honorable dog prefer?"

The manager ordered his deformed, brightly-clad attendant to be silent. To the lieutenant Suriga said, "These are strange days. Possibly Manabe sent the shaggy animal here to perform some of the tasks for which a man can no longer be hired. That is possible." He turned to Koropok. "Is that it?"

"*Ikitai*," whimpered Koropok. "I am afraid. Let me go away." Then he mumbled, "I was to relate to you—"

"Whatever it is," said Suriga, "it can wait." The shrewd manager had no intention of having the pariah say more where others could hear. Manabe was no fool; he was almost too intelligent to be a policeman. "I will talk to you later. In the meantime, you may enter by a rear door."

"I am not sure he is going anywhere," the lieutenant snapped. "I—"

"Oh, surely you will permit it," pleaded Suriga, almost as servilely as Koropok had spoken. "Oh, please! I would not like to ask the lieutenant for the payment for last week, and for Monday night, and for—"

The Japanese lieutenant strode off, his face flushed and furious. A maid giggled.

The disappointed *taikomochi* shrilled, "Why should he not be killed? Do we ever go to the theater now? No! Are we not entitled to enjoyment? And all we do in these days is entertain generals and colonels and admirals and politicians who have little appreciation of our arts—and he will spoil your trade," threatened the jester, grinning evilly at Suriga.

"How?"

"He stinks like an *Amerika-jin*," said the *taikomochi*.

Even the hostess laughed at such an impossible joke; but Davies, walking to the rear, thought, *I've got to watch you,* taikomochi. He feared the warped shrewdness of the jester. Yes, the little devil would bear watching.

Life in the Yoshiwara began for Lieutenant Davies after Suriga listened to his story and summed up the profit to be made from it. But it was the *taikomochi* Tatsu, the jester, who figured out more for Koropok to do than even the countless repugnant tasks assigned to the new servant by the manager, tasks in addition to the telling of the supposed eye-witness tale of the flyers' execution.

Tatsu suggested that the Ainu be arrayed to resemble the bears with whom Koropok had lived in the northern mountains—surely Koropok was as shaggy as a bear, but without the animal's courage. Then Tatsu himself would lead the bear by a chain when geisha were engaged at waiting houses, and the bear, as *hakoya*, should carry the tools of the geisha trade, musical instruments, fans, and all the rest.

What the ugly jester wanted, Davies knew, was someone whom he could order about and strike and publicly insult, someone inferior to the *taikomochi*. Also, Tatsu could and would take from the *hakoya* the tips given to him, and keep them for himself. Lew had no objection to either of these things, and he was delighted at the ease with which he had been made the *hakoya;* but what he did not like was the constant suspiciousness of the warped Tatsu. There was never any way of knowing when the *taikomochi* would pop out, with his shrewd eyes darting about.

Lew was forced to tell himself that it was only the usual suspicion and meanness of the twisted in mind, until one morning when he was scrubbing the woodwork, an old maid-servant came up and frankly sniffed at him, wrinkling her forehead as she did.

She was old and talkative; in her youth she too had been a dancing girl. She said, "*Ichido o me ni kakatta.* When I was young, I had a *seiyo-jin* lover. You do not remind me of him. He was all golden. You are black. Tatsu is a fool."

While Koropok cavorted and began to
sweat, Tatsu would stare at him and snarl,
"You stink like an **Amerika-jin!"**

Davies said nothing. Now had he done anything which might
have aroused Tatsu's suspicions in any way. The one possibility
was that the *taikomochi* had an over-developed sense of smell,
and believed he had detected a difference between the newly
engaged *hakoya* and the Japanese themselves.

Although such a difference had never been established so
far as Davies knew, Lew realized that the *taikomochi's* suspicions,
should Koropok's actions ever be questioned, could cause plenty
of trouble. Lew made no effort to placate the squat Tatsu; he
gave no sign that he knew Tatsu continually watched him.

The one time when this continual surveillance was really bad
was when Davies would wake, on the quilt in the corner where
he slept, to find the jester squatting on his heels and staring at
him. There was always the danger of having spoken in his sleep;
and to have remained awake would have shown Tatsu the fear
of that very danger.

After ten days of this, there were deep rings under Davies'
eyes.

It took this long, also, for the *hakoya* to be trained in his
double duty. The manager himself taught Davies the proper
manner of carrying the geisha implements; Tatsu was the instructor for the bear-dance which Koropok was to perform for
those guests eager to pay for additional entertainment.

Tatsu enjoyed his task. Davies' arms and thighs were well marked where the ugly *taikomochi* pinched him. Invariably, when Koropok cavorted and began to sweat, the jester would stare at him and snarl, "You stink like an *Amerika-jin!*"

It became a joke in the house.

WHAT WAS not a joke to Davies at all was that, in these first ten days, he was never allowed to go outside the licensed quarter. Was he to spend the duration here? He was doing no good, none at all. It would be better to follow up some of the stories he overheard from men grown rich during the war, stories of how munitions factories and aircraft assembly plants were being moved from the cities because the authorities were beginning to feel the tightening of the ring about the empire.

There was even talk of the growing fortifications in the Philippines, to which the army and navy of Japan might one day decide to "advance nearer Tokyo" from Rabaul and Truk; the Japanese were beginning to alter their original attitude toward the people of the Commonwealth, because the time might soon come when the enmity of the Filipinos would prove dangerous.

Hearing such shreds was interesting to Davies… but it was just talk. What was real was that he himself was accomplishing exactly nothing. He had become the fool of a fool. The creature of a jester. A tick's parasite.

To the geisha, he was the least thread in the pattern of their lives. To Suriga, the manager, he was a source of income. To Tatsu….

Before long, everything was routine. Guests, sometimes sober, more often already flushed with drink, would enter the guide house, to be led upstairs to the reception room, made enticing with fresh green mats and flowers in the alcove. As soon as the guests were made comfortable on the matting, maids brought little red lacquered stands, and served tea and cakes. Orders were taken for additional food and for saki, and for entertainment.

In a few moments the hostess herself and two maid-servants

would appear, the latter bringing the bottles of saki, the cups, the tiny porcelain containers where the liquor would be kept warm. And the hostess would explain the unusual attraction to be found only in this place: Koropok.

The geisha and dancing-maids would enter, followed by the *taikomochi* and, behind him, Koropok the pariah. He would shamble in, dressed in brown rags the color of bearskin. His shaggy hair and beard always started laughter from the guests, who enjoyed pulling at both.

The senior, or most important, guest immediately ordered that a tiny bowl of saki be given to each of the girls. Tatsu also received one, but when a bowl was held up for Koropok, Tatsu would seize it too. Did bears drink saki? Oh, no! Men drank saki. Tatsu, amid laughter, would suck down the liquor noisily, and if Davies were not on guard, would wipe out the last sweet colorless drops from the bowl with a finger and then slyly attempt to thrust the alcohol-moistened, broken-nailed finger into the eye of the "bear" when Davies wasn't looking.

"Pain causes him to dance beautifully," Tatsu would explain; and the hint was always taken by the guests.

After many exchanges of bowls between geisha and guests, a singing-girl would take up her *samisen* and the diminutive ten-year-old dancing-girls would posture and sway, with the *taikomochi* hopping up and down wildly between them—while Koropok solemnly waddled around the room, making bear-like noises as he had been taught to do by Tatsu.

At the end, Koropok would go down on all fours. Each of the guests, by this time thoroughly drunk and noisy, had the satisfaction of riding the bear around the room, while the girls clapped their hands and laughed. Once a cavalry captain showed the proper form in riding to an attack, with the shaggy pariah as his steer and the *samisen* as the sword. He used a pocket-knife as the spur.

Davies was well slashed.

BY MIDNIGHT, *taikomochi* and pariah would be alone,

and Tatsu would explain to Koropok the things which had been improperly done.

"*Nani mo g'zarimasenu,*" he would screech. "If you do not do better, we will never be ordered to attend at a waiting-house, where large tips are given by important men. Do not think that Suriga-*san* has not suggested it! You do not growl well. You do not cry out with pain when you are burned by a cigarette. All you can do is eat—eat, and stink like an *Amerika-jin!*"

Once Koropok asked humbly, "Please, honorable master Tatsu, why is my odor like that of the people you call *Amerika-jin?*"

"Because all dogs are brothers," Tatsu snarled at him.

Davies hoped that Tatsu had given him the answer which was truly in the squat Japanese' mind. But there was no way of knowing, nor did the *taikomochi* get over studying the *hakoya* Koropok when Davies slept.

Lew would not have needed to invent stories to repeat in eating-shops outside the Yoshiwara in order to damage civilian morale. Senior officers returned from the southwest Pacific, when sufficiently drunk, dropped words which would have been more damaging than Davies had dared hope. But who heard them? Tatsu the jester, who believed nothing which was said by intoxicated guests. The girls, who did not listen. Koropok the pariah, whom the Japanese considered an animal.

Once or twice the manager had intimated that Koropok might wish to spend a few hours at the pariah village on the outskirts of Tokyo; it was Tatsu who talked this down. Davies would have killed the jester with the greatest of pleasure, because the evil little *taikomochi* was preventing him from carrying out his scheme. But he dared not, unless no suspicion could be pointed toward the *hakoya.* Obviously, it was the *hakoya* who would be suspected, having been the object of the jester's continuing cruelty.

Even so, shrewd little torturings and broken and uneasy sleep were beginning to wear Davies down. It was becoming more and more difficult to control his temper, to play his part, to cavort around with Japanese officers on his back. Worse than this was being compelled to tell and retell the story of the deaths of the flyers—with fabricated embroiderings of how they begged and cringed—before civilian guests who never tired of hearing it.

Manabe, the policeman, was receiving a coin or so each time payment was made to the house for the dancing-of-the-bear and the telling-of-the-dying-of-the-cowardly-bomber-Americans; Davies knew that no escape was worth considering. And a certain stubbornness made him refuse to give up; he had come here for a calculated reason and he wanted to achieve it.

HIS DAY began a half hour before the girls were wakened at six. The rooms had to be cleaned before the taper was lit before the god of luck in the hostess' room. Then while the girls yawned over their hairdressing and read letters and told about the amusing events of the previous night, Tatsu saw to it that Koropok performed all of the *taikomochi's* own menial duties. In return, against all custom, Tatsu assisted in the dressing of the geisha, a task which really belonged to the *hakoya*. Later, Koropok carried the bran-bags and seven body-polishing implements when the household went to the bath. There were dancing lessons for the little *oshaku,* and *samisen* instruction given by the older girls to the younger—and Davies' hour of deviling while Tastu corrected all of his "mistakes."

He was being cursed by the jester when Suriga, the manager, trotted jubilantly into the room. In his excitement, the fat Japanese actually patted Koropok on the head. Suriga's eyes were shining, and only the prospect of money had such an effect on the manager of the house.

"It has come," he proclaimed. "Such an honor as this house has never received. Oh, how pleased I am! Oh, how nice it is! Oh, such good fortune!"

Tatsu grunted, "What do you talk about?"

"About tonight," said Suriga, forgetting to chide the jester for his improper questioning of a superior. "About tonight. *Yoroshi!* It is very wonderful. Our house is honored. We," bubbled Suriga, drooling a little, "have been engaged by the *machiai*, Purple Chrysanthemum, and we will serve and entertain—who do you think, Tatsu? Who do you think? Oh, you cannot guess!"

"If I cannot guess," said the jester sourly, "you had better tell me."

Suriga lowered his voice. "Korogi-*san* himself! The man to whom our revered and great Tojo-*san* entrusts most important affairs. Korogi-*san!* And there is to be a large party, Tatsu! Of officials high in the government. The party," Suriga seethed, "is being given in honor of equally important men from the south, from Manila."

"Oh," said Tatsu. He scratched his chin. "Do the *Filipino-jin* stink like the *Amerika-jin?* Like Koropok?"

"Koropok," said Suriga, patting Davies again, "is the real reason we have received the order to attend. Oh, I understand why this is! When there has been much singing and much saki imbibed, Korogi-*san* will rise and he will say, 'Oh, honorable guests from Manila, here you see what happens to inferior peoples whom the Japanese do not like!' In time such peoples become as animals." He patted Koropok again. "I also think that Koropok will relate his tale of the cowardly *Amerika-jin* flyers, after which Korogi-*san* will then say, 'Yes, that is what took place,' and, because Koropok has not the sense to lie, the *Filipino-jin* will believe every word. Let me tell you that it has been cleverly planned!"

"How do you know all this?" muttered Tatsu.

Suriga said, "I have ears. I was told."

"Why is time wasted on these *kurombo,* these niggers?"

Davies himself was wondering the same thing.

"Because these men," said Suriga, boasting because he was able to answer, "are to be important men in case our unconquerable armies should decide to advance slightly nearer Tokyo

according to Imperial decisions which may not be questioned."
Suriga added, "Some of these men performed a duty to Japan
once, when the war began. They may have another duty to
perform again. Our great Tojo forgets nothing."

Tatsu blinked, spat into a flower vase, automatically ordered
Koropok to wash it, and then stared at the retreating back of
the pariah.

When Davies had gone, Tatsu said, "These *kurombo* from
Manila have seen many *Amerika-jin.* If I were to suggest something which would cause such applause that you would receive
additional payment for our entertainment, would you give me
any of it, master? Would you give me half?"

"No," said Suriga instantly. "What is it?"

"A quarter?"

It was finally agreed that the *taikomochi* should receive a
twentieth of whatever extra might be paid; and the grin on the
jester's face, exposing every buck tooth, was enough to make
Davies doubly alert when he returned.

Lew had no way of knowing what had been said and planned,
but it involved him, because Suriga ran a hand through Koropok's thick, shaggy hair, and through the pariah's dense, black
beard. The manager was also grinning.

"Excellent," he said. "Excellent, Tatsu!"

Davies thought, *What are they up to?* but was careful not to
give the least sign of his growing uneasiness.

He understood why he was to appear in the entertainment
for the Filipino traitors. Firstly, as an Ainu, he would be an
object lesson of what happened to non-cooperative peoples.
Secondly, as a pariah who had supposedly witnessed the deaths
of American flyers, his story would impress even quislings who
might still recall what flyers of the United States had been like.
Thirdly, the Japanese High Command and Tojo wanted to do
everything possible to assure Philippine assistance when the
day came and MacArthur was sending his men ashore under
a canopy of planes....

Surigo had patted him, initially, in sheer exuberance. How about the running of the manager's hand through his servant's hair and beard? Was that the same sort of thing? Was it? Or was it something else?

And what could Davies do about it?

CHAPTER IV

THE POISON

NO DAY ever went more damnably fast, nor left Davies more worried. The entire house was excited and busy, with the girls unheeding of the cries of the vendor of *mistumame*, their favorite syrup-drenched cakes of boiled beans. By early evening everything was ready for the walk to the *machiai*. The departure was watched enviously by Middle Street.

First, Suriga, in a *rikisha*. Next, in order of age and service, the geisha, in long sober crepe robes; after them, the little *oshaku*, brightly dressed, with their red brocade *obi* hanging down to their heels. The brilliance of the geisha's costumes beneath the dull robes had to be guessed at. Every girl had come; those who did not perform were to take the places of maid-servants of the *machiai*.

After them hopped Tatsu, grimacing with importance. The jester was in orange and green. He held tightly to the chain which was looped around the bear-*hakoya* Koropok's neck. What was unusual was that Tatsu carried a large cloth-wrapped bundle, instead of having his slave carry it.

Davies, last in the procession, did not believe that Tatsu was carrying the big package out of consideration for him, although Davies' arms were filled. He carried the silken bags which contained the stringed *samisen*, the hourglass shaped *tsuzumi* drums, and the *mai-ogi*, the dancing fans. He was dressed in the furry brown tatters which were his bear-costume.

The Yoshiwara sucked in its breath at the sight of the strange *hakoya.* Lieutenant Davies, known as Koropok, never lifted his head.

What was in the bundle?

If I knew that, thought Lew, as he passed through the gate and into Tokyo proper, *I could at least be prepared for what is coming.* For a fraction of time he considered simulating a stumble and fall, and seizing the bundle, manage to rip the cloth so he could see what was inside. But Tatsu, as if the evilly warped mind were able to anticipate any such a thing, suddenly carried the bundle in front of him instead of under his arm.

In this fashion the procession reached the *machiai* and was admitted.

Suriga bowed to the manager of the waiting-house, and the pair, both in high good spirits, vanished for a few visitor's-bowls of liquor. A maid-servant led the others through a lighted corridor and upstairs to a large room on the second floor, where the party of men, Japanese and Filipinos alike, had been eating and drinking for several hours.

Davies, for all his head was low, saw the highest official present, Korogi, an intimate of Tojo, squatting at a red sandalwood stand, from which a maid of the *machiai* was serving him saki. The minister wore a kimono, but also European-style trousers, which were opened at the waist. His face was highly

The procession of the machiai *began. First came Suriga, in a* rikisha, *next the geisha; after them,*

flushed as he handed the bowl of saki given him by the maid
to the leader of the traitors.

In that first moment Davies' heart almost stopped.

The principal quisling, whose legs were sprawled out on the
floor, was Felipe; Felipe, a houseboy at the Officers' Club at
Manila.

Not for an instant had Davies feared anything like this. True,
he had lived in Manila; but he had supposed that any Filipino
quisling would be some nasty *politico* despised by his fellow
Filipinos as a cheap grafter... and Davies, as a flying officer,
had never met such men. But Felipe! That was a different story!
Why, Felipe had seen him daily....

If he recognizes me, thought Lew confusedly, *Tojo will need a
new assistant. I can do that much.* Then he told himself, collect-
ing his wits, *I'm the last person a Filipino expects to see in Tokyo.
I'm well disguised. All I've got to do is continue to play my part—and
what a useless part it has become!*

Tatsu whispered hoarsely, "Stand beside me."

From where Davies stood, he could see out into the dimly
lit garden of the waiting-house, where, in autumn, would bloom
the purple chrysanthemums which gave the place its name. He
could see all of the guests, and how the geisha now went to
kneel beside some of them, to serve, while others went to
remove their long robes and be ready to sing to the accompaniment of *samisen* and drum.

the little oshaku; *and finally Tatsu, carrying a
large bundle and leading Koropok by a chain.*

Tatsu held his bundle tightly under his arm and kept it there while he undid the fastenings of the bags which Koropok had brought—and the entertainment of the evening began. Felipe paid no more attention to Davies, than one incurious half-intoxicated glance as at some strange animal.

The pattern of the night was druggingly familiar to Davies. Hiss of silk against silk, as impassive-faced geisha, white with powder, moved on their knees preliminary to striking a few chords and singing, weirdly, with breaks of silence and wide intervals, the expected songs.

> Good evening!
> Thank you, sir!
> Please give me orders
> That is all I know
> Of living,
> And of loving.

The throb of the little drums, the snap of dancing-fans being opened and shut by the smaller girls.

But strangely, Tatsu as yet had not joined in the dances.

Saki and more saki. Polite belches from the Japanese; a few snores from some of the Filipinos. Several Japanese singing with the geisha. A Filipino furtively stroking the arm of the girl who was serving him. His face was familiar....

Then Tatsu suddenly cried, "Observe me!" which was usual enough; but when he leaped away from Koropok, whose chain jangled down to the floor, Tatsu flung the bundle down ahead of him. "This is an *Amerika-jin!*" he screamed. "It is a white man. It stinks. See! I choke it to death!"

The *taikomochi's* hands throttled the bundle realistically. The chain about Davies' neck began to feel tight.

Then Tatsu whirled and, bundle under his arm again, snatched up the end of the chain. "Dance, beast," he shrieked. "Dance! Dance!"

Davies solemnly raised and lowered his feet. Korogi, behind

his sandalwood stand, said sadly, "Once he was a man. His people, the Ainu, refused to cooperate. It is very sorrowful to us. I am glad," he said to Felipe, "that it is so different with you. Premier Tojo is also glad."

To emphasize the words, to prove that he spoke with the voice of Tojo and Japan, Korogi drew out a fan made of flexible metals, silver on one side, gold on the other. A war-fan. An Imperial war-fan. On the silver side shone a gold sun. The orb of the moon, in silver, was on the gleaming reverse.

Korogi fanned his hot cheeks with it.

What a story to repeat I could get out of this, thought Davies, as he continued to play bear. *If only I could get it started!*

He made himself think of this when the Japanese, at Tatsu's invitation, got on his back one after another. There were shrieks of laughter when the most drunken fell off, and when the "bear" was jabbed with pickle-forks from the stands.

The Filipino traitors had sobered and were aware of what the object lesson meant.

It was a full ten minutes before Tatsu, glancing at the quisling leader, said, "When he becomes hot and sweats, he stinks. Does he smell like an *Amerika-jin?*"

Damn him, worried Lew, *he's directing Felipe's attention to me. And when Felipe listens to my account of the execution of the flyers, he may begin to wonder what is under my beard. He may remember the officer who had to shave twice a day.*

It was something which had to be chanced because there was nothing to be done about it now. Nothing.

KOROGI SNAPPED the fan shut, bowed slightly, and opened it again.

"Perhaps you have heard lies about what took place when American flyers bombed children and hospitals in Tokyo," he said suavely. "However, while we Japanese are far too proud to refute such lies, this Ainu was an attendant at the executions at which the Americans acknowledged their guilt and begged for mercy. He has not sense enough to lie. From him," went on

Korogi gently, "you will hear the truth… the sort of thing which happens to anyone who is the enemy of Japan."

Korogi's meaning was perfectly clear to the traitors.

Everyone was staring at the "Ainu."

Then Felipe said, in halting Japanese, "*Doko ka mita yo omoimasu.* Somehow that black beard and those broad shoulders remind me—"

"The name permitted me is Koropok," broke in Davies, beginning his story. "I was ordered by my generous masters to attend the executions of cowardly white men who ignored the warnings of the minister of His Imperial Highness and deliberately fouled the sky above sacred Tokyo. These *Amerika-jin* demons…."

Only Tatsu was frowning; only Tatsu must be wondering why Koropok began the account, this time, before the order was given. Korogi and the Japanese were smiling. Felipe and his fellow traitors were listening closely.

Davies was able to relate the story so mechanically that he could think while he was speaking. Tatsu, for some reason unclear to Davies, was doubtful about the identity of the pariah; why? Felipe, the ex-houseboy, could identify Koropok as a member of the armed forces of the United States, if the Filipino's memory were properly jogged. Right now, Felipe was uncertain.

Add that together, thought Lew, nearing the end of the cruel story so beloved by the Japanese, *and what happened to the flyers will be sweetness and light as compared to what happens to me.* Worse than even that, Davies knew that it would mean the end of his mission, of an American being in Japan.

Outside, as he spoke, the chrysanthemums swayed under the dim lanterns. Here in the banquet room, the geisha continued exchanging bowls of saki with the guests. At the "honor" end of the room, Korogi, full of food and liquor and the heady feeling of controlling everyone in his sight, fanned himself contentedly.

Not once did Koropok give evidence of his inner disturbance but, *What am I to do?* Lew kept thinking. *What can I do?* Plans, he knew, were useless.

He was sure of only one thing: Tatsu intended somehow to strip him of his disguise: but why, why? There was no patriotism nor fanaticism in the warped jester. Was Tatsu counting on the possible reward? The adulation?

The little devil keeps going back to the old fable that there's a difference in oriental and occidental perspiration, was in Davies' head. That myth had been exploded by European scientists. By Germans, Lew had heard his doctor father remark; by Germans who had conducted a thorough series of tests in Japan.

He was at the end of the story. He and the other pariahs, he was saying, now dragged off the bodies of the cowardly white men....

Tatsu, this time, broke in just as he finished, jerking at Koropok's chain as he spoke. "There is one thing more, masters," said the *taikomochi*. "Please to wait. The best is last. I will show you, in a moment, the exact dying of an *Amerika-jin*. Oh, you will find it diverting! You will praise me—"

"Hurry, then," said Korogi. "I have a midnight appointment."

Tatsu yanked on the chain; Davies followed the jester out *at* the room.

The *taikomochi* walked down the corridor. The cloth-wrapped bundle was under his arm, and he seemed to be holding something in the same hand. Davies could not see what this was until the pair were in a small room, when Tatsu turned and faced him. Lew saw then that it was a knife, a long, thin-bladed one.

"I would kill you with it," snarled the ugly jester, "but it is too quick a way for you to die. Korogi will think of something better."

Davies blinked and shuffled his feet.

Tatsu's eyes were bright as obsidian. *He's just about half sane,* realized Davies; and then coldness crept up his legs. Tatsu had ripped open the bundle with the edge of the knife. From it fell the uniform of an American Army officer, a trophy brought to the house by some returned officer-guest. Davies saw the bullet-holes in the blouse.

"I am going to cut your hair, stinking white man," said Tatsu, with the knife held ready. "I am going to cut your beard. Ho! You have not fooled me! Did I not live with the *kwaikofujin* from Germany who knew the truth about sweat, even if the other Germans disagreed with him? Did I not live with him until he took my sister as a wife—and then left her! Did I not listen to you as you slept, and when you cried once, just once in sleep, you cried "*aaaaa*" as if you were choking, and not "*aaiii!*" as we cry. Oh, I heard the despoiler of my sister cry in that manner, when he was lonesome! I—"

Koropok mumbled meekly, "O *ki niia'nu.* I have somehow displeased you, master—I do not understand."

But Davies, as Tatsu gloated, savoring the moment to the full, understood only too well. In a uniform, with the beard hacked off, Felipe would recognize him instantly. Tatsu wanted a supreme vengeance, and would get it when a white man was identified as a spy.

He's got to gloat, thought Davies next. *He's a Jap. He can't help it. And he has everything figured out. He knows just how I'm to be bound, so I can't fight when he cuts my hair. But how does he intend to get me into the uniform? With the threat of the knife? Of course. The Nips think that threatening the Filipinos will keep them in line. They still think that the threat of having killed men who flew bombers will keep more bombers away.*

I've got it, Davies decided.

He stood perfectly quietly while Tatsu sidled up to him, the knife raised. The jester whispered, "I am going to put one little mark on you, dog. I myself wish to see the color of your blood, and hear you cry out—"

Davies smashed him under the stabbing arm.

The bear-chain jangled as Lew jumped forward after that

one fierce blow; but after that, as Davies' hands closed about the *taikomochi's* neck, there was no sound except the tinkling of a *samisen* and the mournful singing of a girl in the *machiai*. Tatsu died very quietly.

Davies picked up the thin-bladed knife and thrust it through the bearskin Ainu belt which was under his costume. Then, without delay, he shuffled out and back to the banquet room. He stood there, blinking foolishly until someone demanded to know what he wanted.

"*Taikomochi*-master requests aid," he said.

Korogi snapped, "Orders from a jester?"

Dropping to his knees, as if overwhelmed by words from the wielder of the war-fan, Koropok whimpered, "He prepares for a new dance. He asks that he who sits nearest you"—Felipe—"return with me, to give advice. Oh, please, honorable master, if I do not bring him, I will be beaten—"

"Even a jester has someone to whom he can give orders," chuckled Korogi. Turning to Felipe, he asked silkily, "Do you mind?"

Felipe, recognizing an order, could not mind.

Davies led the way, shuffling along and never turning when Felipe said, "Were you ever in Manila?" in English. He slid back the panel of the room where Tatsu lay and, cold as ice, brought down the knife.

The traitor jerked, constricted; the blow had gone deep and true. But, unlike Tatsu's dying, this time it was a bloody business.

Davies surveyed the bare room briefly. He moved Tatsu's body a little closer to Felipe's and, shivering, stabbed it twice. He rubbed the haft carefully, finally placing the knife near Felipe's hand. All O.K.—or the best he could do.

You've got to be a better actor than ever in your life, boy, Lew said to himself.

THIS TIME he pushed into the banquet room wildly, mouthing Ainu words, "*Ticksha hok'yak! Bin' cuspo!*" and waving his bare arms. At first the Japanese and quislings stared at him, as at an animal escaped from a cage, while the girls who had known Koropok as the gentlest of persons now cowered. Davies kept on waving his arms.

"Seize him," said Korogi briefly. "He has tasted saki."

"Oh, no, supreme master! No! I—"

The Ainu's arms were pinned to his side by a half dozen Japanese.

"What is the matter with you?" demanded Korogi, slapping Davies' cheek with the fan.

"Oh, master," moaned Koropok, "your guest accompanied me. Oh, yes. But when he stepped into the room—oh, master, Tatsu shouted at him, and…."

"And what?" yelled Korogi. "What?"

"Tatsu shouted, *'Kurombo!* Vile nigger!' And they fight—"

Korogi himself rushed out of the room, followed by Japanese and Filipinos; Koropok stood where he was.

The minutes passed leadenly. What was going to happen next? The quislings, filled with Japanese propaganda concerning supposed American treatment of Negroes, were not going to like this. Nor would Korogi, Tojo's right hand, like it either. *And if I get the chance,* thought Lew, *I can make you more unhappy. If I'm not killed.*

It was a full five minutes before the men returned. Davies could see how the Filipinos were now in a group. Korogi came squarely up to him, and seized the bear-chain, almost choking Koropok.

"What did you see?" he hissed.

Koropok said, swallowing pain, "Master, they fought."

"Who struck first?"

If I say, the guest—Felipe—he will be less on the spot than if a Japanese not only insulted the Filipinos but also struck the first blow. But I came to the Yoshiwara with a purpose, and that's what I've got to fulfill.

"I do not know," said Koropok. "They fought. I ran."

"Did the guest strike the *taikomochi* when the guest *thought* he heard an insulting word?" asked Korogi slyly. "Was that it?"

"They fought," mumbled Koropok again, "I ran."

Korogi flung the iron chain against Davies' face. Blood began to trickle down Lew's lacerated cheek.

Someone was whispering to the minister, "Could we not announce that the pariah dog killed them both, and execute him?"

"You are as big a fool as he," retorted Korogi, He was searching for an answer to the affair; he found it in typical Japanese fashion. Whirling on the Filipinos, he shouted, "A lesson is to be learned from this. You have observed that a Japanese jester is a better fighter than a Filipino soldier. In the future, never forget our utter superiority!"

Korogi snapped open his war-fan brusquely.

"The entertainment will continue," he announced. "I will order fresh geisha. I desire you to enjoy yourselves further."

Koropok shuffled and scratched his head.

"Go away," cried Korogi. "You have had too much to drink. You saw nothing! Did you see anything, Ainu?"

Koropok lifted his head slightly. He blinked. Then he allowed his mouth to open a little, as if he were smiling.

"Even such an animal has a little intelligence," grunted Korogi. "I do not intend to have him say anything which might be in the least at variance with the Imperial official report."

The *hakoya* Koropok said nothing about the deaths at the *machiai*. But when, with Tatsu gone, he was permitted an hour a day for himself, he wandered out of the Yoshiwara and, when questioned, admitted that he saw personages when engaged in his duty. When pressed for details by the always curious temple sweepers, clerks, and professional beggars who patronized the cheapest food-stands, Koropok would allow them to draw him out, reluctantly.

"I have seen," he would admit, "a great person give the Imperial war-fan to—a geisha. I have seen her dance with it. Yes."

Venom. The subtlest of poisons. More than enough to widen
narrow eyes, to make teeth click together. This was utter sacri-
lege. Oh, it was something to cause patriotic men to wonder
about such a leader!

Korogi's forced resignation was handed to Tojo before two
weeks had passed. A tremendous amount of face was lost, and
the rumblings of it were heard clear down to Manila.

The smoking of a filched cigarette, from the case of a Japanese
colonel who had stolen it at Shanghai, was Lew's only possible
celebration. It was an American cigarette, the finest Lieutenant
Davies had ever smoked.

FLIGHT WITHOUT WINGS

IT WAS a hot, white noon, with the sun so directly over-head that there were no shadows in the licensed quarter of Tokyo. Number Nineteen, with its tiled roof and red-lacquered doorway, was as silent as the other guest houses. What few geisha were not at the baths beyond the walls at this hour were sleeping.

A single figure moved in the streets, a wrinkled old vendor who hawked chipped ice which, when flavored with cinnamon oil and sugared red bean pulp, was believed an antidote for heat. Little puffs of dust rose as he walked along a thoroughfare no longer immaculate. In these days of war, none but men and women as old as he were available for sweeping; and the presence of many cigarette butts, orange peels, and shrimp heads proved that their brooms were not vigorously applied. The litter also proved that the Yoshiwara had been crowded on the previous night.

"*Yukinohana!*" the vendor cried hoarsely to closed doors and screens. "Ice with sugar! *Kori-azuki!* Very cool and cheap!"

As he looked down at the melting ice in its cotton-padded container, he swore under his breath. Then his head lifted at the sound of an opening door. It was at Number Nineteen, and he shuffled toward it.

Planes thrummed to the north, sweeping nearer. The vendor knew that they must be Japanese, because *Amerika-jin* pilots feared to fly over Japan, knowing what a miserable death awaited them when they fell to earth.

The planes in flight made the ice-vendor oblivious to noises behind him. There, at an intersection nearer the outer gate, a strutting major had appeared, followed by twenty or more men in close formation. Although the men were being marched in a column of fours, as if conscripts, they were junior officers, pilots in the Imperial Air Force. All were young except the major. He was fat and gray, but there was more spring to his walk.

The vendor was being rapidly overtaken. He had eyes only for the open door at Nineteen, which might mean trade. When near enough, he recognized the figure in the doorway as that of the Ainu *hakoya*, the pariah servant who had been engaged

Knocking the nearer of the astonished soldiers off balance, Davies wrested his bayonet from him and ran him through, while Holmes with sudden fury hurled himself, bound as he was, against the other.

by Suriga, the manager, when no one else sufficiently able-bodied could be found to perform the arduous work at the guest house.

The *hakoya*, without having seemed interested in either vendor or advancing officers, knelt down. With interwoven willow twigs he began to scrub the entrance to Nineteen. He was a short, dark man. He was young, but his face was bearded, as all Ainu are bearded.

His police permit, issued when he had first arrived in Tokyo

"The Amerika-jin,*" the major told the young
officers, "are as soft as* isu-karemu. *They
will melt away before your bullets."*

from a northern province, stated him to be Koropok. The permit allowed him, as a pariah, to repair footwear, labor in slaughter-houses, or bury the dead after executions. He had become a servant here through the sly influence of Suriga, who thereby not only obtained a strong and obedient person, accustomed to degrading work, but one who did not dare to complain when the small pay was not forthcoming.

Koropok the Ainu was actually Llewelyn Davies, a lieuten-ant in Army Air Forces—heavy-set, swarthy, and black-haired like his Welsh ancestors. His disguise had been successful not only because of his appearance, but because he had lived with his father, a doctor, among the Ainu. He had been in Japan since the attack on Manila, and had carried out his initial orders, which had been to direct American bombers to objectives in Tokyo. He would be tortured before he was executed if the Japanese penetrated his disguise. In the meantime, he was doing his best to cause the Nipponese all the trouble he could; and a guest house, where high officers were entertained, was a fine place to hear the sort of things which enabled him to make plans.

He scrubbed away with his twigs, dipping them into a bucket of water, when the ice-vendor stopped in front of him. The Japanese major, Davies also saw, was about to order his men to halt at Nineteen.

THIS WAS something new. Guests were never expected until late afternoon. Could it mean the Nips knew him, at last, for what he was? Were they here, in accordance with their damnable fool-'em-politely-before-torturing-'em *bushido* code, to escort him off? It was entirely possible. The thought chilled Davies, in spite of the heat. He knew that what had happened to Americans, in prison camps, at Yawata, Zentsuji, Moji, about which Japanese officers in their cups boasted so happily, would be just practice for what would happen to him.

Davies managed a casual glance at the major. The officer who was in command was staring down at the "pariah." No doubt of it.

I'll bash in his head with the bucket the instant I'm sure, Lew decided. *Maybe I can get a couple more of the bandy-legged apes.*

But he had to be sure, so he continued with his scrubbing.

The vendor, throat dry, since he dared not lick at the ice and lose any of the miserable profit, croaked, "Ainu dog, go inside and inform the maids that I am here with fine flower-of-snow to sell them."

Davies looked up. He intended to play out his part as the *hakoya,* although the major's face was far too grim for a man who had come here to be entertained. He said, in his clipped Ainu dialect, "I dare not go inside until the cleaning has been done, lord," and then ducked, as if to escape a blow.

"What?" the vendor screamed. "You refuse?"

The man on the steps pleaded, "Honorable vendor, do not strike me. All of the maids," the pariah added, "are at the baths."

"Some must be in the house," insisted the vendor. Then, still unaware of the soldiers behind him, he shrilled, "How dare you refuse me? I have four sons in the Army! All dead except one! Matsuju was killed in the sky! Kuoka died in flames! Kadzune also died in the air—"

The major reached forward, cupped his hand furiously over the vendor's mouth, and then gave him such a kick that the old man went sprawling in the street. Tray, bottles, and ice crashed down. Cinnamon oil ran over the dust like blood.

"You lie," the major snarled. "Any sons such as an ignorant fool like you might have sired would not have sufficient intelligence to be pilots. I doubt if you have sons at all. Because of such words as you have unpatriotically uttered," the irate officer ended with ominous truth, "you could be shot."

Davies glanced around carefully. The danger that he might be under suspicion was not yet gone; the major might have become enraged because an American had heard a bit of how the fighting was going, and how Nip flyers were being shot

The wrinkled old ice-vendor shrilled, "How dare you refuse me? I have four sons in the Army! All are dead except one!"

down. Then what he saw on the faces of the lieutenants gave him a better understanding of the major's rage. Why, the yellow-bellies were afraid!

These babies know what'll happen to them in combat, thought Lew. *I'll bet,* his knowledge of the Japanese told him, *that the major's been ordered to bring 'em to Nineteen to build up their morale.*

Nothing could be more typically Japanese, Davies knew. Someone high in the Imperial government had decided that the flyers needed a big celebration before being sent to fight This would not only build up their fighting spirit, according to Japanese reasoning, but would show them the pleasures which awaited them when they returned as heroes. But the pilots and bombardiers here, Lew guessed, were remembering how few airmen ever came back to Japan. It would take a lot of fancy food and geisha and saki, or Scotch from Singapore, to make them forget what happened when Nip flyers met up with P40s, to say nothing of the ships which were whispered about in Nineteen. New ships. Fast as hell. Armed with cannon.

The major whirled on his column, staring grimly at the lieutenants. One of the flying officers was looking down at the cinnamon oil, which gleamed in the hot sun like a pool of blood.

"Lieutenant Ogawa!" the major said sharply. "A soldier of Japan sees only that which he desires to see! To me," said the veteran of actions against China, "that spot is neither oil of cinnamon nor something which might be blood—unless it be the blood of the enemy. That spot is a fortunate omen. It is the sun!"

Right in the dust, too, thought Lew, his grin covered by his beard and his bent head as he scrubbed away. *Right where it belongs.*

"Lieutenant Ogawa," ordered the major, "sing!"

Shoulders squared, the thin lieutenant had no need to ask what song the major meant. Without pause, but in none too steady voice, he began:

Umi yuka ba mizuku kabane,
Yama yuka ba kusa-musa kabane,
O Kimino!
He ni koso shiname
Nodoka niwa shinaji!

The major, unsatisfied with the nervous rendition, puffed himself up. "Let us all sing," he commanded, stiffening to attention even more than before, so that his belt creaked where it cut across his paunch.

Screens were slid open, and the heads of girls not at the baths appeared as the column obediently shrilled the words and monotonous minor tune of the patriotic song, with the fat major singing at the top of his lungs.

Give my corpse to the water.
If on sea I strive;
Give my corpse to the mountain,
If on land I strive;
Oh, holy Emperor, for thee alone I live,
And never die in vain!"

As the din died away in the stifling air, it came to Davies with renewed force that some of these airmen didn't like the idea of dying. What all of them would have preferred, Lew decided coldly, was to bomb defenseless cities and villages, or slip up on one or two P40s when the odds were fifty-to-one in their favor. But those days were over. These babies were beginning to learn what they were up against, and they didn't care for it.

"Now," said Major Taksei, rubbing his hands together, "you are prepared to enjoy yourselves here. You are in a proper frame of mind. What is wrong with you, Lieutenant Ogawa," he went on, like a dog refusing to give up his bone, "is the time you spent in America, learning to be of assistance to Japan. I think," Taksei chuckled, as a sign to the lieutenants that he was about to say something very funny, "that while away from Japan you must have eaten too much *isu-karemu.* The cold juice of cow-animals ate away some of the courageous iron in your belly. *Isu-karemu!* Oh, what a horrible thing to eat!"

And how I'd like a big gob of it, thought Lew, *on a scorcher like today!*

The old ice-vendor had come to his knees, but dared not move off lest he attract the attention of the major. All that remained intact of his outfit was the tray. Everything else was broken.

"THE *Amerika-jin,*" announced Major Taksei, "are as soft as *isu-karemu.* Up in the sky, they will melt away before your bullets. Oh, you will be forced to chase them in their inferior planes, because they will not face you. They have no more courage than—than this Ainu dog."

To emphasize the comparison, he pushed the *hakoya* called Koropok expertly with his foot. Davies fell sidewise. The bucket of dirty water was spilled, to splatter on the major's highly polished boots.

Damn it, thought Lew, as the major belabored the shaggy head of the house-servant with small fists, *why did I do that? But did I mess him!*

He whimpered, *"Dan' sam' ni mosh'wake...* Oh, pardon and forgive, master! Oh, do not beat me! Please do not beat me!"

"It is like this," Taksei, breathless, said when he gave the pariah a final clout, "that the *Amerika-jin* beg for mercy. I say this because I know. I saw them being herded from Bataan. I have seen them where they are imprisoned." He stopped suddenly, as if a notion had come to him, and then smiled from ear to ear, making the little clucking sounds which showed that he was pleased with himself. "I myself have seen that magnificent sight of a broken enemy," announced Major Taksei, "and you shall see it also,"

Davies guessed what the major had in mind. Taksei intended to show the lieutenants that they need not fear combat with such men as the prisoners. Japan had used identical reasoning ever since the days when American seamen, shipwrecked in sailing-ship days, were caged and displayed in order to prove to the people of Japan that foreigners were no more dangerous than animals.

Suriga, manager of Nineteen, had been peeking from the cover of a screen. Now that the major was obviously in good humor and laughing loudly, Suriga believed he could safely put in his appearance.

He was all bows as he stepped through the doorway. "*O agari nasai yo,*" he invited servilely. "Please enter to avoid the heat."

"You have been slow in appearing to do us honor," the major grumbled, not bothering to return Suriga's bows. "You are also unpatriotic. You have permitted your maids to go to the bath house to enjoy themselves, when they should have been here, ready to entertain our brave officers."

"I will order them to return at once," Suriga promised. Although he had seen exactly what had taken place, he continued, "If that fool of an ice-vendor had not fallen over his own clumsy feet, I should buy his wares-of-coolness for your enjoyment. Oh, how I regret his clumsiness! I—"

"Shaved ice," said the major, about to lead the way inside, "is no drink for fighting men. It is too similar to *isu-karemu.*" He glared at Lieutenant Ogawa, who had lived in America. "I ask you," he demanded, "of what good is *isu-karemu?*"

Davies knew that the lieutenant was supposed to say, "It is vile and worthless, and not fit for the men of Japan." But there was a curious glitter in the young officer's black eyes, and for a moment Davies wondered if the pilot were about to rebel against this goading which caused him to lose face.

Then Ogawa said, "If I had a captive American pilot or bombardier, and it were terribly hot, and he were thirsty, I would let him see *isu-karemu,* of which all Americans are fond. Then I would throw it in the dust!"

"That is excellent," applauded Major Taksei. "Under such circumstances, I would not even object if you ate the *isu-kare-mu,* very slowly and as if with enjoyment, so the American

would suffer more greatly. Oh, the things I saw when we captured them at Bataan! I have hopes for you, Lieutenant Ogawa!"

Ogawa bowed gratefully.

The major, glancing down at the ice-vendor, began clucking
again, as he had when a previous notion had come to him. "Keep
that old fool here until I want him," Taksei told Suriga. "You,"
he said to Ogawa, "may have your wish sooner than you suppose!
Now, let us all go in and have some cold *biru*."

"Beer?" asked Suriga. "That is difficult to obtain—"

"And it had better be cold," snapped Taksei. "We will have
some bottles while you send for your maids."

Suriga nodded. Then he said, "Koropok! Go and put on a
house jacket. When you have done this, come to me for orders."

"Koropok" looked up dumbly, and the manager repeated what
he had said. Davies slowly placed the twig brush in the bucket.
He stood up. As he shuffled, pariah-fashion, around toward the
rear of the house, officer after officer took a kick at him. Major
Taksei was glad to see that the lieutenants' morale was improv-
ing.

Lew, in the tiny hole where he spent his few sleeping hours,
made no effort to hurry. By the time he reported to the principal waiting-room of Nineteen, a place of cool green mats with
flowers in a bronze pot in the alcove and one *kakemono* above,
the maids who had been sleeping were already serving the
officers with Nunebeki beer. The major had already emptied
several bottles, between which, to show his strength, he had
swallowed cups of Scotch. His round face, in the heat, shone
with perspiration, and the maid who knelt beside him kept
wiping it off with a cotton towel. The top button of his tunic
was unfastened.

Suriga, bent almost double at Taksei's left, beckoned to
Davies, who shuffled across the mats. As Lew came to the
manager's side, he heard the major say, "Yes, we will do something about this shortage of *biru*. I can help you." Taksei's voice
lowered, but Davies heard, "Those little boats, you know!

Perhaps the very little boat which brought you this excellent beer leaves again tonight for more—"

Then Taksei saw the servant Koropok.

FACE FLAMING, the major shrieked, "What are you doing here, cow-face?" and put a hand on his holster.

"He has come for his instructions," soothed Suriga and gave them instantly before the major could take further action, because another servant as sturdy and stupid as this one could not easily be found.

"Go to the bath house where you have been before," the manager said urgently. "Inform the honorable oldest-maid to bring everyone here."

"*Watakushi... n' wa' wak'rim'senu,*" mumbled Davies. "Somebody will beat me. I am not sure what you order, lord. I—"

"Where is this place?" demanded Taksei.

"Not far," promised Suriga. "The maids will soon be here—"

"*Where* is it?"

"Just beyond the street Kyomachi, honorable Major."

"Hmm." The major glared up at the pariah. "How many words can you read, Ainu?" he asked. "Come! Tell me!"

"Read, great lord?" whimpered Davies. "Words? Oh, please do not beat me again. I am not able to read words."

Taksei took out a notebook and pen. Whistling, he wrote on one of the pages. He grinned when he read over what he put down, tore out the sheet, and folded it several times. After sealing it with a *sen* postage stamp, occupation variety, he wrote on the outside also.

"Explain to the stupid animal," he said to Suriga, "that after he has summoned the maids, he must stop at Shoyuji Prison, and deliver this message to the commandant. It is near Kyomachi, as you know."

Taksei dropped the note to the floor. Suriga picked it up humbly, and then let it fall again. With the formalities observed, the manager said, "Koropok, go to the bath house. Speak with the oldest-maid. On your return, present this paper to the soldier at the gate of the place-of-prisoners. He will conduct you to the personage to whom the paper is directed. Go quickly."

Davies cowered away from the note. "I am afraid," he whined. "Beat me, but do not make me go! If I go to such a place, I will be forced to remain there!"

"You see?" Taksei shouted to the lieutenants. "Even a dog of an Ainu understands what it means to be inside one of our prison camps! That is way to scare the *Amerika-jin,* believe me! Why, all we had to do was behead a few of their bomber pilots, and they have been afraid to attack Tokyo again! Fear! That is the big weapon! And we know how to use it!" He began to sing a snatch of a Korean song.

> *Whul whul na-n'un goigol sai-to!*
> *Ta je-jak-i itkut man-'n*

Then he shouted, "And we have taught *them* fear, I can tell you!"

Suriga repeated to Koropok what must be done, and he did it so kindly and so often that Davies guessed the manager hoped to profit from illicit beer brought into Tokyo from the outside. When Lew, head low, finally mumbled that he would do exactly as ordered, lieutenant Ogawa, at the major's half-drunken command, was teaching the others an American song. They would sing it again, together, the major shouted, when the war was won—just as he sang a Korean song as proof of the fact that he had assisted in conquering that once-arrogant country.

Davies backed out of the room. Since he used the rear doorway at all times, it seemed safe to stop at his hole, now that everyone was waiting on the guests. The outside of the note merely said that it was to be delivered by an Ainu to the commandant, by orders of Takao Taksei, major. The poorly gummed stamp was easy to slip off. The message was so informal that Davies knew the senior officers were friends. It requested that by four in the afternoon, when the day was hottest, American

A "Damn!" was jerked involuntarily from Davies as a hand suddenly jammed his head into the basket's filth.

officers, pilots and bombardiers be in the Shovuji Prison yard so that Taksei's charges would be able to look at them.

Taksei had written it this way: "*Tanoshimi ni omoiashita ni...* I am looking forward with pleasure to seeing the American devils frying in the sun, thanks to you. However, my dear companion, I promise to provide a little unusual entertainment of my own. It is all for a patriotic purpose."

Davies' mouth was a hard, thin line under his black beard. American soldiers were to be tortured, in order to boost the morale of Japs! There was obviously nothing he could do about it; but it came to him, as he wasted a precious moment before starting, that people at home ought to know about it.

Could I get away and tell 'em? thought Lew. *Could I?* Everything which America meant to the gaunt lieutenant swirled up to blind him, to tighten his throat. How about the little boat— it must be some sort of power craft—which slipped into the bay with forbidden beer and luxuries?

There was no time to figure anything out. Davies paused long enough to get the bit of sharpened lead from his bearskin Ainu charm-bag and make an accurate copy of Taksei's signature on a scrap of newspaper, before leaving. Outside, he shuffled to the shaded pit where the tightly woven garbage baskets swarmed with shining green flies. He carried, as the excuse to come to the single place where he believed it safe to hide his scrap of paper with its signature, the crumpled wad of newspaper from which he had torn the piece.

Lew went through the formality of lifting a lid, to drop the newspaper inside, when, without previous sound or warning, he was shoved and tripped. A "Damn!" was jerked involuntarily from him. As he fell, a hand jammed his head down into the basket's filth and held it there.

Both of Davies' hands flashed into desperate action. His right, which was in the wide basket along with his head, managed to scrape fishbones into the crumpled newspaper; his left, on the ground, slid the folded scrap under the basket which only he filled and emptied.

After the one instinctive ejaculation, Davies became Koropok the pariah again, allowing whomever had slipped up on him to bang his head around at will and finally, to haul him to his feet.

IT WAS Ogawa, the lieutenant who had lived in the States. He was, Lew saw, about three-quarters drunk and four-quarters nasty. Worse, he was suspicious. His eyes glittered and his red tongue ran over his lips.

"Do not deny what you said," Ogawa hissed.

What did I say? Davies wondered uneasily. As Koropok, he looked frightened out of his few wits. He didn't remember saying anything. So he said now, hoping Ogawa would give him some inkling of why he was suspicious, "Whatever I said, lord, was to honor all lords and masters—"

The Japanese flying officer was staring at him. The drunken face had become horribly shrewd.

Does he see behind the beard? thought Davies. *He has lived in America. This isn't too funny. What's he going to do?*

Ogawa snapped in English, "You said 'Damn!'"

No muscle of Davies' face moved. He merely stood as before. *It didn't work, did it?* he thought, watching Ogawa's discomfiture at failure of the trick. Davies' reply was ready; but, as

Koropok, he waited for the Japanese to speak in a language which a pariah could understand.

It was a full half minute before Ogawa said, this time in Japanese, "Where did you learn such a word as you used? Tell me, or I will beat you!"

Davies said humbly, "Oh, lord, I said only *'Dam' or' ga i'*, to tell myself that whatever a lord does to me is his right."

He's thinking that's actually what he heard, Lew was pretty certain, as Ogawa muttered to himself. *It is just about what a pariah would have said.* Then, to make doubly sure that the Nipponese' last remaining doubts would be dissolved in anger, to make Ogawa forget everything else, Davies said, "Please, lord, I must hurry away. I must obey the orders of my master and your master."

"Suriga is your master," Ogawa howled, "but I have no master except the Emperor. A major is a higher officer. How dare you say such a thing?"

Davies did not reply.

"Wipe your face," commanded Ogawa. "Use your jacket! Clean off your beard! Get the garbage-filth off your cheeks!"

As Lew did as he was told, he mumbled, "Oh, lord, I would have cleaned myself before taking the paper to the lord at the *Amerika-jin* prison—"

"That is not what I meant," grated Ogawa. He waited until Davies' face and beard were less nauseating. Then he grabbed the beard with one hand, yanking at it, while with his other he slapped the American again and again.

The Japanese was working himself up into a fanatical rage. He snarled, "When I shoot down an American pilot, this is what I will do to him! I will degrade him! I will pull out every hair on his head one by one, and then behead him!" He gave Davies one last furious slap, and then doubled his fist. Lew waited until the drunken, infuriated Japanese swung. He dared not counter, although the slanting chin was a beautiful target. He ducked instead, and Ogawa sprawled over the garbage basket. It overturned and Lew had all he could do to refrain from picking it up and slamming it down on the head of the Japanese.

His own head was whirling. He could, he knew, go inside and report to Suriga how the lieutenant had assaulted him; Ogawa would be punished, but so would Koropok. It would serve no purpose. Davies' orders were to do only such things as would make trouble for Japan. *But I won't forget you,* Lew promised.

He could taste sweat on his lips, and the taste of decaying fish from the basket. It was a long way from being ice cream.

The front street shimmered and blazed in sunlight. Davies could hear the nasal singing inside Nineteen, and the shouts of the men. Their visit to Shoyuji Prison, at four, would precede a wild evening at Nineteen when they returned.

Near the entrance to the licensed quarter were soldiers and sailors, examining the girls in the showrooms barred with wooden lattices. When a man selected a girl, she would hand him her long bamboo pipe and, smoking it, he would follow her inside. Saki stands were open here, and stalls where crushed fish and taro sent up their unpleasant odor in the heat.

Davies received the usual number of pushes and kicks, and again and again wiped spittle from his jacket. He was passed through the gate and hurried toward the proper bath house. A dozen wild ideas passed through his head as he thought of the Americans in the prison camp, but not one of these schemes was worth the damn which had come so close to breaking his disguise. What could a single man do? Why, even if all of the fellows at Shoyuji could get away, they would be tracked down within an hour. If only people at home could know what the Japanese were doing to prisoners....

The facts should be told by a soldier who had experienced what Japanese *bushido* was like. A prisoner ought to tell about it, a prisoner who had been held in Tokyo. How could such a person get away? Davies didn't know.

He himself, a familiar and despised figure, might manage to escape, but that was different. He knew his way around. He could get to the smuggler's boat and, after taking care of the man or men aboard, do his own navigating. And, in some way or other, he might put Taksei's signature to use.

Lew let the notion carry him away as he walked nearer Kyomachi, allowing himself to think what it would be like to be home. Home! His own people. Friends. Cigarettes. Dinner. Ice cream. Talk. He wouldn't play around long; just long enough to get the hang of the new ships.

I'd like to fly one of those babies the Nips call the forked-tailed devils, he told himself. *I'd like to be over Tokyo in one.*

He swallowed hard, gave a twitch to his bearskin belt, and approached the bath house. His orders were to remain in Japan, damaging the Japanese in every possible way, right here where the conceited sons were positive not one American lived outside of a prison. Orders were orders. But even so, when a man had been here since Manila's fall, he couldn't help but think of home.

CHAPTER II

HE REACHED the bath house, and shuffled inside. The cashier, knowing him and his errand, waved him on to deliver his message.

As "Koropok" walked along a steamy corridor, girls in loose bath gowns passed him, having already bathed; other girls, carrying towels and stark naked, waited a turn at the tub. Hoping that Nineteen's maids would be finished and dawdling in the dressing room, Davies continued past where bathing was in progress, past where dumpy bodies were being polished with rice-bran bags, to the cooler room where many maids and women sipped cherry-flower water and giggled as they listened to Honorable Oldest-Maid's stories.

Koropok, delivering the order from Suriga, broke in on the *neisan's* account of a girl and man who had performed *shinju,* the suicide for love. He shook his head at the demand that he

*There in the glaring, burning sunlight, Davies
saw the American flying officers who had been
taken prisoner. One of them with red hair cought
his eye—could that be Rusty Holmes?"*

carry the maids' cloth bags back to Nineteen. When the *neisan*,
angered at the refusal, said that she would have the bath house
manager compel an Ainu dog of a pariah to do as she said,
Davies was forced to tell her that Suriga had entrusted him
with a message which must be delivered immediately to the
place where foreign soldiers were imprisoned.

In Davies' ears, as he left, was the venom of the women. "If
I had my way," a maid called Yoshiko from Nineteen said, "there
would be no *Amerika-jin* prisoners. Let all be beheaded, as were
the barbarians who dared to bomb Tokyo! I myself," the girl
cried, "would delight in plunging a knife into the heart of an
Amerika-jin. I would consider it to be my duty!"

It was hotter than ever outside. Davies guessed the time as
being between one and two as he shuffled along Kyomachi; and
as he walked, he began to plan. Whether or not he could get
an American out of Shoyuji Prison probably depended on too
many things to be workable, but he intended to check carefully on each one of them. First of all, it depended upon his
ability to forge Taksei's signature and write a message in the
exact manner of the major. Secondly, it depended on the attitude

of the commandant. Thirdly, Davies had to determine the exact location of the beer-smugglers' boat. And, lastly, he had to *know* a prisoner, or two, or three. They must be men who could handle a power boat's engine, and one of them had to know navigation.

Would the commandant send a whole squad to guard a couple of prisoners? Davies wondered. He didn't think so. The Nips figured that one Japanese was superior to a dozen unarmed Americans. *But my orders,* Lew remembered, *are that under no circumstances am I to risk detection except for a major accomplishment.*

Then, as he saw the ten-foot plank boards of Shoyuji Prison, he grinned in his beard. Perhaps this also might be possible.

Two infantrymen were on guard at the prison gate. The spectacle of an Ainu, a pariah, approaching them was more than enough to bring their rifles pointing at Davies. He held out the message; and while one guard went behind him, pricking his jacket with the bayonet, the other guard snatched the paper. He read swiftly, then tooted on his whistle. The corporal who strutted out grabbed the message away from the private just as the latter had taken it from Davies.

The corporal drew his revolver. He walked behind Davies. "Go in the direction I indicate," he said, and prodded Lew through the gate. "Walk slowly," the corporal warned. "One fast step and I blow you apart."

Davies obeyed.

For some twenty feet there was a plank board fence on either side of the four-foot-wide runway. At the end was another guard post, manned by six soldiers and a machine gun. As Lew passed through it, the sun seemed more violent after the shade of the runway. On either side now was a five-foot barbed-wire fence, obviously electrified as the Japanese had learned to do to protect themselves in Formosa from the natives who so hated them, and with such good cause. Behind the wires were low wooden barracks; between barracks and fences were open spaces, prison yards, on which the summer sun beat down fiercely.

The yard to Davies' right was completely empty. He guessed instantly that it was for privates and noncoms, and that they were earning their two and a half cents a day by laboring on the docks, in the shipyards, at ironworks—whether they wanted to work or not. Davies knew only too well, from the things he had overheard at Nineteen, what happened to men who became too exhausted to continue.

In the other yard, to the left, in the glaring, burning sunlight, were prisoners in ragged dungarees—officers, bearded, thin to emaciation and doing nothing. Just sitting—sitting in the sun, the blazing white sun, and brushing flies from their hands and faces and bandages.

Flies hung like silvery-green gauze in the stifling air. Davies could hear the buzzing, like a high and distant flight of planes; and where the flies were thickest, shimmering like silk, was the infirmary.

Davies' eyes were no longer those of a terrified pariah. They were unnaturally bright, fever-bright. In his head was, *Damn them, damn them, damn them!* and it was not the flies which he cursed.

A prisoner with red hair, face concealed beneath a red stubble, caught Davies' eye. He dared not stare; but wasn't it Holmes? Rusty Holmes? While Lew, walking almost too slowly to satisfy the corporal, tried to identify the bomber-navigator who had been in Manila, another prisoner stood up, thrashed with flailing arms at the biting torment of the flies, and then ran toward the scant border of early afternoon shade at the barracks' edge.

A Japanese bayonet sent him staggering back into the sun.

L E W ' S   T E E T H bit deeply into his lip, but he walked shufflingly ahead like the pariah he impersonated. He could see the red-haired prisoner's hands double to fists. *I mustn't let him be shot,* Davies thought swiftly. *It's Rusty, all right.*

A quick glance told Lew that all the guards' eyes were on the man with the flaming hair. The corporal, behind Davies, must also be watching Holmes.

"Eyes in the boat, Rusty," called Lew. "Hold everything. It's Davies."

The corporal's gun didn't explode. Guards peered this way and that in the blinding sun, trying to see who had cried out. Rusty Holmes' hands remained clenched. A shiver ran through him, but he didn't turn his head.

A guard, unable to tell who had raised his voice above the permitted whisper, began to beat one of the prisoners.

"Damn them," Davies' lips formed. "Damn them to hell."

Inside the commandant's office a fan buzzed. A captain of Major Taksei's age sat at a desk, listening to his aide read the infirmary report. When he saw Davies, he said, "He looks almost like officers of the Royal Welsh—" as, with a plump hand he accepted the message from the saluting corporal.

A broad grin spread over his face as he read. He chuckled to his aide, "Major Taksei! Oh, what a clever joker he is! I can tell you stories about him, when we were in Korea… And now, with a single stroke, he will use Americans to kill Americans! How subtle! With one arrangement he will degrade prisoners and instill new courage in our pilots! I would do anything," the captain ended, "to comply with a request from my old friend and superior."

While the captain brushed the characters in reply to Taksei's note, Davies listened to the fan. It buzzed like the flies.

"We must be ready for the major by four," the captain said to his aide, folding the sheet and handing it to the corporal. "There are prisoners in the infirmary," snarled the captain, "who are being too kindly treated. Have them in the yard. If the *Amerika-jin* prisoner doctor protests, inform him that I am considering removing him from the hospital entirely. That will silence him."

He shot a fat finger at Davies.

"If you delay by one small moment in returning to the honorable major," roared the captain, "I will fry the last ounce of fat off of you here in the sun. Do you hear? And when you are dead I will flay you, and make boots out of your hide. You will wish that you were an *Amerika-jin!*"

It was not necessary for Davies to simulate trembling. He was shaking, though with deep anger, not with fear.

They've got to know at home, thought Lew. *Even if they won't believe such things are possible, they've got to be told.*

He could think of nothing else all the way back to Nineteen.

A hundred duties awaited him, from the moment he delivered the captain's reply. Every girl, kitchen-maid as well as returned geisha, was engaged in entertaining the lieutenants. "Koropok! Hot water! Koropok! You are slower than an American bomber coming back to Tokyo! Koropok! Koropok!"

The matting in a room was ruined by spilled tea. Koropok replaced it. The charcoal on which to broil bits of fish was consumed. Koropok ran for more. A pilot howled for ice, and Koropok was sent to find a vendor. The lieutenant desired to place ice around a bottle of beer, as he understood the Americans did, so that he could practice what he would do when

Washington was captured. Major Taksei shouted for this and for that, but kept an eye on his watch. He was here on duty.

Davies began to doubt whether some of the lieutenants would be able to walk to Shoyuji Prison, and *rikisha,* in these times, were difficult to obtain. Ogawa, in particular, seemed so drunk and sleepy that his maid—who was Yoshiko, the pudgy girl who wanted American blood, had pillowed his head in her lap.

A dozen times Koropok was sent to Suriga's office. He knew, on his fifth visit, where the power boat which smuggled luxuries to the capitol was docked. Suriga was a careful manager. He wrote everything down, leaving nothing to chance.

Suddenly, chillingly, as Davies straightened up, he saw that the girl's eyes had opened. She was staring at him open-mouthed. She had seen him with the ink-pot and brush!

Bit by bit, Davies did his planning. He believed it would work, and it would be a real pleasure for him to do it. One thing remained to be solved: how, if prisoners escaped from Shoyuji Prison, could he remain undetected as the person who had engineered it?

He remembered his orders. He believed that information about the treatment of American prisoners in Japan warranted his own detection, arrest and execution—and he was not able to think of any way to prevent this from happening.

"Koropok! Where are you? Oh, how the stupid animal stinks! Wash yourself, Koropok! How you sweat! Koropok! Koropok!"

Then it was twenty minutes to four, and Major Taksei gathered his lieutenants. Some needed support, even after their faces were repeatedly washed, and they were strongly dosed with green tea in which chickweed had been infused.

Ogawa, however, was so weakened by the eating of frozen cow's milk, Major Taksei said, that the pilot would never awaken until morning. Taksei intended to recommend that Ogawa be ordered into the infantry, and would have suggested a more severe punishment for his not being able to go with the others save for the fact that it was Ogawa who had spoken of offering *isu-karemu* to the Americans in the broiling sun, and then throwing the filthy stuff into the dust of the prison yard.

Of course they had none of this *isu-karemu*, but Ogawa, before saki had made him forget his duties, had told how shaved ice could be pressed together and colored pink or brown so that it would look like the horrible American food. Koropok's final task had been to bring every ice-vendor in the neighborhood to Number Nineteen.

And then it was a quarter to four, and the house became silent. Ogawa slept in his room, head on Yoshiko's lap. She herself, having taken cup for cup with Ogawa, slept also, her back against a screen. Suriga counted the profits in his office, with his *hakoya*, Koropok the Ainu, crouched at his feet. Major Taksei had paid for the night for Ogawa, since it would be an ill thing for the hundreds of soldiers in the district, staring into the show-windows, to see an officer in the lieutenant's condition. Taksei had no objection to an officer becoming drunk. Certainly not. But it could not be allowed to interfere with duty.

It was breathlessly hot and still in the tiny cubicle. Suriga puttered slowly at his accounts. So many whiskey-sodas, so many bottles of saki. Taxes—oh, a large total! So many girls. In a way, the manager envied Koropok, the Ainu dog, who had no worries, who thought of nothing.

Four o'clock, thought Lew. *They'll be paraded. They'll keep up their chins, too. Even the sick.* He swallowed the ache in his throat, but it was still there. There was no way in which he could keep out of mind what was taking place.

CHAPTER III

THE YELLOW sun beat down on Shoyuji Prison, on the fierce yellow men, and on the yellow dust of the prison yard where the prisoners were dying. There were no buzzards overhead—only flies, waiting.

Do they know at home? wondered Davies.

He had the means of escaping, himself. He was positive he could manage it He also believed that there was a good chance of getting two or three men out of Shoyuji. Why not escape with them?

Someone in Nineteen laughed shrilly at Oldest-Maid's account of the actions of the lieutenant she had entertained. It was high, shrill laughter… and Japanese, at this very moment, were laughing at the gaunt prisoners. Both of Davies' hands were so tightly clenched as he envisioned what was taking place at Shoyuji that his nails cut into his palms.

Then he forced himself to relax as he awaited whatever orders Suriga might give. His job was here. It was here, doubly, because of what he had seen, because of what he knew was taking place now. The Japanese had to be pulverized into dust, until they

were no more than the yellow dust into which they were grinding down prisoners, hungry and sick alike. Only they couldn't
grind down such men, Davies knew. It wouldn't work. Those
were *men* in Shoyuji.

Not until six o'clock did Suriga finally give his *hakoya* permission to eat and then rest, although Koropok must be alert to
answer any demands made on him. Davies gobbled down his
plate of rice and fish, and then went out to scrape a bit of
fishbone into the garbage basket. He dropped his plate clumsily. When he stood up with it in his hand, he also had the scrap
of paper with Taksei's signature, which he palmed in the hand
which carried the plate back to his sleeping-place. Only such
care in little things had kept him undetected. Care in little
things—and he had to be most careful when everything seemed
to be going well.

In his tiny room, he used a sheet of notebook paper filched
from Suriga's office and similar to Major Taksei's notebook
paper, on which to write a message of his own. The paper might
be traced to Suriga, but this would not be damaging to Davies.
The message he brushed on the sheet was, like the major's,
addressed to the commandant of Shoyuji. Lew was proud of
the signature at the end.

He now reviewed his plan, step by step. He would go to the
prison and deliver the note. It must look to the captain as if his
friend, the major, had written the letter; it must look, later, to
Major Taksei as if the message had been composed by Lieutenant Ogawa. Davies felt that he had done both things.

"Dear friend and comrade," the message said, "lend me three
prisoners, including the red-haired American I observed."

Major Taksei would have seen the red-headed Holmes,
Davies knew. Not only was Rusty's bright head instantly dis-
cernible, but it made him the butt of crude Japanese jokes. The
captain would understand why Taksei wanted to devil Holmes.
On the other side of the picture, Rusty would be on his toes.

"I have a lieutenant," the forged letter continued, "who desires to prove his courage. What he does will be an excellent thing for the others to witness. It will also be amusing to me. Therefore please order the prisoners, together with whatever small and unobtrusive guard you feel is needful, to follow the pariah who delivered my earlier note." Davies had ended, faithfully adhering to Taksei's bombastic and boastful manner of writing, "It is my opinion that when the story of what happens is learned, your name and mine will be in every mouth."

That last, thought Lew, *will make the captain smell promotion.*

He had one more thing to do, and now was the time for it, as the hot summer evening darkened from purple to black, with no lights anywhere, because of the fear—in spite of all the boasting—of the *Amerika-jin* bombers.

Quietly, Koropok shuffled down the long corridor to the room where Ogawa and the girl Yoshiko were sleeping. Under his tattered jacket, Davies carried the ink-pot and brush which he had used. He entered the room without a sound, saw the sleeping pair, the saki bottles and bowls, the food stand, the chopsticks, porcelain spoons, knife, bowls. He was about to hide the writing implements under winter quilts in a cupboard, where investigation later would easily disclose them, when an additional way of proving Ogawa's guilt occurred to him. He dipped the brush in ink, kneeled beside Ogawa and made a tiny ink-spot on the Japanese' thumb.

Davies had the story he would tell later all ready: The honorable lieutenant had sent for him. The honorable lieutenant had given him a message, which he, Koropok, had delivered. He knew nothing else. As to what happened after he delivered the message, everyone would know that.

As the American straightened up, he suddenly saw that the girl's eyes had opened and were staring at him. The ink-pot was in Davies' left hand and the brush in his right; and because the maid had seen them, her mouth popped open in the fraction of time necessary to put both objects down.

Davies' hand stopped a scream, turned it into a muffled

outcry. In doing so, he knocked against Ogawa. The lieutenant groaned, blinked, swallowed—and was awake. Even his buzzing head must have told him that something was wrong. Japanese-fashion, he looked for a weapon, and found it in the food-knife of thin steel. He had it just as Davies was aware of his movement; he stabbed just as the American turned, still with a hand clamped on Yoshiko's mouth.

Ogawa's blow at Koropok's back missed, and the Japanese was carried forward on his knees. He would have fallen from the force of the blow if Yoshiko's neck had not been in the way of the blade. Davies' hand, on the girl's mouth, became hot with blood; instinctively he shot out his other hand to tighten on Ogawa's throat. His fingers were iron now, and into them went all of the restrained anger because of the things he knew. When he relaxed them, Ogawa was dead.

So was the girl.

Davies did not curse himself for having done the last little thing in order to prove Ogawa's guilt to investigating Japanese authorities. Instead, desperately, he began to figure out what must be done. He heard Oldest-Maid singing.

> *Agemaki ya,*
> *Tonton!*
> *Hiro bakari ya,*
> *Tonton!*

Her song for despairing lovers coincided with what Davies decided to do with the bodies of the girl and man.

THE BLOODY knife, with the evidence of Ogawa's fingers on the haft, he left undisturbed. He placed Ogawa and Yoshiko's bodies chest to chest, on the matting, and bound them tightly together with the girl's sash. Next, he looped a cotton towel about Ogawa's neck, and slipped chopsticks through the cloth.

By using towel and chopstocks as a tourniquet, the Japanese could have killed himself. The pressure of Davies' fingers would be additional evidence.

Davies twirled the cloth gently, careful not to tighten it about the dead neck, lest the fact show up at post-mortem. This must look like suicide. Like *shinju,* the death-for-love. It must be thought that Ogawa, having lived in America and therefore performing an unusual *shinju,* had bound the willing girl to him, and stabbed her as he tightened the tourniquet.

Everyone would know that Ogawa had been very drunk.

There was blood and ink on the matting. Davies wiped off ink-pot and brush-handle, but did not bother to hide them. He emptied every saki bottle.

Lew knew how the authorities would reason out what had happened. Ogawa, they would decide, originally had good intentions, intending to kill the *Amerika-jin,* particularly the powerful red-haired devil, to prove his courage to his companions and Major Taksei. Forgery was bad, but was excusable when patriotic. It was unfortunate that Lieutenant Ogawa, whose belly was accustomed to weakening *isu-karemu,* and not to saki, had not been able to make himself a hero.

Davies took a last look around. Here were all of the evidences of much drinking; and he himself, when questioned, would admit that the lieutenant's words to him, Koropok, had indeed been difficult to understand, but that he dared not disregard an order from an officer who served the great Emperor.

Do that right, Lew told himself as he left the room, *and you'll save yourself a beating.* What he had most to fear, he knew, was that the Japanese would cut him down during their first insane moment of wild fury.

The only person he met in the corridor was a thirteen-year-old *oshaku,* a dancing maid, who reached up and jerked at his beard as he passed. Intentionally, Lew dropped the message, making sure that the beady-eyed girl would say that Koropok, after having come from Yoshiko's room, had been carrying a letter.

Outside, the district was stiflingly hot, dark and perfumed. The canal Sanya-bori, at the end of which should be the smug-

Once the prisoners were on the boat, Davies
felt sure they could clear the anti-sub net
and escape to sea under cover of fog.

glers' boat, gleamed like black jade as it wound through the
licensed quarter. To the south and east, toward Kyomachi and
Shoyuji Prison, there was evening heat haze, dark and thick.
Some where over the inner bay the haze would become summer
fog. It was always so.

He walked slowly, his head far in advance of his feet, and
ducked away from the blows of marines and soldiers standing
near the showrooms; he ascended the stone steps beyond the
quarter, where lanterns no longer illuminated the face of the
old shrine there, and the door to the interior altar was opened
and closed hastily by worshipers, lest the light of the hundred
candles flaming there before the paunched god attract American bombers.

From the slight elevation, Davies marked the course of the
canal, clear down to the stretch of mud at the end where only
boats of light draught could be berthed. The canal Sanya-bori,
previous to war, when the dredgers were not needed elsewhere
to keep channels free for war shipping, had been far busier than

now. Barges and sampans had crowded it then; now only small *choki* were tied to the muddy bank. The spot where the power craft should be was partially covered with haze.

Once the prisoners were on the boat, Davies felt sure that it could slide down the bay—sticking near the shore to take advantage of the fog and also in order to miss the anti-sub net—and to sea. Should a patrol see it, the patrol officer would have already accepted many a bribe, because in no other way could such a craft operate. The patrol officer would be counting the cut he would get when the boat returned laden. Such Army and Navy graft went clear up topside, Lew knew from the stories he had heard at Nineteen. Fortunes had been made, here and in the occupied countries.

As he neared the prison, it came to him that plenty of Nips were going to be unhappy, should he be successful. As he walked, and as he remembered what had happened in the hot prison yard, his hands clenched.

He was not surprised that the party of lieutenants and Taksei had not returned to Nineteen after the sadistic performance in the prison. The major and lieutenants were undoubtedly gorging themselves in a restaurant. That was good Japanese custom. What he did fear was that the captain, the prison commandant, might have gone with them, and this worry rode on his shoulders all the way to the gate of Shoyuji. But Davies had to act now, this night, or not at all.

It was a needless worry. The same procedure as before was gone through with: Koropok the pariah was again prodded through the gate and along the tunnel, and to Captain Mikimura's office. The sergeant on duty sent a soldier to the captain's quarters with the note. In almost no time at all Mikimura appeared, all smiles. He gave orders for his junior officer to be found and brought here. When the lieutenant came from his rounds, Mikimura was rubbing his hands.

"*Umaku itteru ze,*" he said. "What a lovely thing Major Taksei has decided! What a pleasure it is to assist him! Read this letter, and consider the requests as my orders. How generous of Major Taksei to include me in the story!"

The junior officer giggled as he read. "The large red-haired one," he said. "Oh, it will be a pleasure to get rid of him. He is a troublemaker. I only wish I might see what Major Taksei has in store for him! As for the other two prisoners—"

"Let us liquidate a pair of strong ones," said Mikimura. "The sort who refuse to be starved to death and who curse us. Sergeant! The records!" The captain grabbed the record book of punishments and pawed through it. "Number 24,429," he said, "is a man whom no punishment has civilized. Also Number 447. He has been long here, but thin as he is, he continues to live. Send him also."

When the sergeant went to get the three prisoners, Mikimura purred at Koropok, "Where do you take them, Ainu?"

Davies ducked as if expecting a blow. "Oh, great lord," he said, "I know nothing. I came from Nineteen. I return to Nineteen. That is all I know."

"That is what I thought," said Mikimura. "Oh, what a night they will have… including the prisoners! I wish I could go and witness it!"

So do I, thought Davies. *Nothing would suit me better.*

THE THREE Americans were brought to the commandant's office. The faces of all three were gaunt, and their bodies emaciated; but they gave Mikimura stare for stare until the captain snarled, "You are to leave the prison."

The red-haired prisoner, Holmes, had given no sign that he now knew the black-bearded pariah to be Davies. He said, "We are to be exchanged?"

Mikimura was about to scream at him, until the humor of the situation occurred to the Japanese. "Exchanged!" he said. "Well! Of course! Congratulations!"

Davies stood with bowed head while the junior officer gave a corporal instructions. The corporal and two soldiers were sufficient guard. The corporal was to take the prisoners to a certain place which the pariah would indicate, was to receive a receipt for them and then return. That was all.

Holmes knows something's up, thought Lew, as the hands of the prisoners were being tied behind them, ropes cutting into flesh, *but the other two believe that this is their finish.* He didn't know the other prisoners.

"*Kat'ku ii-tsuketa zo!* Carry out orders," Mikimura snapped. "Go!"

As the little party went out, shouted farewells came from the barracks. There was the sound of blows, too, but these only made the yells the more cheerful and encouraging.

Shuffling on ahead, Davies was leading the way along the city's lower section, where the water-ways and canals had to be crossed by innumerable bridges, and where it was silent, deserted and dark.

The corporal demanded, "Why do you go on these alleys, Ainu dog?"

Koropok had the answer. "I only follow the great officer's orders," he whined. No soldier would dispute him in that.

When he neared the mouth of Sanya-bori Canal, inky-black and heavy with haze, the time had come. And so Koropok the Ainu paused and turned. He dared not speak a readying word in English for Rusty's ears and for the other two; it was too likely that the soldiers surely had heard English at the prison. But because Holmes was watching him, the brief nod of Davies' head ought to warn Rusty that this was it. He saw Holmes' elbows nudge the Americans on either side, indicating that Rusty was warning them also.

The two soldiers' rifles, bayonets fixed, were on their shoulders. The corporal had a hand on his holstered revolver. The soldiers were to the prisoners' left and right, and slightly to the rear; the corporal was beside Davies.

Ainu-fashion, Koropok grunted, and started to face forward again, as if about to walk ahead. As he turned slowly, his fist crashed against the noncom's slanting jaw with the exploding fury of two years' restraint.

Knocking the nearer of the astonished soldiers off balance, he wrested his bayonet from him and ran him through. Before Davies could bring the gun to bear on the other, Holmes had hurled himself, bound as he was, on the Japanese, to knock him to the ground, his rifle firing harmlessly into the air. Then Davies killed him with his mate's bayonet. The corporal died last, without knowing how.

"Listen," said Lew, as he slashed off the ropes. "Walk with me as I tell you. Grab the guns. That's it. Somebody'll have heard the shot, but will think it's just some fancy air-defense. The Nips do it all the time. If they pot a few civilians, it's O.K. with the military. If... This's the first time I've... You fellows... It's been two years...."

"Shut up," Davies whispered. There was the power boat. A cabin job. Locked. No Nip would take a chance at being caught in the boat if a disgruntled official felt he hadn't been given a big enough cut. "That's it," he said. "Break the lock. Take a course along the north shore. Close as you dare. There'll be maps in the cabin. It's got gas. Japs are great on being ready. It has a mast, too. The course is up to you, Rusty. There must be sails for that mast. Be sure," said Lew, because it was paramount in his mind, "to tell people at home what it's like to be a prisoner of the Japanese!"

"You're coming with us," all three protested.

Davies shook his head. "No can do," he said. Home! He cut through arguments with a swift explanation of the things which they must do until they were out of the bay, ending with, "You'll make it. But don't be taken alive." Then he grinned. "There's one thing you can do for me."

"Anything!"

"I've got to stay alive. I have orders, so it's official. Here's what you must do. Crack me over the head. A real clout with the revolver-butt. There must be a wound. Then, while two of you ready the boat, the other fellow must drag me back and dump me with the dead Nips. If anyone's already there, which is improbable, put me as near the spot as possible. It's got to look to the police as if I were left for dead. I'll be O.K. if you do this. If you don't," Davies said, "the Nips will slice me apart inch by inch. No story would work."

"But… Lew.…"

Davies turned away, so that he faced Tokyo. The stink of the canal was in his nostrils. Dark Tokyo. Fearful Tokyo.

Holmes' big, thin hand was on Davies' shoulder. It pressed down hard.

"You know best," Lew heard Rusty say huskily. "Be seeing you."

Pain crackled in Davies' head. There seemed a great whirling, blazing red sun before him, and then everything darkened, to become a blue sky spattered with many stars. Davies did not know that he was smiling as the stars vanished, as everything became black as the night, and Rusty picked him up.

BELT OF STEEL

THE DUSK of late summer pressed down on Tokyo, and on the women who were walking slowly along the curved street which led to the temple. Their gray or lavender kimonos, worn threadbare, blended into the evening. They walked in silence. A few old men were in the crowd, and they walked silently also.

Long paper lanterns hung from poles fastened to the shop eaves. Paper bells replaced the little metal ones which formerly had been attached to the bottoms of the lanterns; the tufts of stiff white feathers still ornamented the ends of the poles, not being needed for the melting-pots. The lanterns would have been taken down by children of the shopkeepers, in past years, and been carried to the temple, where children and parents alike would have prayed for small future happiness. But now no lanterns could be lit nor carried, lest even such a small firefly gleam attract the attention of what Japan dreaded—the *Amerika-jin* bombers.

Now, too, there were more women on the street than had walked on it toward the temple a few months ago, when the temple courtyard had been white with dropped petals from the *garyo-bai,* the sleeping-dragon plum, whose contorted branches and ugly stunted trunk writhed above the stones. The women had not come then, as on many previous spring evenings, to marvel at the blossoms, just as now they were not on their slow, silent way to admire the reflections of the great lotus leaves and the lotus seed pods in the placid temple pool, nor to watch the carp.

They were coming to pray. For the dead.

And when fall comes, thought the bearded man dressed in the tatters of an Ainu pariah, who shuffled along with the crowd, *they won't be coming to see the turning-red-of-the-maple, either. And there will be more of them coming by autumn, because there'll be more dead Nips.*

The dark man in the short blue jacket grinned in his beard. The Japanese women were on their way to pray for husbands and sons who had died in battle for the Tenno, the emperor. Each month their number was increasing.

A radio in one of the shops began blaring. "It is impossible to live under the same heaven with the enemy of our lord!" snarled the metallic Japanese announcer; and the people on the street and in the shops dutifully repeated the pledge of the savage forty-seven Ronin to avenge their master's honor.

So did the bearded man.

A change had taken place in the several years since the stocky "pariah" named as Koropok on his police permit had slipped into Japan disguised as an Ainu. Then it had not been necessary to whip up patriotism, nor to console women, because the dead were American dead at Pearl Harbor, Wake, Manila.

What was happening in the war was altering the expressions of the women, who walked sorrowfully and downcast toward the temple; and it made a wonderful difference to the bearded man as well.

Until comparatively recently, his eyes had been grim, far more so than when he had left Manila to attempt to direct American bombers in a mission over Tokyo by indicating new objectives. But he was able to allow himself, now, the realization that the Japanese were beginning to lose some of their assurance of victory, and this made him, for the briefest of moments, look like the Llewelyn Davies who had flown a P40 for MacArthur.

Davies no longer constantly feared detection. He was ac-

"O.K., boy,"
whispered the
prisoner and
Davies lifted
his fellow
American and
slung him out
of the ring.

cepted for exactly what he seemed, a pariah, a scorned outcast servant in Tokyo's licensed quarter, whose sole occupation was going about his master's business—Koropok the Ainu.

Lately, he had managed the escape of American airmen from a Tokyo prison camp. He knew that they had rejoined their comrades, and his, and that they had related their terrible account of torture, because the Tokyo radio had screamed a furious denial. However, in an effort to lend realism to their disavowal, the Japanese government was at last agreeing to permit food and medicine to be brought from Vladivostok, where it had waited for over a year, to the sick, starved, but still dauntless prisoners.

Intelligence could now be positive that Lieutenant Davies was alive and free. Was G-2 figuring how he should be damag-

ing Japan's war machine? The growing nervousness and tension within the empire made anything difficult.

What I'm doing, thought Lew, cringing in simulated terror from a shopkeeper's blow and protecting his face from spittle, *is marking time, damn it!*

HE WAS carrying a message from Suriga, the manager of Number Nineteen, to Baron Kumikawa. Davies had read the zigzag characters before placing the folded sheet in his bearskin Ainu pouch; the message had nothing to do with war. Even if it had, and even if the information had been vital, Lew knew of no way in which it could have been conveyed to Intelligence. None.

The note was merely an assurance that Suriga was honored with the opportunity of sending *geisha* and pretty young *oshaku* to the baron's party, and that the honorable lord could count on some unwatered Scotch whiskey which had come direct from Singapore. Davies knew that the baron could afford to give his guests the finest entertainment, because Kumikawa was a director in the Greater East Asia Commercial, Religious, and Educational Association, which had the concession for the sale of opium in China and the Philippines.

Davies could see, over the heads of the Japanese, the high iron gate and brick wall of the baron's Tokyo dwelling. According to Yoshiwara gossip, Kumikawa was so high in favor that he had profited well. It was even said that Tojo himself smiled on the baron; and when The Razor smiled, in those days, it was gold in the purse!

Nearer to the procession now, Davies saw that some of the girls, unmarried, had in their hands long strips of paper, *tanzaku,* which, also according to gossip, they would tie to the branches of the ancient plum, to ask heavenly aid in securing husbands instead of being sent to some far island for the pleasure of all soldiers. That such petitions were being written seemed to Lew proof of what was happening.

"*Banzai!*" shrilled the radio. "*Mo yoroshii zo!* Excellent news!"

The crowd paused to listen.

"Our valiant soldiers," Radio Tokyo boasted, "have cleverly enticed the brutal and cowardly Marines of the United States to the small and unimportant island called Nakushima. Many of the enemy have been ruthlessly killed for their arrogance in leaping into our carefully prepared trap. Our soldiers performed in traditional manner, and have now become deathless heroes for ten times ten thousand years. *Banzai!* Accord all honor to them for having died gloriously in defense of His Imperial Majesty! *Aaaaaa!* The *Tenno!*"

When the crowd had cheered dutifully and began to move ahead again, it was in greater silence than before. The sound of the clapped hands of worshipers at the temple could be clearly heard, so complete was the quiet.

Davies knew that another American attack had been driven home. Where was Nakushima? He had no way of knowing; the Japanese had renamed everything which they had grabbed at the war's start. But when the man disguised as an Ainu glanced around to see how the people had reacted to the announcement, it appeared obvious to him that the island must be nearer Tokyo. Otherwise, why the frightened eyes, the licked lips, the bowed heads?

Lew's glance showed him something else, which instantly stopped his jubilation. Three dapper gendarmes, the dreaded police of Japanese military intelligence, were making their way through the crowd. The trio were walking in the same direction as the others, but slightly faster; and they were moving slantwise toward the gutter where Koropok the Ainu shuffled along.

Those devils aren't going to the temple to pray, Davies thought. *Have I slipped up anywhere? Are they after me?*

The gendarmes were obviously on duty. Each had a hand on his revolver butt. Lew knew and feared them. They had the soft, purring ways of cats, the penetration of pawnbrokers, and the morals of *geisha.* Not even Japanese officers of the line could match them in cruelty. Torture was their main method of obtaining confessions. Lack of success in an investigation often resulted in the murder of innocent persons so that the gendarmes would not suffer loss of face. Such persons had "failed to show a proper respect for officers of His Imperial Majesty."

If they're not after me, thought Davies, forcing himself to keep his hands unclenched, *who are they after?*

The Kumikawa gate was near. Lew walked imperceptibly faster, shambling like an Ainu. He could see the ancient gatekeeper, who knew him to be from Number Nineteen; a word from this *hakonin* to the baron, regarding the arrest of someone bringing a note to Kumikawa, might save Davies from being taken off for questioning, unless the gendarmes had a real reason for arresting him. *If he ran,* the American knew, *they would shoot him down just to get rid of an Ainu, even if they had no interest in him.*

The gendarmes were closer. There was the possibility that they were following someone behind Davies, but he did not dare so much as turn his head, because it would take no more than that to give the gendarmes an excuse to report that the Ainu dog named Koropok was implicated in the affair.

Then Davies had the answer.

"Four hundred thousand sixty," a squeaky old voice whispered behind him. "Lieutenant Davies. Do not turn 'round."

Davies' heart almost stopped. Was he being trapped? No. The number was that on the dogtag which he had once worn.

"Take in your hand what I give," the voice said.

Something flat and thin, a folded piece of rice paper, was shoved into Davies' hand. His fingers closed on it; and at that moment the gendarmes rushed, knocking the temple-pilgrims aside in their sudden haste.

In Lew's head flashed, "Trapped!" but he had already slipped the paper into his bearskin pouch, substituting for it in hand the message from Suriga to Baron Kumikawa. Then his arms were pinioned by a gendarme.

The Japanese swung him around. Davies now saw that the man who had whispered to him was as old and feeble as his voice had indicated. He wore a bedraggled kimono, much too large for his shrunken frame and obviously not his own. It was of filthy cotton, of the same grayish white as his thin goatee. He was a Korean.

He did not look at Davies at all.

THERE WERE such men in Tokyo; Davies had seen them before, hostages for the behavior of grandsons in labor battalions. If a young Korean escaped, with the hope of joining China's guerrillas, it was with the knowledge that his revered ancestor would be suspended by the thumbs until there remained just enough life to execute. Even so, Davies had overheard officials who were guests at Nineteen complain that the old fools died willingly if their grandsons fought against Japan. These sad old men were locked up each night, but were permitted to hobble around during the day, when the spy-conscious Japanese hoped surveillance would result in something like this.

The Korean was actually smiling. "I am very old," he said. "What is pain? Nothing. What is death? Less."

A low moan was forced from the old Korean as sly fingers twisted at an agonized neck muscle. The laughter of the crowd as the Korean's goatee waggled up and down caused the gendarme who was applying the torture to swell with pleasure. Not to be outdone, the gendarme who had seized the "pariah" wasted no time in kicking Davies in as many places as could be reached.

"What did he say to you?" the gendarme shouted. "Speak!"

Davies mumbled in slurred Ainu dialect and with hanging head, "*Kon' imi wak'-rim'senu.* I do not understand."

"I will bring you understanding," said the gendarme. His fingers slid up along the tattered sleeve, assuming a hold which, if Davies had moved or struggled, would have burst a tendon. Because the stocky, bearded man stood motionless, all Shohei, the gendarme, could do was to kick the unresisting pariah again.

Shohei's companions, in true Japanese fashion, jeered at Shohei's discomfiture, their laughter, however, being proof to Davies that none of them fully realized the great importance of their bag. Their comments so infuriated Shohei that he sought a means of recovering face. He must show everyone how clever and powerful he really was, and do it instantly. Intending to throw the Ainu to the ground, where the swarthy pariah could be jumped upon, an action which would bring admiration and applause, the gendarme hastily twined his leg around one of Davies', at the same time placing an arm over Lew's shoulder and across his chest.

Lew gave readily to the pressure, recognizing the familiar wrestling hold. But something he was unable to control made him stoop suddenly, somewhat the way a cringing and frightened pariah would crouch—and the gendarme, caught by the unexpected response to the hold, went sprawling on his face.

Davies did his best to look like an Ainu who had not the slightest idea of what had happened. But though he stood with hanging head, dumbly, he was cursing himself for having given in to the impulse.

That does it, he thought. *I'll be taken in for a beating. I'll be questioned and searched. Perhaps it could have been avoided. What got into me?*

He knew only too well what it was, as Shohei scrambled wildly to his feet and glared at him; he had given in instinctively, because of the indignities he had suffered for so long, to the desire to see a uniformed Japanese go sprawling headlong into the muck of the gutter. But to have done this now....

The note must be destroyed before the search. Davies didn't want to destroy it, unread. His fingers itched to take it from his bearskin pouch; instead, he clutched the message from Number Nineteen tightly. *Keep your head,* he told himself. *Hold tight.*

The other two gendarmes were not smiling now. Shohei squealed, "Ainu beast! *Kuma!* Hairy bear! Dirty bear! *Kuma! Kuma! Kuma!*"

The old gatekeeper came shuffling up.

"Who called?" he asked.

"Nobody called," snarled Shohei, slapping Davies across the face. "I named this animal for what he is. *Kuma.* A sickening hairy bear of an Ainu." He slapped his captive again. "*Kuma!* What a disgusting name! I—"

"My master," said the gatekeeper softly, "is Baron *Kumi*kawa. I do not think he will like what you say. Do you?"

The name stopped the gendarme's tirade. He blinked and licked his lips, and his nostrils wriggled like a rabbit's, as he searched for abject apology. He had plenty of time to select his words, because the old gatekeeper was not pressing him; but the manner in which the porter was smiling told Shohei that the excuse and the apology had better be very good.

As he began, "O honorable and venerable retainer of a great personage, please accept from me my deepest regret that I—" At this moment one of the women temple-goers shuffled timidly up to him and, bowing deeply, touched his arm.

"Honorable officer, please to listen to—"

"Go away," howled Shohei, flinging off the hand. "*Abunai yo!* Do you wish to be arrested for interfering with duties?" He made his voice deferential again. "O honorable and venerable retainer of a great and renowned personage—"

"The old one in the white kimono," said the woman, "gave something to the Ainu-*jin*. A paper. I saw it."

The gendarmes who had been holding the old Korean both wanted to rush over to the pariah; each released his grip at the same instant; each had to grab his victim again. Shohei, recovering from his mental paralysis, finally seized Davies' hand, ripped the paper away and opened it.

"It is in code," he announced to his mates. He had puffed up like a mating toad. No longer need he fear his superiors' reprimands for his unfortunate use of the word *kuma*. Nor would he, as punishment, be sent to fight against the *Amerika-jin* savages known as Marines. No. Instead, he would be rewarded.

Oh, the captain would mention the protest from Baron Kumikawa, but would smile because of this great accomplishment, this apprehension of the Korean and the Ainu. How envious his fellow gendarmes would be when he was promoted! He would shortly be their superior, and therefore they would never dare say anything concerning the way in which he had slipped accidentally just as he was about to hurl the pariah down to earth. Oh, what face he had regained!

Shohei was so happy that he slapped the Ainu again and again.

WHILE HE slapped away, grinning all over his face, and while his companions shoved their own captive over to where he and Davies were standing, and while the woman waited to receive the gendarmes' permission to continue to the temple, Yagi, the gatekeeper, had been placidly reading the paper in Shohei's hand.

"*Nani!*" he snorted. "Code! What nonsense! The message is an expected one from the honorable brothel-keeper Suriga to my lord."

"Do not talk about nonsense," Shohei cried. "I understand all about codes! A common word is used, and the common word has a different meaning. When a fool like you sees *geisha* written it means nothing! But to the enemy it means battle-ships! It is plain that the number eleven does not mean eleven *geisha* at all, but eleven ships of His Imperial Majesty which this filthy Korean and filthier Ainu wish to destroy! What do *you* know about codes?"

"Nothing," admitted Yagi. "All I know is that my lord, Baron Kumikawa, intends to give a great party, and that this pariah, employed by Suriga-*san*, brings information concerning proper entertainment for the affair."

One of the other gendarmes asked, "Is the Ainu known to you?"

"He is," said the gatekeeper. He looked at Davies; and as he looked, he began to grin. But he said nothing.

Davies, watchful and cold, wondered what was in the old gatekeeper's head. Yagi was scratching himself the way he did when greatly pleased.

Shohei's face was crimson. "There must be more to this message than is obvious," he argued, as he saw his promotion vanishing. "Can you deny that a woman informed me that she saw it given the Ainu by the Korean?"

"She probably saw a girl hand a *tanzaku* to some other girl who had no paper love-petition to tie on the temple's tree," said the third gendarme.

"But—"

"Shohei," the third gendarme said, "how could the Korean give the pariah a note which had already been given the Ainu by the brothel-keeper? And if it had been anything in code," the gendarme muttered, just loudly enough for Shohei to hear, "you talked too much about it."

To save what little face seemed now possible, Shohei pleaded, "At least we must take the Ainu to the captain for questioning. Did you not see how he resisted me as I ran to arrest the Korean?"

The gatekeeper was clearing his throat; but it was the third gendarme, wanting no part in the reprimand which would follow Baron Kumikawa's protest, who began to speak. "No," he said. He lowered his voice. "First, you are so clumsy that you fell on your face, despite your training in wrestling. Next, you insulted a great lord. To top everything, your actions have delayed patriotic wives in going to the temple. I am afraid you are in trouble, Shohei."

"But this Ainu dog—"

"Is known by the gatekeeper to be a messenger. The Ainu carries the message. Do you think that Baron Kumikawa associates with the enemy, Shohei?"

The second gendarme growled, "The crowd grows. Soon common policemen will come to see what is wrong." He tightened his grip on the Korean's frail arm. "It is time the crowd moves on, and that we return with the Korean."

And heaven help him, thought Davies.

It must have occurred to the pair who were holding the old Korean that although their mate would be held officially responsible for what had happened, their own conduct before the civilians had brought no applause. A quick word was passed; the gray Korean was knocked down. While one of the gendarmes shouted, "Oh, you dare resist us, do you?" the other kicked the old man in the stomach.

Davies tried not to look.

When no cheers rose from the street, which was by now packed from side to side with additional pilgrims, all of whom were going to pray for the dead, Lew heard the gatekeeper mutter, thinking aloud, "This is not good. Fortunately my lord Kumikawa understands the situation."

It was so silent that what the Korean moaned, in Japanese, was plainly audible. "You may kill this body," the old man groaned, "and you may cut this flesh into a thousand pieces. But the soul will remain to cry out. *Mansei!*"

The kicking, Davies knew, was mere preliminary. The Korean was under suspicion. When the old man was really expertly tortured, could he remain silent? The Korean must have been given an exact description of the Ainu pariah known as Koropok, and the Korean had been told the serial number of Lieutenant Llewelyn Davies. By whom? By the person who had given the old man the message which was in Koropok's bearskin pouch. And... *what was in the message?*

Would the contents be wrung from the Korean? Wouldn't the old man, in agony, tell everything he knew when he was questioned?

At that moment, Davies had the answer. The Korean had been jerked to his feet. He was actually smiling. "I am very old," he said. "What is pain? Nothing. What is death? Less." The smile did not wane as he added, "There is only me;" and, as the words were uttered, he did look at Davies for a fraction of time.

It was apparent to Davies that the gendarmes' defenseless victim was informing him that no confession could be wrung from one who feared neither death nor agony. By "There is only me," the Korean undoubtedly meant that the man whom he knew to be an American must expect no other contact.

Shohei struck the old man across the mouth with his revolver butt. The Korean continued to smile. In prayer, through crushed and bloodied lips, the old man began to chant, "*Po che choong sa'ng... choong sa'ng....*"

"Monkey talk," said Yagi. "*Mionichi ma' naorimasumai!* He will talk differently soon. Come deliver your message. And remember I saved you!"

Why didn't Yagi take the message and deliver it himself? Something was in the wind. "I am grateful," mumbled Davies humbly, following the gatekeeper. *I've got to have a look at the paper in my pouch,* worried Lew, *and then destroy it.* He swallowed slowly audibly, repeatedly, as if nauseated. "Please forgive me," he whimpered, "the bottom of my stomach is rising."

Yagi grabbed his sleeve. "If you vomit here, such defilement among worshipers will cause arrest. This must not happen. Hurry!"

Here was more proof to Davies that the gatekeeper intended to make use of him. How? There was no way of knowing.

The unlit lanterns stirred on their poles as the temple bell sent its brazen sound rocking down the street. The women, at the summons, pressed ahead rapidly, carrying gatekeeper and pariah with them. The pair were almost at Baron Kumikawa's iron gate when the voice of the Korean reached them, amazingly strong and vibrant.

"*Po che choong sa'ng!* I appeal to the four hundred thousand and sixty divinities to find some way to avenge me! I pray to the four hundred thousand—"

The voice stopped; the echo of the bell hummed on.

Davies could only hope that the gendarmes, made furious by the defiant outcry, had killed the Korean. Quick death was the only merciful thing which could be hoped for, for the brave old man. The answer to the appeal for vengeance addressed to No. 400,060 must be in the communication which Lew chafed to read.

CHAPTER II

MESSAGE FROM HOME

YAGI UNLOCKED the gate, pushed the Ainu through and, coming after him, locked it from the inside. Beyond the sanded court was Baron Kumikawa's great mansion; to reach it, thick clumps of shrubs had to be rounded.

Here was another world, a complete contrast to the street of shabby shops. To the right, concealed from the outside, was picture-book Japan. A lake lay ahead, a miniature one, dotted with miniature islets connected by stone bridges. The water, in the evening haze, wound about little rock-strewn hills and disappeared in dark, blue-black, rippleless threads between tiny promontories. Beside a bamboo thicket was a wooden pavilion for tea-ceremonies and garden-viewing. Crows on its roof exchanged signals with those on the house-top.

"*Ki' to i' ni*," said Yagi. "Behind that small building you will find the place where the bottom of your stomach can come to the surface. Waste no time." The gatekeeper gave Davies a shove. "I will wait for you here."

It was difficult for Davies to shamble off like a pariah, and to stumble a few times on the flat stones of the path as if he were unaccustomed to such magnificence as was underfoot in the baron's garden.

Inside the *benjo* it was dark. Davies made certain that Yagi had not followed him; then, stooping down, he opened his pouch, took out the folded paper, and cupped it in his hand. Something from home! A word to Llewelyn Davies, and not to the outcast who had been slapped and kicked and starved since Pearl Harbor—who, for all that time, had been alone in Japan.

Carefully, swiftly, Davies unfolded the thin sheet.

The light was failing; but to Davies each word stood out on the paper like ink on white silk. Like ebony on silvery lacquer. But also like the handwriting on the wall, written so long ago, and difficult to understand.

WERE YOU RIGHT, OR WAS I?
ANDY

That was all. That was the entire message.

Davies' fingers automatically shredded the paper. The portion of it containing the one sentence he chewed and swallowed; the rest he dropped into the *benjo*. Andy. Andy Craig. The amateur strategist, transferred from a fighting unit of P40s over to G-2 just before Lew's departure from Manila.

Andy! What would it be like to be sitting with him now, informing him what was going on in Tokyo and Japan, telling him of those things which a servant at Number Nineteen over-heard when drunken officials talked? What would it be like to speak in English to a *friend*, and to drink an American drink and smoke an American cigarette—to be an American again!

A request for information, Davies realized, had to veil the very purpose of the question, lest the message fall into Japanese hands and reveal to them what might be intended. The request had to be cryptic. But this one was so broad, so vague, so apt to concern itself with any one of a hundred things, that it brought no hint as to what Intelligence must desperately want to learn.

I've argued with Andy about everything under the sun, thought Lew. *This must be about the war, of course. It must be about something Andy's sure I'll remember, and where we really went to town.*

It came to him, as he turned to leave the *benjo,* that the problem was academic, because the Korean, the go-between who had somehow received the communication, and who had been supposed somehow to transmit the reply to the United States, was as good as dead. An answer couldn't be delivered to G-2; the old Korean had told Davies that no other contact could be expected.

But he asked me to find a way to avenge him, flashed through Davies' head as he stepped into the hot darkness, *and he meant that I should do it by carrying out the instructions in the message.*

Surely only desperation brought about by failure had forced the Korean to hope for what was impossible. Even if Lew knew the answer, it was ridiculous to believe that he could get it to G-2. It couldn't be done.

The swift Oriental night had lowered over the garden. The miniature lake was a sheet of shining ink, as were the jagged tiny bays; the peaks and promontories had lost form. The islands, with their dwarfed trees, had to be guessed at. An enormous whiskered carp leaped, gulped a night-fly, and splashed back; the circles which it made on the surface could not be seen, either, although the sound of diminutive wavelets lapping against the shore was singularly real.

I T W A S then, perhaps because of the bays and islands, that Davies, with his mind back in Manila with his fellow officer, remembered the particular argument to which Craig must be referring. There was no doubt; Lew was positive, and it fitted in perfectly with the sort of thing which Intelligence would want to know. The mere fact that G-2, at this time, was interested, brought a deep, warm feeling to Davies, because it meant that the armed forces of the United States were closing in—closing in to bomber range.

The argument had been a hot one. All modern strategy had been on Andy Craig's side. On Davies' side had been knowledge of the Japanese.

What would the Japanese Navy do when war came? That had been the argument. It was Craig who insisted that the Nipponese battle fleet would attack with fury and recklessness, following up immediate successes; it was Davies who disagreed. The Japanese, Lew had insisted, would hold the heavy units of their fleet near Japan. The battle fleet would not be risked early in the war. Great restraint on the part of the admirals would be necessary; but they had shown such restraint before, following their initial and treacherous attack on Russia in 1904, and, because it had been successful then, they would repeat the operation exactly, monkey-fashion. Japan's heavy ships-of-the-line, under Togo, had skulked and been held back, despite all taunts of cowardice, until there was perfect opportunity to annihilate the Russian fleets. It had worked then, Davies had argued, and the Japs didn't change easily. They would use an identical strategy against the United States.

"The Japanese fleet," Lew remembered having said, as he started now toward the waiting gatekeeper, "will hide in safety behind Japan proper, just as it did when they fought Russia. I'll bet a bottle of beer that their admirals are committed to a policy of waiting until they get our battle fleet where they want it. Then they will strike, hard. And I'll bet another bottle that the big Nip ships will be anchored at the very same fortunate place where they hid while waiting to finish off the Russians. They'll anchor off Tsushima Island."

According to what Koropok the Ainu had overheard at Number Nineteen, from one word on one night, from a location whispered in drunkenness on another, this was what had happened. The Japanese fleet was at Tsushima.

All I've got to do, thought Lew somberly, understanding to the full now the desperation of the old Korean, *is to get the information to our side.* He drew a painful breath as his lips formed, "It isn't possible." It was absurd to even think about it.

"*Atsui ni komaru,*" said Yagi, advancing to meet the shadowy figure of Koropok. "You are to have the privilege of prostrating yourself before the great Lord Kumikawa, an honor of which you will boast to any descendants you dare to have." Yagi placed his hand on Davies' shoulder, and then squeezed the muscles of the pariah's upper arm. "*Mah!*" he ejaculated. "You are like a bear! Good!"

The gatekeeper began to chuckle again, and by the time the pair reached the house, he was laughing and rubbing his chin. He beat down the protests of the maid-servant when the *jochu* objected to taking him and his forbidden-to-enter companion

"You are to have the privilege of prostrating yourself before the great Lord Kumikawa," Yagi said, advancing to meet the ragged Koropok.

to the baron, who was engaged with guests. Yagi insisted that he himself had admitted the honorable visitors, and that it was they who had asked him to bring the Ainu to the baron.

This Davies was sure was untrue. Obviously, the old gate-keeper was a trusted retainer, and privileged to take liberties.

Baron Kumikawa's residence was in foreign style. The carpeted hall along which the *jochu* led the way was lined with glass cases containing a collection of china, from primitives the color of Chinese pit-clay to magnificent crested Spode taken at Singapore. There were pianos, paintings, and divans in the rooms off the hall; and when the girl, after bowing to a closed

door, opened it timidly, Davies heard the metallic rasping of the reception of a high-frequency broadcast—from the States!

"*ZZnnzbrkk!*... American, Sixth Army... mmMacArthurrrz-kzk... *brk!*... *KkmmzkzzfffFourth* Marineszzzzzzbrk!... the capture of this airfield assuressk!... *bbbzk!*... now seven hundred miles from Japann*nzzzzbvk!*..."

Within bomber range! No wonder Intelligence wanted to know the location of the Imperial battle fleet.

There were a half dozen Japanese in the room where Yagi bowed, kicking sidewise at the pariah to make him prostrate himself.

"Japanese *deadrkdrkzz... zkzbrk!*... seven thousand killed and... *zzzzz...* nine hundred taken prisonerrrrzzzzbkbk....

"*Mo yoroshii,*" ordered the fattest of the Japanese, who was sprawled in a big chair. "That is enough. Shut it off."

While one of the guests jumped to do Baron Kumikawa's bidding, Davies observed this man to whom the gatekeeper had brought him. An opened silk kimono exposed the great paunch and chest, singularly like a Japanese wrestler's. Kumi-kawa's black, sly eyes were cold and restless; he had a cruel button of a mouth. Baron Odagiri Kumikawa, the confidant of Tojo the Razor. A shrewd man.

His scrutiny of the bearded pariah known as Koropok was so keen that the American began to wonder if the baron had penetrated a disguise which had become almost automatic. Kumikawa waited until the *jochu* was padding down the hall before taking his eyes from the man in tattered jacket. Then he turned to the gatekeeper and smiled.

"*Wakarimasu ka?*" the baron asked the fidgeting retainer. "What is your opinion of the news the Americans have broad-cast tonight?"

Yagi grinned broadly, since his master knew he had not un-derstood a word of the *Amerika*-jin lies. "If the news is good," said Yagi, "it will soon be even better. If it is bad, our final victory will be more sweet"

Kumikawa snarled at his guests, "You need faith such as my retainer's. *Aa!* Your attitude of fear has filtered down to the people. *Makoto mi o sewa da!* Such advice you give me! Why do I bother with you? You, Tsumuri, had the effrontery to suggest an elimination of celebrations, and instead wish to inform the subjects of His Imperial Majesty that it will be more patriotic to continue at work! A fine way to make everyone believe that we are winning! *Mah!* Even my old gatekeeper has far more sense!" Kumikawa took a great gulp of Scotch and soda from the glass beside him, burped politely, and then added, "I do not know why he has offended my nostrils in bringing a hairy Ainu here, but he has a reason for it."

"A good one," said Yagi promptly. "A fool of a gendarme was about to arrest him who is the messenger from the honorable brothel. In fright, the Ainu made a little shrug of the shoulders, and such is the strength of his arms and body that the gendarme fell flat on his face. It came to me that an Ainu dog, a pariah, a less-than-nothing, might have a place in your plans, O Lord."

THE BARON'S mouth rounded to a bright red O, and then he began to laugh until his ponderous body quivered like a bowl of yellow fish-jelly. "Yagi," he said, when he was able to speak, "I only wish that my councillors here had a little of your intelligence. *Ho!* How the people will love such a spectacle! An Ainu!"

Love what? Lew missed no word.

"From the manner in which the women walked to the temple," said the gatekeeper, "it is time something is done. Their unpatriotic sorrow is clear proof that duty to *aaaa!* the *Tenno!* is being forgotten."

Tsumuri, the wizened Japanese connected with Radio Tokyo, snarled, "Were they beaten for such disloyal conduct? It is to be hoped that the gendarmes made arrests as an example. If I had my way—"

"Beat-kick-slap is your way," broke in Kumikawa disgustedly. "That is all you know. Morale is *induced*. It comes from subtleties." The baron's appraising eyes returned to the stocky figure of the pariah. "You can wrestle?" he asked.

Davies, as if unaware that the question was directed to him, remained silent, head and hands hanging.

"Call the animal by name, Lord," suggested Yagi. "Koropok."

Davies turned humbly toward the gatekeeper.

"Koropok," Kumikawa repeated, and when Davies' eyes faltered up to his, the big baron demanded, "where did you learn to wrestle, Koropok?"

"*Dan' sa' yorosh'k'rba,*" mumbled Davies, in clipped Ainu dialect, apologizing for his very presence. He fumbled for the message which ordinarily would have been given to a servant. When it was out of his pouch, he held it forward fearfully. He muttered, "My master Suriga-san will beat me because I am slow in returning to his house. O Lord, will you beat me also?"

"Nobody will beat you," promised Kumikawa, snatching the note and reading it. "*Geisha* and whiskey, all as ordered," he announced. "I will enjoy both after consummation of my plans." The Japanese rose heavily to his feet, and walked closer to Davies. "I will take care of you, Koropok," he said, grinning evilly.

"Thank you, Lord," said Davies.

"*Chikusho de saye mo on wo shiru,*" chuckled Kumikawa. "The beast has a sense of gratitude; but his muscles are more important." He grinned at the gatekeeper, Yagi, who grinned in toothless response. "When I teach him a little of the art of *shiroto-zumo,* he will wrestle well enough to hurl down whichever starved American prisoner we drag into the ring with him. This will certainly encourage our people. It will be a climax, after they have already witnessed the ease with which our own wrestlers are able to smash Americans. You agree?"

So that was it. American prisoners pitted against professional Japanese wrestlers, who would bang them around for the amusement of the throng. No—it was going to be done for more than mere entertainment. It would show the weakness of

American soldiers—officers, probably, and introduced as such. It would raise drooping Jap morale. It would get minds away from deaths and defeats. And Davies himself, as he was realizing, was to aid in this; he was to be the final unanswerable proof. When a despised Ainu pariah, a spat-upon dog, was seen to be superior to an *Amerika-jin,* how the Japanese would scream, and how their spirits would rise!

"Now," said the baron, waddling back to his chair and draining his glass, "you gentlemen were inclined to listen to Tsumuri, who was all for more punishment. Let me ask you: were you right, or was I?"

While the visitors caroled agreement with the baron, who had been advocating subtle entertainment, Kumikawa's repetition of the words which the Korean had given Davies brought Lew's problem into focus again. How could he answer it, with the Korean under arrest and as good as dead?

Were you right, or was I? Were you, Lew Davies, right in saying that the Imperial battle fleet would be anchored off Tsushima, waiting the proper opportunity to strike, or was Andy Craig right in arguing that it would attack fanatically at the first threat to the Empire? Davies had been right, and knew it; but what could he do about it now? Nothing. And American bombers were in range!

Tsumuri, having lost face, attempted to regain some of it by elaborating on the baron's idea. Smiling all over his face, he wheezed, "*Warui wa iawnai!* How encouraging it will also be to our brave soldiers when they listen to the account! Oh, how I thought of this immediately! I myself will arrange it. Our radio will take the story to them, wherever they may be. How they will laugh when the pariah is named as victor! How they will realize the weakness of Americans!"

"You are forgetting," Baron Kumikawa snapped, "that our soldiers know a little something about the Americans, too, these days."

Again, in spite of Davies' concentration on the problem

which transcended any question of morale, the man known as Koropok had missed none of the talk. If Kumikawa, keenest of the Japanese, had been watching the pariah closely, he might have seen a gleam in the bearded man's dark eyes, which vanished as swiftly as it came. Was there, after all, a possibility of carrying out the order from G-2? A word, one word, could be the answer. Could it be managed?

Davies muttered, "Koropok would like to kill an *Amerika-jin,*" to start things. He began to tremble, acting well, as if suddenly aware of his temerity in speaking without having been questioned by a Japanese.

"You will have your chance," shouted Kumikawa, waving back the other men who would have slapped the Ainu across the mouth. "With your muscles, and what I teach you, who can say that some prisoner will not die in your bear's grip? *Hai!* It is a good thing that in my youth I took part in amateur wrestling in summer-heat! And I was a good man at it, too!"

"I would like to kill *Amerika-jin* soldiers with a gun," Koropok mumbled. He let his shaggy head rise. Then, heart beating faster as he began to plan, he started it by banking on his knowledge of the Japanese. "Koropok," he said, touching himself on the chest, "wants to kill *Amerika-jin* in battle."

Japanese curiosity, as Davies had figured, rose to the bait. Every person in the room demanded, "Why?"

"Because an Ainu is better than those white beasts."

Tsumuri cried, "You see, Kumikawa-*san,* the value of our propaganda!" The Radio Tokyo official was so delighted that he said to Davies, "We will inform the Americans what you have said, Koropok. More, word of your victory over one of their men will be heard by them. Our magic will bring them the words."

Deep in his beard, now that the groundwork was prepared, Davies, said, "O, Lord, in the mountains from which I come it is the custom for the defeated man to admit that he must eat dust."

Would it work?

"I like the idea," said Kumikawa, "but whether or not those stubborn prisoners will admit being beaten is a different matter. I know this much," he added, cutting off what Tsumuri was trying to say, "the fancy performances of Radio Tokyo, where an American loyal to Japan imitates a prisoner's voice, is laughed at in the United States. It must be the voice of the prisoner. Possibly a little persuasion by gendarmes may be advisable, Tsumuri."

"It can be arranged."

"Good," said Kumikawa. He dismissed the meeting with, "Now I will take my walk around my garden and contemplate beauty. You," he said to Koropok, "are to live in my house. Suriga will not object. In one way or another, a brothel-keeper always manages a profit. Let him sleep in your room, Yagi."

And so Koropok came to the mansion.

CHAPTER III

BARON KUMIKAWA'S SCHEME

IT WAS strange to be in a house even in the least corner of it, where there were beds instead of quilts, although the pariah, like the servants, slept on the floor. It was strange, and disconcerting, to smell coffee in the morning, for the first time since arriving in Japan. The baron liked *kohi* on arising, having lived abroad; he liked a steaming bowl of it, and also *hammu-ekk* and *bif-tekki* and something with bones known as *ram cha-ropps*. He read books in English and German; he listened to shortwave broadcasts in both languages; and there was danger in this house, Davies knew from the start. The traveled, shrewd Kumikawa was certain to test Davies masquerade with the acid of his intelligence.

Baron Kumikawa, Davies learned from the beginning of instruction, was engaged in playing with a new and enjoyable toy. The toy was not just a stupid pariah, but an idea: Kumikawa, now fat and middle-aged, intended to utilize the stocky, hardened body of an Ainu to carry out the directions of the baron's mind. The baron would make of the pariah a robot wrestler, mechanically able to carry out the holds of Japanese wrestling, *zumo,* and mechanically able to meet and answer the holds when they were employed by an opponent.

Koropok's training began on the first morning, after a breakfast in which meat was included, since a Japanese wrestler's diet was different from that of other men. After eating, Koropok

"You are forgetting," Baron Kumikawa snapped,
"that our soldiers know a little something
about the Americans, too, these days."

was taken by Yagi to the bare room where the baron exercised with weights and pulleys.

"*Abunai yo!*" warned the gatekeeper, squatting down comfortably and picking his teeth, having investigated portions of the pariah's own meal. "Take care! The lord is so strong that with a touch of a finger on your neck he can send you to your ancestors, if you have any. Obey him in all things, Koropok. He is generous to a fault. If he should reward you with a coin or two, remember that if it had not been for me the gendarmes would have tortured you."

"If the honorable master should do as you say," said Davies, "I will prostrate myself, and beg him to give the coins to you or you will beat me. I—"

The gatekeeper, after blinking and deciding that the Ainu must have spoken innocently, said, "Say nothing. Merely give me any coins."

When the baron arrived, smoking a pungent Cairo-made cigarette, and wearing a cool cotton kimono, the business of making a wrestler out of an Ainu began. Yagi's post at the gate had been taken over by a *jochu.* The gatekeeper was to act as sparring partner during early training, although later Kumikawa mentioned that an actual wrestler might be engaged when Koropok knew a little.

Kumikawa's little eyes surveyed Davies from head to foot when the body of the white man was naked. Although the morning was already hot, Davies was cold under a keener scrutiny than he had ever faced in Japan. But the baron only said, "He is no weakling. Fasten his belt, Yagi," and Koropok was quickly belted with the soft, thick cloth worn by Japanese wrestlers.

Simply, the baron began to explain *zumo,* Japanese wrestling. Had Koropok ever witnessed a contest? Oh, once Koropok had been a sweeper-at-contests, and had been able to see a little? Excellent! Then he knew that there was a square ring, didn't he? Good again! He knew that victory went to the wrestler who was able to shove or push or carry his opponent from the ring?

"Yes, Lord," admitted Davies.

"*Oide nasai!* Come here! See how I suddenly slip my hands down to your belt, and, as you brace yourself, I suddenly seize the knot behind your back, and—*yoh!*—up and backward you go!"

If there had been a ring, Koropok would have been out of it, as the pudgy baron lifted him and carried him backward. Kumikawa was puffing from the exertion, but he was laughing.

"I am not so old as I thought," he gasped to Yagi. "Now, belt yourself, and we will see if Koropok can repeat the operation."

And so the training began. There was the arm-grip and the leg-to-leg and head-to-neck—over and over and over. When these became automatic, Koropok also had to recognize the ejaculation or word of encouragement from the baron which was the signal for employment of a particular grip.

"Enough, for the day," said Kumikawa at last. "He is less stupid than I feared. We are really getting somewhere."

You are, thought Davies, *but am I?*

To accomplish what he intended, Lew knew that he must do a good job of what the baron wanted. Kumikawa had to be convinced that even an Ainu could defeat an ailing American beyond the slightest doubt, for the edification of a Japanese audience. Nor must Kumikawa lose interest, become bored, and decide not to go through with his plans.

If this happened, Davies knew of no other way whereby the answer to Andy's note could ever reach Intelligence.

AT ABOUT the time Kumikawa shortened his training periods with Koropok, Yagi suggested the employment of an old professional wrestler, a *toshiyori* who had taught younger wrestlers before the war. This Kumikawa vetoed. Instead, he found a fat rice-brewer, shaped like a wrestler and weighing over two hundred pounds. He did this, Davies believed, because he had decided that a professional might properly claim some of the credit in the manufacture of a wrestler. However, the actual tugging and pushing and grunting, as brewer and pariah butted one another around in their search for grips, revived Kumikawa's flagging interest.

It was Davies, a little later, after the baron had missed a morning's bout, who muttered that when he had been a *geta-*mender, before being engaged at the honorable brothel, he had seen boys wrestling on summer nights, and it would be helpful if he could again witness the courage and skill of Japanese boys....

Kumikawa jumped at the idea. The radio news was not good. One of these days, the baron believed, Japan's fears of bombing would come true. It was a wonder it had not happened by now; and it made the baron uneasy. The enemy was now within land-based bomber range. Why did they wait? Had they a particular target in mind? A terrible annihilation? The fortunate thing was that the Americans could receive no information as to where, precisely, to strike. Kumikawa had scorn for the gendarmes; but they did follow everyone, and arrested so many that they were bound to net the wishful Koreans and Formosans along with the innocent people. Not that anyone could get word from Japan to America.

Most fortunate of all was that the battle fleet was in security, and refused to risk combat until an attack was made on Japan proper, or until the Americans could be wiped out at sea, as had been done to the Russians.

Kumikawa knew the expressions which he saw on faces in the streets. Did Radio Tokyo think that the evidence of death could be talked or sung out of the minds of mothers and fathers and wives? Perhaps he himself was no smarter, intending to furnish them with morale-building entertainment....

The baron was at this low when Koropok made the suggestion. The baron jumped at the idea merely to be doing something different. He, and his crony-retainer Yagi, and Koropok, went to the poorest part of Tokyo, down stinking narrow alleys, where men and women alike stood stark naked at evening in their doorways. The quarter was swampy; armies of mosquitoes attacked anything human.

"They are like the *Amerika-jin*," complained Yagi of the insects. "They do not attack where we have the right to expect them!"

And there are many of them, thought Kumikawa. *Too many?*

There was an opening at the end of an alley barely four feet wide. Here, on the street, boys of seven and eight competed. The ring was marked off by ropes on the earth; four sticks were the corner pillars. The sky was the roof. Once a nude woman rushed into the makeshift ring to smack the boy who had defeated her own. The umpire was a *gorotsuki,* a crippled black-mailer who lived by threatening thieves and gamblers. His every decision was vehemently questioned. Kumikawa remained silent only during the first bout; after that, he yelled and protested like the most ragged *rikisha*-puller, sweating and red in the face.

An hour ago, he had lounged in a chair, sipping a highball. He had listened to world affairs over the radio and made notes. He had conferred by telephone as important men asked his advice. Now, he was one with the crowd.

"Pull off his arm!" he screeched, as one urchin tried to shove another out of the ring with an arm-grip. "Pull harder!"

The veneer was pretty thin, Lew realized. He, for his part, watched trick and counter-trick, because the baron would certainly speak of them; and it came to the American, watching the monkey-see-monkey-do Japanese boys, who imitated exactly what they had seen before, that there were shrewd and maiming holds and slaps about which Kumikawa had told him nothing. Why? It occurred to Davies, as he looked, that after the Ainu had defeated the American, the audience would have the additional pleasure of watching some gigantic, heavily-muscled and paunched wrestler half kill that selfsame pariah. *If I can get my answer across,* thought Davies, *they can do what they like.*

"Next week," Kumikawa hissed in his ear, "you yourself will be in the ring, Koropok! Thousands will watch what you do to an *Amerika-jin!* And millions will hear him when he is forced to admit his defeat. Are you ready for it?"

"I am ready," said Koropok.

He had spoken more firmly than he intended; but this only pleased the excited baron. "*Mah!*" he ejaculated. "You even talk like a man now! I have done something to you." He began to shake with laughter. "But will Suriga like your future behavior at Number Nineteen? Oh, what a joke that will be on him, when you go back to work for him again!"

Two interpretations of this were possible. One was that Koropok could work again when he was returned to Nineteen, but would be less submissive. The other, toward which Davies inclined, was that Koropok would be so thoroughly pounded, bruised and possibly maimed by a Japanese wrestler, that, when Koropok crept back to Number Nineteen after the performance, it would be a long, long time before he could work at all:

"I am glad I came," Kumikawa grunted, when he tired. "It is proof that intelligent minds can be made to forget the war."

H E O R D E R E D Yagi and Koropok back to the mansion, while he himself sought more soothing entertainment. Along with it, he accomplished the following results: sale of cigarette, orange, shaved ice, and beer concessions for the Great Wrestling; a considerable cut, cash in advance, from the *zumo-jaya*, the tea-house nearest the wrestling hall—because if he had not made the contest possible, they would have had no guests—and an equal amount from the licensed quarter, which, on the night of the wrestling, would do an increased business. On his way home, highly satisfied, he stopped to visit the retired *toshiyori*, the wrestling instructor from whom he had learned many tricks, and not only talked him out of an embroidered heavy silk wrestlers'-apron for the Ainu, but out of a few coins as well, which would put the *toshiyori's* name on the program. It was too late to arrange for a percentage of program sales that night, but the baron would remember to do it in the morning.

He slept well that night. All had gone like clockwork, even if once or twice he had wondered if it were worth the effort.

He slept far better than his protégé, Koropok the Ainu. In Davies' ears, as he twisted on his quilt with Yagi snoring near him, was the sound of thousands of ugly Japanese voices, thrilled at the spectacle of the defeat of Americans by powerful Japanese, and by even an Ainu pariah; American soldiers—fed just enough to remain alive, matched against bull strength and savage trickery.

If the previous weeks had dragged, the final week flew. Koropok was taught the ceremonial preliminaries in such a way that his mistakes would cause laughter. His execution of grips and holds were tested and retested, and also his responses to Kumikawa's coded directions. And then… then, he was on his way to the hall, to the *Kokugikwan,* and, seemingly without the passage of time, he was in a room there, surrounded by Japanese whom the smiling baron had invited to examine the Ainu. The reason for the invitations was almost immediately obvious: the baron was willing to wager that he could pick the exact moment, from the start of Koropok's combat with an American, when the latter would be hurled from the ring.

Davies was in better physical condition than before the baron had started the training; but he was horribly nervous, and knew it. To add to his disturbing doubts, he overheard enough talk to start cold sweat: the heavy units of the American fleet, he heard, were becoming more and more bold, and their battle formations were being plotted by submarines which made no effort to pick off single ships, because before long the entire fleet would be annihilated. The Americans were acting similarly to the Russians, and, as in the Russo-Japanese War, one of these days the Japanese would have the American fleet where they wanted it. Then there would be destruction, after which Japan would move back, island by island, across the Pacific, to the American mainland and victory, to a peace signed in Washington.

Kumikawa finally bowed the other Japanese out of the room. Squatting beside Koropok, he gave him last instructions, a repetition of what he had already ordered. He said at the end, "Rest with closed eyes, Koropok. I know a thing or two of Ainu customs. Before the Ainu go to kill bears for fat and food and skins, it is your tradition to pray to your *kamui,* your god. Do so now, in silence and with all reverence. Pray that your god put strength into your body."

Smart. Davies understood what Kumikawa was about; he was allowing the pariah to hypnotize himself with the idea of victory.

The little room off the great wrestling hall was quiet. Yagi squatted in a corner; Kumikawa calmly read *Japan's Volkswirthschaft und Staatshaushalt* and smiled to himself as he figured from it another way to increase his fortune. And Koropok, in a padded kimono, heard the sounds which filtered into the room.

Japanese laughter. Shrill shouts. As the hall packed from the central ring to the four walls, the noise grew and grew, and out of it rolled the thunder of beaten drums which, in peace, would have been pounded on the top of a drum-tower. The *yagura daiko* pealed like thunder; and when the roaring stopped, abruptly, Davies heard one shout "*Banzai!*"

It was a full minute before the waiting audience, in proper silence now, heard the announcer shout, "On the east, Hitachi-yamaaaaa! On the west, Sunomogoriiiii!" Those would be the first two wrestlers, professionals. Davies, with his eyes closed, envisioned the two fat Japanese with the umpire standing between. When the umpire's fan was lowered, the wrestlers would rush forward.

Deliberately, coldly, the American reviewed in his own mind what he had to do. If his plan were imperfect, it was the only one possible. It might not work. He wondered what his own reaction would be, were he put in the place of whatever American would face him in the ring, in Tokyo, faced by an Ainu….

It was a full half hour before Baron Kumikawa marked his place in the book with a convenient cockroach, handed it to Yagi, and said, "It is time."

Koropok stood up also, and shrugged out of the kimono. He was naked, save for the embroidered vermilion-and-green silk wrestler's apron and the thick, plaited cotton wrestler's belt. He had legs like a running guard's, a lean waist, wide shoulders. He tingled from head to foot.

"Come," said the baron.

CHAPTER IV

TOKYO ROSE

THE NEXT sound Davies heard was the exultant roar of the audience, packed by thousands into the hall, in the center of which, raised above the floor, was the ring. But the outcry, the derision, was not for him.

The howls and jeers were for the three Americans who had mounted to the rope-bordered, pillared ring. One was tall and thin and dark, with a newly healed wound slanting across his cheek. The second was shorter, slight also, with light hair. The third was a true *seiyo-jin*, a red-haired barbarian. As Davies looked up at them, his heart began to pound—with cold, calculated rage, with hot sympathy, and with a great pride.

Not one was afraid.

The Americans were scarecrow-gaunt. Everything possible had been done to make them the objects for Japanese laughter. Their wrestling-belts were of cotton, but strands of red, white, and blue had been twisted through the proper white. Their aprons were of sacking. All three were thin to emaciation.

Davies knew none of them.

While the crowd howled, Kumikawa and Yagi escorted

Koropok toward empty chairs at the corner of the ring where a black-cloth-wrapped post represented the winter-corner. Each pillar about the ring was named for a season; these were the traditional *shihonbashira,* the four pillars of wrestling. In the middle of the ring was a fourth horizontal projection, much lower and thinner than the others, and the object of stares: a microphone. What the Japanese was hissing and spitting into it could not be heard here, but Lew knew that it was being recorded for short wave broadcast to Japanese troops.

When this announcer had finished, gendarmes flanked two other employees of Radio Tokyo as they stepped into the ring. One was a middle-aged white man. The other was a woman, young, attractive, expensively dressed, white—Tokyo Rose. Davies, before he sat clumsily in his chair, as an Ainu would sit, saw the girl move over to the American prisoners where they stood quietly together. She smiled and spoke. She extended her hand graciously.

None of the prisoners accepted it. Good kids, thought Davies. Did they realize what faced them? Davies was pretty sure that they did.

The renegade broadcaster, Tokyo Rose, said something to the three prisoners, in anger. Then she slapped the nearest of the men, the one with red hair. While the audience yelled approval, the American staggered. One of his companions steadied him. Red stained his face, but his lips remained firm.

The hall was stifling hot. There was in it the bitter scent of orange, and the biting odor of black tobacco, and the sickish-sweet smell of Japanese bodies sweating in anticipation. To what happened next Davies shut his eyes, but he could not help hearing what took place.

"On the east," bellowed the umpire, "Kaigetsuuu! Champion! Oh, what do I see on the west? *Dare-mo-nai!* Nobody! Nobody with red hair!"

Davies heard the Japanese' feet stamping; there was a pause, a grunt. A moment of silence. The thud of a falling body.

The audience roared, the high shrill venom of the women piercing the yells of the men—civilians, soldiers, sailors, Royal Marines. Davies heard also the excited treble of Tokyo Rose as she spoke into her microphone. "Can you hear the Japanese nation applauding a Japanese hero, Americans? Don't fight! Disobey your officers! If you continue fighting, you will be made prisoners, while men at home steal your wives. Your fate will be that of these men here. And just think: even a pariah, an uncouth and uncivilized Ainu, can master your officers! Listen! In a moment we are going to broadcast the match between an American officer and an Ainu!"

Kumikawa touched Koropok on the shoulder.

"It is time," he said. "Do you remember everything, Koropok?"

"I am forgetting nothing," said Davies softly.

Then he was in the ring. The baron removed the costly apron after the audience goggled. Davies went through the preliminaries while the entire hall laughed, because the Ainu, instead of gargling with water, spitting it out, and then purifying his body with pinches of salt, did just the opposite. He put the salt in his mouth; he sprinkled water on his body.

His every preliminary posture was wrong. Oh, this was going to be a sight, something to relate for years! How clever was Baron Kumikawa!

Davies avoided looking at his opponent directly. The prisoner was the slight, blond American, outweighed by thirty or forty pounds.

The umpire's fan waved, and dropped. Davies shuffled forward, stamping his bare feet incorrectly. The other American watched him quietly and, as the baron shouted the veiled command for Koropok to grapple and Davies came in, the prisoner lashed out with a left which caught Lew squarely on the nose.

Good kid, thought Davies again. *Nice going, pal!*

The prisoner's left flicked out again in a sharp jab.

"On the whiskers, Fitz!" shouted the tall, dark prisoner.

*"Don't try to put anything
over, Lieutenant,"
warned Tokyo Rose,
as Fitz stepped
reluctantly to the mike.*

But Davies, as the fat baron danced up and down, let the other American's quick right cross slip past, and then had both hands behind the blond prisoner's back and tight about the belt, which brought the slighter body against his.

"Hug him, bear!" encouraged the throng. "Kill him, Ainu!"

It looked as if this were exactly what the pariah was doing. Baron Kumikawa had his watch in hand, mindful of his bets and waiting to give the order which would result in Koropok lifting the prisoner and hurling him from the ring.

Davies said in the other American's ear, "Listen. I'm Llewellyn Davies. Here on duty. Believe me. I've got to go through with this. When it's over, you're going to speak into a mike. I want you to say—"

The prisoner squirmed desperately, trying to free an arm. He could not. "Go to hell," he said.

"When you're given what you've got to say," said Lew, pounding his feet as if anxious to end the struggle, "add this sentence. Say, 'Davies was right, Andy.' Say that. 'Davies was right, Andy.' That's all."

"Go to hell!"

As Kumikawa shouted that which would send the prisoner across the thick rope on the floor and out of the ring, and Koropok's grip tightened, Davies said, "Don't be a damned fool! If the Nips wanted you to say that, it'd be in the script they give you. And don't make a mistake. They may kill you for what you add. But it'll be on the way to G-2… Now I've got to give you the works."

Kumikawa was chattering; if Koropok delayed, the bets would be lost. The crowd was shrieking and yowling. For one fleeting, infinitesimal ticking of time, black American eyes and blue American eyes met.

Then, "O.K. boy," whispered the blond prisoner. "Davies?"

"Davies," said Lew. "Thanks, kid."

He lifted his fellow-American; he slung him out of the ring. But before he was himself able to leave, the baron had scrambled up and stood beside him.

"You are now to be accorded a great honor, Koropok," ha said "You are to be allowed to wrestle Hana-arashi, a great champion. Oh, how fortunate you are, Koropok! What a wonderful chance for you!"

A chance to be torn apart, Davies knew only too well.

Would the American called Fitz say those four words into the mike, which, when monitored, would be the tip-off to G-2? Did the kid believe that the stocky, bearded pariah was also an American, disguised, on duty? If Fitz didn't, Davies couldn't blame him. But he prayed, *he willed him to believe.*

RADIO TOKYO'S official, Tsumuri, was in the ring. The young blond prisoner, after having been doused with cold water, stood naked and dripping beside the scrawny Japanese, with both Tokyo Rose and the male renegade near him. The mike was raised so as to be at the proper height for the *Ameri-ka-jin* prisoner.

Davies, squatting wrestler-fashion, heard Tokyo Rose say, as the audience was quieted, "Have some sense, Lieutenant. If you refuse to read the script into the microphone, you will be tried for insubordination, and you know what a trial means here. Your head. Be nice and do your stuff."

The prisoner shook off the hand which she placed on his forearm.

"If you refuse," said Tokyo Rose, "the rations of every American prisoner of war will be cut in half."

"What do you want me to read?" asked the prisoner.

The male renegade handed Fitz a sheet of paper, at which he stared. His head shook slowly in refusal, slowly as if wavering. His eyes wandered slowly, taking in the strange scene.

When they reached Davies' black ones, they seemed to light, and his tight lips loosened for a fleeting second in the most fragmentary of grins.

"I guess I've got to do it," the young flying officer said wearily.

"Don't try to put anything over," Tokyo Rose warned. "A record is made of what you say. The *record* is broadcast. If you get funny, Lieutenant, another recording will be made. After that, you will be properly punished, of course."

Davies knew despair. The Japanese would never permit the broadcasting of a word which was not in the script. He himself hadn't figured on anything but a live broadcast, going directly over the air.

"I want to add something," the prisoner said quietly, looking up from the sheet of paper in his hand. "I'd like to say, 'Davies was right, Andy.'"

Tokyo Rose snapped, "Why?" while Tsumuri listened.

"Davies is an officer friend of mine," said the prisoner, emphasizing the word friend, "who said that Japan couldn't be attacked by air."

Before Tokyo Rose could turn to Tsumuri, the radio official said, "*Sonnara yoroshi.* In that case, it is all right."

"American boys," said Tokyo Rose into the now live mike, "wherever you may be, this is Rose, an American girl just like those girls of yours at home who are being stolen by the 4F's. And I want to introduce to you Lieutenant Bill Fitzhugh, a boy who was shot down in combat, who didn't have a chance against superior odds and superior skill and superior planes...."

And then Davies heard Fitzhugh's quiet, distinctive voice, which would be identified at home as being truly his; heard the young lieutenant admitting, from the script, the strength of even the pariahs in Japan, men not considered good enough to be in the Imperial army or navy; and, at the end, heard Fitzhugh's slow voice, as the script read, "We can't win, fellows."

Then, as Tokyo Rose smiled at him, he added distinctly, as levelly as before, "Davies was right, Andy."

Tsumuri and Baron Kumikawa were so delighted with Fitzhugh's performance that, as a reward, he and the two other prisoners of war were told that they might watch a true Japanese champion of the ring, Hana-arashi, in action.

Although the pavilion blazed with light, its windows covered lest a gleam attract the long-feared bombers, traditional lamps were lighted atop each of the pillars in honor of the champion.

The audience sighed and leaned forward. Oh, what a sight they were going to see! Oh, this was something!

Tubs of water and bowls of salt were placed at the bases of the east and west pillars. A different umpire mounted to the ring, a Japanese whose fan's handle was tufted with crimson silk, indicating that he was of first rank, as a wrestler of Hana-arashi's class deserved. The *yobidashi,* crier, followed him, and immediately began to shout Hana-arashi's history of victories.

Then Davies saw the ponderous Japanese wrestler climb up and into the ring. A big man, his combed-back hair and top-knot glistening with camellia oil, his apron, of white silk, embroidered in gold and green, with a heavy gold fringe sighing metallically around his thick ankles.

The wrestler's countenance seemed stupid and dull; but the little eyes set deep in the round brown face were keen and alert and as black as rare tomb-jade. Hana-arashi's three hundred pounds of body was round like an elephant's, and there would be terrible strength in the short heavy arms and the strangely developed big, projecting belly. Around it was the plaited wrestler's rope.

It won't be long now, thought Davies. *The lest opposition he gets, the easier it will be on me.* But he doubted whether Kumi-kawa wanted it that way. *I'll probably get the works,* he said to himself.

When Hana-arashi purified his mouth, the crowd roared. When he spat, the throng screamed. When he sprinkled pinches of salt over his belly, the Japanese women became ecstatic. And when the Ainu did everything wrong, excited laughter rolled up to the rooftop.

Kumikawa was going to draw the match out as long as possible, Lew realized, when the baron began whispering to him. Davies, watching his opponent, decided that this wasn't going to happen.

He had completed his job. To hell with giving the damned Nips a show. If Intelligence picked up what was to be broadcast, he had done as important a thing as was possible. Nobody had a right to insist that he become entertainment for Japan, for the small brown apes, as the Chinese called them.

"Hana-arashi will come out raging," whispered the baron. "He will come close, and push his belly at you. When you fear that it will push you out of the ring, he will reach behind you to grasp your belt. It is at that moment that you must slip quickly to the right. Remember now!"

"I will remember," said Koropok.

HANA-ARASHI'S DISCIPLE wrestler who accompanied him had removed the magnificent apron. The champion stood with legs spraddled and raised his arms high above his head. He shouted, "*Yoh! Yoh!*" and brought his powerful hands down crosswise over his belly, where they thudded as if on a drum.

He was ready. His lips curled back disdainfully.

"On the east, the great champion Hana-arashi," cried the umpire, fan waving in a circle. "On the west, what? Koropok the Ainu!" Down came the fan.

Instinctively, after the long rigorous training, Davies met the sudden charge of the big Japanese and gave to it. He heard, or thought he heard, above the din of screams and shrill, venomous shouts, the words, "Get him, boy!" But this could have been his imagination, and not the voice of a half-starved but still defiant prisoner of war.

The camellia oil's scent was overwhelmed by the odor of Hana-arashi's sweating body. Davies heard the baron's shouts; he heard the squeals of the umpire and of Hana-arashi's disciples, all big men; he heard the wrestler's exhaled, "*Yoh!*" as the ring shook to the three-hundred-pounder's feet.

He felt Hana-arashi's enormous belly touching his own; he replied with proper, automatic foot-movement. The Japanese' stubby arms would be slyly seeking a belthold. If Hana-arashi failed in the grip, which was what Kumikawa, betting on time, intended, there would be a second hold, more crippling, and a third and a fourth, each designed to maim and torture.

The audience was becoming crazed with the sight of complete Japanese domination, of Japanese size, of Japanese superiority, of Japanese courage.

Something deep stirred in Davies. Something not to be resisted. He did slip to the right. He saw the glitter of Hana-arashi's eyes as the wrestler's fingertips touched the belt. Then, with his own feet planted firmly, with the muscles of his legs like iron, with Hana-arashi's face inches from his own, Davies' right shoulder drooped slightly. His right hand balled to a fist and, without pause, he brought it up in one fierce, terrible blow against the Japanese' chin.

He moved back as if pushed back. Hana-arashi seemed to be following him, while the audience goggled because the pariah had escaped the famous hold. But the Japanese' second step was his last. Eyes blank, he fell face forward, hit belly-downward, and slowly rolled from the very impact to his back.

Koropok stood as if dazed by what had happened; the pavilion was so quiet that the sound of a lamp's sputter was like a machine gun. Then Hana-arashi's disciple wrestlers, first to recover among the startled spectators, swarmed over the pariah all at once.

Darkness came to Davies mercifully soon.

What took place between that time and the dragging of Koropok back to Number Nineteen was never clear. The next thing he knew, he was kenneled in his hole beside the kitchen, valuable to Suriga only because he was cheap and no able-bodied Japanese could be had for Nineteen's dirty work.

Sometimes guests at Nineteen would be escorted to see this pariah who had been in the ring with Hana-arashi at a time when the champion wrestler was assailed by a momentary sickness; that was the story. Tokyo did laugh at the account of how Baron Kumikawa lost thousands of yen, being unable to per-

suade those men with whom he had wagered that Hana-arashi's
strange illness should have canceled all bets.

Tokyo soon forgot this. The story was being whispered that
now American battleships had thundered against the Philippines. But this fact, to the Supreme Command, only meant that
the arrogant enemy was being coaxed nearer Japan, where before
long an over-confident American fleet, like Russia's fleet in the
past, would be at the mercy of the lurking Imperial Japanese
Navy....

Davies was hobbling painfully about on the night when the
admiral entertained at Number Nineteen.

It was Davies, carrying his bowls and bottles, who first saw
one of the admiral's aiguilletted aides rush in from the street,
brushing aside the maid at the entrance. Davies knew, as he
saw the desperation on the aide's face, that something had
happened. And he knew from the single agonized word which
came, muffled, from the room where the admiral was informed
of the news, what it must be.

"Tsushima!"

And it was Koropok the Ainu, the pariah, who later scrubbed
the blood from the matting in the room where the admiral had
performed *seppuku*—a fact which, like the bombing of the battle
fleet, could not be kept forever from the Japanese people. It
took a lot of scrubbing: but this was a labor of love.

LOST FACE

IT WAS in Number Nineteen, and dark with the velvety blackness of early morning. The entire household slept, the dancing girls and singing girls and the withered old maid-servants and the one remaining manservant, the pariah known as Koropok the Ainu. The nightly guests, Japanese officers and Tokyo officials, snored away, full of saki and Scotch from Singapore and brown Sumatra beer. On thick quilts the manager slept restlessly, as if remembering even in sleep that another increase in taxes would further reduce his profits.

None were disturbed by the *whirr-clank-clank-splash-whirr* of the dredge which worked night and day on the nearby canal, keeping the mud-bottomed waterway open for the barges which assisted Tokyo's beltline railroad in pouring war freight to the wharves. If the scoop dripped mud and slime when it emerged, it sometimes deposited more than ooze when the steel jaws dropped the contents to the mud-scow: A man and woman bound together by the woman's sash. *Shinju,* love suicide. A soldier, hands self-tied, as if he preferred death here rather than at the hands of *Amerika-jin* marines. Bodies of girls were scooped up; and if some had killed themselves because their husbands would never return, others had died in the canal rather than accompany those parties ordered to lonely islands where soldiers demanded comfort. And bodies of babies. Many bodies of babies.

Before long, shouts would demand that Koropok—who

looked like an Ainu bear and who, according to the yells, also
slept like one—awaken and commence his duties in this house
in Tokyo's licensed quarter. From then until long past midnight
the stocky, bearded man would be kept working as the least of
servants. The more degrading the tasks, the surer he would
perform them, particularly when guests could enjoy the degradation of a person of inferior race.

The outcast who slept in foul quilts often wondered what
the Japanese would think if the time ever came when they
learned that he, Nineteen's seemingly servile *hakoya,* instead of
being a despised pariah, was an enemy capable of resistance. In
his disguise as a timid Ainu, among which people he had lived

as a boy, he had been able to cause the Japanese plenty of trouble without being suspected. The slightest suspicion meant that he would be killed, slowly.

Now, Llewelyn Davies, called Koropok, slept. He smiled, as if envisioning the new bombing attacks on Japan's vitals, the steel mills. Perhaps the pilots and bombardiers were again being briefed for attacks, contemptuous of the frightened threats

Kudzumi flung water at Koropok's face. Cold water. "Oh, what a great thing I have unearthed! An Amerika-jin!" *he cried excitedly.*

made by hysterical Radio Tokyo, and only made grimmer by
what happened to prisoners. One of these days the bombers
would be fighter-escorted, by ships different from the P-40s
which Lieutenant Davies had flown at Manila.

Lew stirred. If he had been anywhere save where he was, he
would have glanced at a watch; now, waking came by slap or
kick. He no longer worried about detection. He was secure at
Nineteen, accepted for what he appeared to be. It was a far safer
place than any pariah village on Tokyo's outskirts, where gendarmes ranged daily in dreaded pairs on guard, lest some peaceful Ainu, driven mad at last by the torturing Japanese, might
rush to railway tracks and, by throwing his starved body under
the engine-wheels, delay a shipment of munitions. This had
never happened; but the authorities, knowing what had been
done to Formosans and Koreans, Chinese and Ainu, watched
nervously for any sign of vengeance.

No one watched the *hakoya* Koropok at Nineteen. It had
been the finest spot for harboring the single American on the
loose in Japan, and Davies, black beard grown thick, face gaunt,
had made the most of it.

His cotton sleeping-kimono was so tattered that even the
oldest maid-servant did not want it as a cleaning-rag.

As he slept, the dredge in the canal which ran through the
licensed district clanked away. Into the rhythmic sound was
blended another, similar, and approaching. Footsteps. Not that
ox clacking *geta* on the street, nor of straw sandals within the
house. The sound of booted feet.

A harsh summons, with each *k* like a cough, spoke in the
entrance hallway. The awakened manager's sleepy but unctuous
response only caused Davies to burrow deeper into his molting
quilts. When Suriga, the manager, protested, "*Sore wa domo
chito shinjiraremasenu!* I can hardly believe it!" to what was said
to him, Davies heard nothing at all in his heavy pre-dawn sleep.

"*Wak-k-k-karimasu k-k-k!* Take us to him!"

The heavy footsteps advanced along the corridor, past the

kitchen, to the hole were Koropok kenneled. A flashlight cut a yellow circle in the smelly gloom. Davies, face away from it, did not stir.

Standing over him was a gendarme officer, one hand about the flash, the other on the butt of his holstered automatic. Behind the thin-faced officer were two of his men, the dreaded government police, one with handcuffs waiting. All were immaculate in dark uniforms and shining boots. The beaks of their stiff caps had a vulture-like droop. Behind them was Suriga, his round and oily face rolling from side to side above his naked chest, his eyes popping, his mouth shut only because of the universal fear of the gendarmes.

THE OFFICER'S lips curved in a thin smile as he looked down at the sleeping *hakoya*, the Ainu dog. He said nothing, nor gave any order, as if words were not needed for what was to be done; then he stepped back slightly, nodded to his men, who grinned also, and without further preliminary he kicked the sleeping American as hard as he could. Almost at the same instant the pair behind him jumped forward and dragged the kicked man to his feet, twisting his arms behind him. The flashlight burned into Davies' eyes.

For the smallest fraction of time he was without thought, and every muscle was rigid. The pain in his back where he had been booted told him the method by which he had been awakened. Then, *This is it!* thought Lew.

He made no resistance.

The thin-faced gendarme officer was staring at him intently. "*Dok-k-ko k-k-ka de mita yo ni o'masu,*" he muttered. "I have seen him somewhere."

You have, Davies agreed silently and with sinking heart. *You worked in the Luneta Bar in Manila. You're Kudzumi, the fellow we called K-k-k-katy.*

Suriga said, "Assuredly you have seen him. He has acted as messenger to important personages. Oh, he has often gone to the residence of the baron himself." The manager made a dutiful little bow. "The baron has declared himself pleased because Koropok would run all the way. Oh, the baron is not going to like this! No! When he learns about it—"

"It will be too late for him to do anything," snapped the officer. He continued staring at the man known as Koropok, while Davies waited. At last Kudzumi grabbed the American's black beard and gave it a furious jerk. "Do not lie," he snarled. "Where have I seen you?"

Davies stood with lowered head, not because it was proper Ainu-fashion when in the presence of a Japanese officer, but because Kudzumi's hold on his beard forced his head almost against his chest.

He said, in clipped Ainu dialect, "*Shir'senu goz'asu.*"

"You do not know? You are a liar!"

"Correct what displeases you in me," mumbled Davies, "but I do not know where you, a great lord, has seen me."

Kudzumi grated, "Where have you lived? Quickly! We waste time!"

Davies told him, naming the Ainu settlement in north Japan which could be verified. He knew he was under arrest. But why? Because of what he was, of what he had accomplished? It didn't look like it. Suriga would do everything possible to retain a husky and unpaid servant; but what did K-k-k-katy mean by saying that it would be too late for the baron to help Nineteen's manager? *If I were merely to be held in jail,* Lew knew, *the baron could pull wires. So either I'm to be executed chop-chop, or shipped off somewhere in a hurry.*

T H E R E   W E R E   faces in the opening to Koropok's cubbyhole, awed and curious and frightened—the girls of the household. When it was light they would be herded to the bath and to the hairdresser's, but not again by the *hakoya* Koropok. The youngest *oshaku*, barely thirteen, whispered a question to the honorable cook. The thin gendarme officer, eyes still fastened on the swarthy, bearded face of the "Ainu" as he strove to recognize him, let go his grasp and whirled around.

"Tell me something about this dog," he shouted, "and I will bring my custom to this house. I am a generous man!"

The little *oshaku* said, "He is not very clumsy sometimes when he carries trays with bottles and bowls. Sometimes he is more clumsy. Once an honorable guest was made angry by his clumsiness. Once—"

"Be still!" Kudzumi stared at Davies again. The Japanese said, aloud but as if to himself, "Drinks," while Lew, cold as ice, waited for recognition.

Outside of Nineteen, the dredge clanked away. *Clank-clank-whir*rrr*rr-splash.* A vendor of *hamanabe,* of clam flesh, lifted a cracked old voice from the eating shop just beyond the district. A two-motored plane on patrol began its dawn flight; and although it was Japanese, it sent the vendor scurrying.

Inside, the sound brought trembling. Oh, the *Amerika-jin* were inhuman; nobody knew when ten of their giant dragon-

The officer looked down at the sleeping Ainu,
Suriga's round, oily face peering over his shoulder.

flies, or fifty, or a thousand perhaps, might be bringing death to Tokyo. Inside, the maids cowered, the two gendarmes tightened their grasp on the Ainu, and their officer's face puckered in thought until it was like that of a puzzled monkey.

What more does the ring-tail need? wondered Davies. *He's sure to catch on now. Not even a Nip can be so dumb.*

Pinioned as he was, Lew believed that he had a chance of reaching Kudzumi's gun, to go down fighting. It seemed impossible that the former bar-boy in Manila could fail to put two and two together and get the right answer, which was that the Ainu "Koropok" was an Air Forces officer. The time to make the attack would be at the exact moment of recognition; Kudzumi would ejaculate something, and the pair of his men holding Koropok would, as they looked hastily at their superior, be bound to relax their grips slightly. Which would be enough.

You've had your share of luck up to now, Davies told himself. He did wish that he might have continued with his partially-formulated plan to cripple a new and important plastics factory near the district; it would have been fine to hurt these devils just once more. But being killed here would be far better than torture, and he hoped to be able to take K-k-k-katy with him when he went.

Davies' downcast head did not mean that he wasn't watching the Japanese. *How in hell can he miss?* thought Lew, as the officer's face remained puzzled.

Suddenly Kudzumi, realizing that everyone was watching him, and that he had expressed a doubt which he had not been able to solve and had therefore lost a great deal of face, shouted, "*Sore ja i-k-k-ko!* Let us go! If there is anything peculiar about him, I will learn it later." He fumbled for notebook and pencil, and began to write, after handing the flash to one of his men. "*Hak-k-koya* of Number Nineteen," said Kudzumi, writing. "Ainu." He paused. "What is your name, Ainu?"

Davies' mouth said, "K-k-koropok-k-k."

Damn! thought Lew. *Oh, damn, damn, damn! It just popped out!*

"What?" screamed Kudzumi. "What? You mock me?"

The gendarme officer flung himself on Davies, beating with his fists against the pinioned man's face. Davies could have reached the gun, but made no effort to do so. K-k-k-katy still believed him to be an Ainu; and as such he would merely be beaten and arrested. O.K., provided he remained alive in Japan.

KUDZUMI SHRIEKED for his men to throw the hairy animal to the floor—and the kicking began. At first it was a wild, impassioned business, during which Kudzumi howled with rage, aware that the girls of Nineteen would relate the story of the mocking for the amusement of military officer-guests, who would laugh because a gendarme had lost face. Then, as Davies protected his head as best he could with his arms, Kudzumi controlled himself, although his hatchet-thin face was contorted and, hot as persimmons in sun, the same fiery red.

Deliberately, to the accompaniment of the excited indrawn breaths of the maids and the manager's mumbling at this spoiling of his human property, Kudzumi proceeded to kick the pariah Koropok into insensibility.

For an instant Davies wished he had fought. But what good would it have done to shoot one ring-tail gendarme? That wasn't why Lieutenant Davies was in Tokyo. *He must have been ordered to round up pariahs,* Lew guessed, *and he doesn't dare kill me unless I resist.* But as the kicking continued, Davies realized that the gendarmes could lie, and the girls would testify to whatever they were told.

Pain vanished. The room became bright. Skyrockets, pinwheels, yellow and green and silver, whirled before Davies' closed eyes. Must be Fourth of July at Manila. Luneta Bar. Light flashing off glasses polished by K-k-k-katy. By K-k-k-kudzumi. The brown bug. Lew's lips moved silently in a Manila song:

C-c-c-cootie,
Horrible cootie!
You're the only b-b-b-bug that I abhor;
When the m-m-m-moon shines
Over the barracks,
I will scratch my b-b-b-back until it's sore.

After that, not even Llewelyn Davies' lips were able to move.

Early as it was, the district turned out to see the Ainu *hakoya* of Nineteen being dragged by the gendarmes along the street lined with ornately carved buildings. Oh, what a beating Koropok had been given! Why? Undoubtedly because he was fearful of being sent somewhere in uniform, where he would be shot by an *Amerika-jin* bullet or blown to bits by shells from an *Amerika-jin* ship, or, worse, be stabbed by those *Amerika-jin* marines who fought like the fiends of hell. Did he not appreciate such an honor, which included the saving of the life of a Japanese soldier who otherwise would have died? Oh, Koropok really deserved a terrible beating for such ungrateful conduct. And he had received it, as all could see.

His limp body was placed in the first two-wheeled cart found outside the gates; and while the old *kurumaya* who rented and pulled it grumbled at being impressed, because gendarmes always pocketed the fee which a man earned, he did his objecting under his breath. One did not provoke the gendarmes.

The leaven of distrust worked away in Kudzumi all the way to the building into which the younger and stronger Ainu were being herded. Again and again the officer stared at the relaxed face of the man sprawled in the *kuruma.* It told him nothing. If there were anything unusual about the Ainu, Kudzumi wanted to know it before he turned the pariah over to the gendarmes captain; Kudzumi wanted the credit. What he did not want was to be laughed at for a ridiculous suspicion.

Then he thought of something worth trying. "Stop," he ordered. "One of you go into that shop. Bring a bucket of cold water. Make haste."

When he had the bucket, he had not made up his mind exactly what to do. Should he snap a question at the bearded man, when a drenching aroused him? Or should he listen closely to whatever the pariah might say?

"He makes me think of somebody," Kudzumi muttered, half audibly. "He is similar in appearance to a Welshman. Black. Bearded. Could I have seen him when I was on duty in Singapore? Shanghai?"

Kudzumi tried to imagine the *hakoya* in the uniform of a Welsh Fusilier, but to no avail. In true Orient-fashion, he refused to recollect that the beating had been given because he had thought that an inferior had mocked his method of speech.

The old **kurumaya** *who pulled Koropok's limp body in his cart grumbled at being impressed.*

The Japanese never recalled disgraceful happenings, but forgot them instantly.

Kudzumi flung water at Koropok's face. Cold water.

"Ouch," mumbled Davies. "Damn!"

Kudzumi missed neither word. His eyes lit and burned. "So that's what you are!" he snarled, as he danced up and down with excitement. One of his hands gripped the half-conscious man's bare shoulder like the claw of a dredge. "Oh, what a discovery! Oh, what a great thing I have unearthed! An *Amerika-jin!*"

How Llewelyn Davies guessed fuzzily what he must have said, not even he himself understood. Perhaps it was because, as consciousness came, he was about to repeat it. He whispered again, so exactly similar in sound, "*O cha,*" which always sent a maid at Nineteen scurrying to bring tea for an arriving guest; and he added, "*Dann',*" clipping the word *danna,* in the manner of an Ainu speaking Japanese. With that word, meaning lord, he would have bowed to a guest coming to Nineteen... "*O cha. Dann'.* Tea for the lord."

Davies could see that Kudzumi was no longer positive. "*Kann' shi' k'sare,*" Lew pleaded. "Please have patience with me. I am only a stupid Ainu. My body believed it was at my master's honorable house at Nineteen. I—"

"Throw him out of the *kuruma,*" said Kudzumi disgustedly, with the coughed *k's* crackling. "He is a complete fool."

While Kudzumi strutted toward the building into which other Ainu were brought, one of the gendarmes was about to kick the pariah some more, until his companion reminded him that the outcasts were to arrive in a living condition and able to work in lands where weakened men would die too soon; an additional beating might send the spirit of the pariah down to whatever gods he dared to have. So Koropok was allowed to limp weakly ahead of the gendarmes.

Davies had heard what the gendarme said. He was terribly bruised, but what was hurting most as his head cleared was the probability that his usefulness in Japan was at an end. He would be shipped off in a labor battalion. Where? What difference did it make? He couldn't do anything about it, either. There was the feeble hope that Suriga, Nineteen's manager, might pull wires to recover his *hakoya*, but this would take time. Even if Suriga managed it, the average life of a Korean or Chinese or pariah Ainu, on some island, was measured in weeks.

I wish I could've done something about this new plastic, thought Davies, as he stood with hanging head before a gendarme captain. But there hadn't been time.

THE CAPTAIN was barking questions as each Ainu was shoved in front of his desk. Beside the gendarme officer were several army lieutenants, one of whom directed the answers to an army sergeant. When it was Davies' turn, a lieutenant hissed that it looked as if the fellow had been beaten. Oh, yes, agreed Kudzumi instantly, the ugly dog had said impolite words to his master when leaving his master's house, and with the result which could be seen. If proof were needed, Kudzumi's two gendarmes would testify to it.

"*Warak-k-k-keredo shik-k-k-kata g-g-g-ga nai,*" said Kudzumi. "We were unable to prevent it."

"We waste time," grumbled the captain testily.

Davies answered his questions, and the sergeant wrote. Koropok. Ainu. Age not known, but about twenty-five or thirty. Occupation, *hakoya*. Police record, none. Papers in order. Family, none.

"Koropok," the captain said. "*Ha!* A word has been received by telephone. It is suggested that we wait a little in his case."

Davies thought, *Suriga!*

The antagonism between gendarmes and army flared. The lieutenant said, "So you can have him attempt to escape? No! We need men with strong arms. Your orders are to certify to us those men we wish. Well, I wish him."

The captain was angry. The orders were exactly as the lieutenant had stated, but the captain had just been asked, as a favor, to delay the matter of assigning the Ainu named Koropok, but that had not been an order. An order for it would come before long, the captain supposed, because Suriga knew important men. And the captain would have liked to put Suriga in his debt; oh, there was fine entertainment to be had at Nineteen, and, as the manager had intimated, all free, too.

"Do you desire me to get in touch with my superiors?" asked the lieutenant, as the captain sought to find a way out.

"No," the captain said.

He would have gladly blamed Koropok for the whole affair, but could do nothing to the damnable pariah. Kudzumi! That was a different matter.

"I believe," he said, holding down his anger, "that your usefulness here is at an end, Kudzumi. Hold yourself in readiness for new assignment." A notion came to the captain, and he grinned maliciously. "A new assignment," he repeated.

Koreans were marched to the docks to lie chained below decks with the pariahs.

Kudzumi, face draining of color, bowed low before his superior.

"I will take the Ainu Koropok," the lieutenant repeated.

The sergeant's lips formed the word he wrote. Taiwan.

Taiwan—Formosa. And that, thought Davies, is that. It didn't make much difference whether he was worked to death in the coal mines or in the camphor jungles. It was a death sentence, either way. He knew utter despair.

What followed was like a bad dream. Rough clothes were given the pariahs, some of whom would be shipped to islands where, when the Americans came, the Ainu would be killed by the Japanese at the very beginning of the attack.

The strongest were quickly marched down to the docks, to labor in Formosa, and Davies, that night, lay chained below decks, body to body with Ainu and Koreans.

The coastwise steamer rolled as it hugged the rocky shore, and the pariahs were terribly sick. After following the protective inland water to Nagasaki, the ship joined a convoy, and with it scurried for the Loochoo Islands. From a word here and there dropped by the guards, Davies learned to his grim satisfaction that the Japanese, in their own back yard, were afraid of American subs. What would happen to the chained men, including Davies himself, in case of a torpedo attack, the bearded Koropok knew only too well. At first he wondered if even that wouldn't be better than death in Formosa; but a fellow didn't want to die until he had to.

The pariahs suffered silently. They had suffered all of their lives. Once their fathers, and they as children, had lived in freedom in the wild craggy peaks of north Japan; once the Koreans had lived gently in a gentle land. By now, both had been beaten down. Of all the men chained on the ship, only one thought about fighting, chained and finished as he was.

I'll bet, thought Davies, *that before I'm worked to death I get me a couple of nice, fat, nasty Nips.* A gendarme for choice.

Kiirun Harbor. A train. Taihoku, and out of Taihoku. Rice

on the bottom land, and graves. Sugar-cane and beans and sweet potatoes. Indigo. Bullock and coolie-carts. Pole-burdened carriers trotting chop-chop fashion along narrow trails. Water-buffalo. Japanese women in drab kimonos, and Cantonese women, and Foochow field-women with three long pins as head-dress, and Formosan women, brown and slender, in trousers, jackets and mushroom hats, shoveling ballast along the railway.

Davies saw none of this. He and other pariahs were in a box car, ventilated only at the roof, where a guard sat, rifle poked through the hole. He came down only once, to stare in the gloom at a half-alive Korean who had been unable to eat anything since leaving Japan. He stared at the dying man solemnly, said, "*Komatta mono da.* He is worthless."

The guard cut the sick man's throat with his bayonet.

No one moved or spoke. No one moved even when the guard

There were brown slender Formosan women
shoveling ballast along the railway.

turned his back and clambered up the ladder to his post on the car's roof.

Only the man called Koropok had hands which were clenched to fists.

He thought, *Getting rid of just one Jap like the guard would be something.* He cursed the guard as silently as the Korean had died; and then he cursed himself. *Quit being sorry for Lew Davies,* he told himself bitterly. *Quit wanting to keep on doing big stuff. Do what you can, wherever you are. Kill one Jap. Hell, an infantryman is just as important as a bombardier, even if a bomber can kill a hundred Nips. What you need is a powerful kick in the pants.*

For a second, wild notions came to him, such as organizing the pariahs and Koreans where they were sent to labor, and killing their guards and escaping to the hills, where they could descend on the Japanese by night. But when he looked about at the beaten-down men, he realized the hopelessness of such a plan. But, damn it, he would find something to do, somehow. It would be far better to be killed in the performance of his duty than to die, exhausted, working for the ring-tails.

Davies felt better after that.

CHAPTER II

THE SKY-TIGERS

WHEN THE train stopped, the Ainu and Koreans were checked and then chained together and marched through the street of a small mountain village. The trail on the eastern side of the village started gradually, narrowed, and then steepened. In five minutes the ascent became difficult, and Davies wondered if there were no easier way to wherever they were going. It seemed impossible that anything could be transported along such a steep and mountainous way, or over the slender, swaying bamboo-and-rattan bridges by means of which the ravines were crossed.

Signs in the village, and marks on rattan-tied bundles and crates there, had told Davies where he and the others would go. To the camphor jungles. It was said in Tokyo that when a Japanese was sent to the Formosan hills, sooner or later his ashes would be sent back to Japan, but without the ash of his head being included in the little black and silver lacquered box. His head would remain in Formosa, a trophy of the savage native Taiyals, whom the Japanese were able to include in the East Asia Co-Prosperity Sphere only when dead.

Few soldiers could now be spared as guards to protect camphor production from the attacks of the savages. But when the war was won, Tokyo promised, the native Formosans would find out what the Koreans had already learned. Oh, the nasty savages would pay a price for their uncivilized behavior!

Soon Davies learned why the chained men, including himself, were being hurried at bayonet point up the difficult trail where each surmounted ridge showed only a higher and steeper one behind it. He had found it out by the time he saw the first long-abandoned Taiyal huts, hovels of slate slabs overgrown by ferns which grew taller than the roofs. The reason was simple, and very Japanese. Those men in the gang who were unable to keep the pace, who fell from weakness brought about by con-finement and insufficient food, were immediately unchained. They were stripped, unresisting, of their coarse new clothes. Then they were stabbed and, as they were dying, were tumbled down into a ravine.

"This is how I would kill an *Amerika-jin* pilot!" a guard would scream, as his bayonet ripped at a fallen Ainu. And, "This is what an *Amerika-jin* marine can expect from me!" another would squeal, hopping up and down as he stabbed.

Only the hardy ones, who would last a while and repay Japan for the food which must be given them, finally reached the jungle camphor-camp.

It was in a clearing. The path led to a guarded, electrified barbed-wire fence; inside were crude low buildings and, in sheds with open sides, the camphor-stills with their iron *namsho-type* stoves. Not all of these were smoking, nor were there great piles of camphor chips waiting to be fed to the retorts. The camp was short of workers. It needed men, to cut down the giant trees to the east of the camp and deeper in the jungle, and to carry the sacked, pungent chips back to the stoves for distillation. It needed men to take the pure-white camphor, exactly resembling snow, and the exudations—the red, brown and white essential oils—down the none-too-easy miles to the hand-cars.

Such a man was Koropok.

Another man, now also considered expendable, was standing inside the ten-foot-high fence. The first words which Davies heard, as he shuffled with the others through the gate, were, "*K-k-k-kita k-k-k-ka?* Is he here?"

He means me, Lew was sure. *So I get the works.*

Kudzumi, standing beside the guard officer he was relieving, was shoving up the lowered head of every chained man, looking for one in particular. The Japanese was no longer in the immaculate uniform of a gendarme. Because of his brief service, his new khaki had not been tailored to his thinness; there was too much of it across the shoulders, and around the middle and not enough in the leg, and his face, from the moment he had arrived, dared anyone to comment.

He had been on the same ship as the impressed Ainu and Koreans; he had come part way to the camp in a hand-car pushed by Chinese and then, the final miles, along the easier way ordinarily taken. Even this less steep ascent had been unpleasant for the stuttering ex-gendarme who, despite his thinness, had enjoyed many gendarme prerogatives and had lived luxuriously. Being a Japanese, he did not blame himself for this new assignment. Nor did he blame his superior, which would have been unpatriotic, as well as futile. He had someone better to blame: Koropok the Ainu.

The officer whom he was relieving was all smiles, because he was getting away alive; but to Kudzumi this cheerfulness said,

"Oh what a fool is Kudzumi, now assigned to the worst place in the Empire! What face he has lost!"

What the retiring guard officer did actually say, and mean, was, "You are fortunate. I wish I had been sent men as strong as these." Perhaps the officer thought to soften what was obviously a blow to the former gendarme, for he added, "Doubtless you will make a name for yourself here."

"I will make a name for myself," said Kudzumi, each *k* like a whip's crack, "but not in the way you mention. Oh, how I will force these animals to sweat! How I will make them wish they had never been sired!"

To Davies, as he shuffled nearer in his place along the chained line, it sounded exactly like the boasts of the men who had killed the faltering ones. His turn, he was sure, was not far off.

The retiring officer shrugged. There was a problem, he stated. If the laborers were badly beaten, they would not work. And if they did not work, there would be no camphor, which was in demand for some new celluloid compound which would assist in winning the war, and which was being shipped out of the camp in too small quantities. "If there is any falling off in shipments," the officer said, gravely, "let me assure you, as one who knows to his sorrow, that somebody in Tokyo will want to know about it. Because if—"

"Are you intimating that I do not know my duty?" demanded Kudzumi, turning away from the slowly-passing line of chained Ainu and Koreans, and causing Davies to hope for a short respite before the Japanese discovered him. "Is that what you are saying? I do not permit such a statement I—"

"You are no longer a gendarme," the other said flatly, "nor am I an Ainu. So speak more politely, if you please."

"*N' moshi wak-k-ke,*" said Kudzumi. "Please excuse me." What lost face! Then, resuming his examination of the arriving gang, his eyes blazed. He began to shake with contemplation. His "*Ma!*" of satisfaction rocked him.

He had seen Koropok, now in striking range. He slapped

him with all his might; and because the Ainu and Koreans ahead of Davies continued shuffling along, all in line and chained together, Kudzumi, frothing, was forced to follow the procession to keep up with his victim. As the former gendarme raged and slapped and kicked, he began to inform Koropok what was going to happen to him.

THE RELIEVED officer muttered, "*Kono baka yaro.* How the damned fool gabbles! He is a low-class fellow. I am glad that I do not serve with him." The officer wondered what an Ainu could have done to have aroused such vindictive anger. It was none of the officer's affair; but if Kudzumi had been less nasty and impolite, the officer would have explained, in a round-about and subtle manner, that a performance such as this was causing Kudzumi to lose face in front of the guards. "He is a regular gendarme," the officer muttered, and strode away.

The last thing which he heard was Kudzumi's, "You will go to the most dangerous places, you Koropok! Oh I will not kill you myself! Oh, no! Once I gave you a bit of what you deserved, and my patriotic action was not understood. Now, when you die horribly, it will be the savages who kill you!"

Davies, head spinning, managed to flinch like a beaten animal at each furious blow. His own anger was burning blood-bright within him; if he had been loose, nothing could have held him off the ex-gendarme. Kudzumi's last performance was to grab the thick, black hair of Davies' head, as if trying to tear it off.

"The savages," jeered Kudzumi, "will admire such a hairy, dirty head as this, Koropok!" He gave a final tug as he screamed, "The one sort of head which they desire more is that of the filthy, cowardly, uncivilized *Amerika-jin!*"

A stolid guard, removing the chains and replacing them with the short chains by means of which each impressed worker was fastened to the log beside which he slept, stopped more of the tirade. Kudzumi demanded what was being done. When he was told, his orders were that daylight remained and therefore the dogs should be taken into the jungle and worked until dark.

"Anything less than that," shouted Kudzumi, to recover face, "would be unpatriotic."

The guard, dumb Japanese field-worker that he had been until sent to Formosa, had sufficient sense to be glad that he was assigned to duty within the camp. He would not have cared to be in the jungle at evening, when a shadow could be a shadow, but could also be a Taiyal prowling for a head.

The tired gang was divided into groups. Two guards were to accompany each of the Ainu and Koreans.

Inside the guarded, electrified barbed-wire fence were crude low buildings and, in sheds with open sides, the camphor-stills with their iron **namsho-***type stoves.*

The camphor trees near the camp had already been cleared away. The wilderness, the jungle, was like nothing anywhere in the world. Davies had never seen such a mass of twisted and entwining plant life, impenetrable save where the trail had been hacked, and shutting out the sun. Earth seemed unnecessary for growth; there were innumerable varieties of parasitical plants, drawing life from the growths to which they were attached. Some of the rattans and other strange creepers wound erratically from tree to tree, binding all together in as unbreakable a chain as the one which was again holding the impressed workers. The rattan itself, sometimes as long as five hundred feet from root to tip, was covered with sharp, hooked thorns. Davies could see why the Japanese had been unable to rout the Taiyals, the native Formosans, out of such a wild place.

Gradually, as Davies' gang was driven ahead, the mass of ferns, creepers and wiry grasses thinned, and an occasional camphor, leaves soft and shining, could be seen, an outpost of the forest-jungle beyond. The path now slipped around the side of a cliff, and the two Japanese guards became doubly alert, as if here there had been the twang of an arrow or the hiss of a knife. The pathway was scarcely wide enough to afford foothold, and one of the Koreans pressed his body in fear against the rock wall. Just as a guard leveled his gun at the slim Korean, the man gathered his store of courage, squeezed his bundle of chip-sacks more tightly to him, and managed to continue, his face like parchment.

Poor devil, thought Lew.

He had made up his mind to this: for Davies, the *shi-ju-pun,* the camphor-camp, would be the finish. *The cavalry,* thought Lew, eyes on the unbelievable path, *will never come over the hill and rescue you, fellow.* Balanced against personal desire to square accounts with Kudzumi was the fact that the destruction of the least amount of camphor would be a more honest carrying out of orders than the killing of one Japanese. Less camphor, less plastic.

Davies tried to tell himself that if he took care of Kudzumi it would cripple the camp's production; but this wasn't true. Kudzumi, with his rages and self-pity, would do production no good.

Chained as Koropok would be each night, what could be done at all?

As he almost made a misstep, with jagged rocks far below, he told himself, *You keep your eyes open, boy. That's all you can do.* He meant this in more ways than one. He had to wait, even if nothing came of it.

Camphor trees, of insufficient size for cutting, were becoming more numerous. Through their tops Davies could see densely forested hills, a foreground for a mountain with wavelike peaks crowned with snow. Beyond that mountain must be the slopes down to the Pacific, beyond which lay the chain of the Marianas. South was the Bashi Channel, Luzon, Manila, from which Lieutenant Davies had been sent... so long ago. Manila, where K-k-k-katy, the polite and smiling bar-boy, had done his stuff so well for His Imperial Majesty's Intelligence.

It was sheer relief for Davies to swing his axe, when the guards finally selected a tree suitable for cutting. The bite of steel into wood, the clean pungent smell of camphor, the start of his own sweat, made a fellow forget things. It made him remember things, too: kindling at home, coffee and bacon and eggs sputtering. Home, home, home....

"A good worker, that pariah," one of the guards remarked to his mate. "He has seen an axe before. Our output should be good. Perhaps you and I will receive some reward because of what we accomplish here. Yes, I should like a cigarette! I wonder why our new commander is angered with him?"

"In some way the Ainu must have caused the honorable commander to lose face," the other guard surmised. "How? Who can tell?"

"This is a fine country in which to lose face," said the first; and, although both giggled, they saw to it that their weapons were ready.

The camphor tree on which Davies and another pariah were working was a splendid one. Fully thirty feet in circumference at the base, it towered high into the late afternoon sun. The tree was not being immediately felled. Chips, from as high as the axemen could reach, were being clipped from the standing giant; the tree would fall when enough had been cut away.

Some of the other weakened pariahs chopped at their trees as if, as one guard said, they were paring fingernails. Before long the lash was applied.

Bite of axe. Sweat. Sun and jungle silence. A lowering sun and a greater jungle silence. Bite of axe….

When the tree shivered at last, and fell, the sound of its death roared and thundered up to the mountain and back, and the jungle came alive.

Long after the guards had sent the weakest of the workers to fill sacks with leaves, from which oil was distilled also, strange birds of brilliant plumage continued screaming in the jungle. A red-bellied king crow screamed a stuttering *k-k-k-kaw chee-djeee!* until Davies' tired face relaxed into a grin. He wished that the commander, K-k-k-kudzumi, could have heard it.

WHEN THE sacks were filled, the guards nodded at the same instant. It was not yet dark. A strange aliveness had been born in the jungle, which caused the guards to finger their guns and to shout for all of the work-gang to join them for the return to the camp. Only one man was missing, a small, smooth-faced Korean who had been wearily stripping leaves from the upper branches of the felled camphor tree. When the men sent out to look by the uneasy and fearful guards finally found him, his body had been gashed by a spear. A hurled spear, judging from the wound. The Korean's head was gone.

"He looked like a Japanese," a guard shuddered. "That is why they removed his head, although it was a small one."

The other guard, licking his lips, said, "These Taiyal savages have never seen bearded men like the pariahs."

Davies, plodding back toward the camp, laden like the others with sacked chips, supposed that this was true. The return trip was not fun. It took everything he had, after what had already happened to him, to maintain footing on the difficult trail, to keep from being torn from it by creepers or hooked by immense thorns. And when he returned to camp, Kudzumi would be there waiting for him, Lew knew.

In this Davies was correct. After the workers had been counted and fed, they were chained to logs in a dark area of the camphor-camp, where they would sleep until pre-dawn. But Kudzumi had selected a special sleeping-place for Koropok, the former *hakoya* of Nineteen. A log had been rolled between two camphor stills which would be worked all night. It would make no difference which way the night-winds blew; smoke would swirl around Koropok and sting him. It would make no difference which way he turned, right or left; flames from the stills' fireboxes would glare into his eyes. If he moved to his back, he could not shut out the overhanging light by which the retort-feeders worked. He could not turn on his face. The chains were so fixed that this would not be possible.

Kudzumi came during the night to admire his scheme. As the camp commander stared down, he muttered to himself again as he had at Nineteen in Tokyo, "*Dok-k-ko k-k-ka de mita yo ni o'masu.* I have seen him somewhere. I wonder," Kudzumi went on in a sufficiently audible voice for the chained American to hear, "what the dog would look like without that beard?"

Kudzumi would have called for a razor, and shorn him on the spot, but to remove the beard of an Ainu might be serious. Not only Koropok, but the other hairy imbeciles would cover their pleads with their arms because of the exposure. Not an Ainu would eat, nor work, nor move. Kudzumi did not know why this was, but it was true. It had something to do with animal-gods which the damnable Ainu worshiped. If the ugly Ainu refused to eat or work, no camphor would be produced. Kudzumi was not yet ready to bring about his own demotion.

It came to him, as he stared down at Koropok and weighed the possible action, that another demotion might mean assignment to some island a little nearer to the *Amerika-jin* than Formosa. Not that even Formosa was so far away any more. But practically to ask for such an assignment, by failing to ship camphor, would be exactly like performing *seppuku*. As Kudzumi spat at the chained Koropok and then moved off, he could almost feel the pain of the thin, sharp knife which should be ripped up diagonally in making the first belly-cut.

My father, thought Kudzumi, *was a saki-brewer, and not a samurai. What right have I to aspire to such a noble death?* This reasoning was face-saving.

In the morning, Davies' eyes were red and burning, and during the long, hard day, it became less easy to keep his axe swinging to wedge off the chips of camphor. At the end of the day's work, another member of the gang was missing. This time his body was not found at all. There was no trace of what had happened. Nor was the vanished camphor-worker a Korean, resembling a Japanese. It was the tallest of the Ainu who was gone.

That night, one of black sky and enormous blazing southern stars, Koropok fell into what passed for sleep. Sheer exhaustion numbed him.

Then Davies supposed that he was half-dreaming, half-mad.

"A good worker, that pariah," one of the guards remarked to his mate. "He has seen an axe before."

There was a whistling in the sky. No other word described the approaching *sssssszzzzzzsssss*. The sound increased so swiftly that Davies began to understand the speed at which it came. In all his life he had never heard anything like it. *Sssssszzzzzzsssss!* Like the terrific swinging of a saber through air? Like flashes of lightning? *Sssssszzzzzzzsssss!* Then it was gone; but the camp was awake.

Bombers? American bombers? No. Shouts and curses told Davies that American combat planes had passed low overhead, hopping over ridge and mountain. And already another sound was coming nearer, the dull deadly rumble of the bombers which followed. Soon the noise was so huge that the forest shook, and thunder seemed to be smashing the eastward mountain into rocks and boulders.

There were hundreds of them, thought Lew Davies. Where were they going? What was their objective? Why did the fighters hedgehop? Suddenly Davies' lips formed, because of his knowledge, "Let them all return safely, please. If any of the men must die, let it be in the crash. Don't let the Japs capture anyone."

Behind the giant bombers came more fighters, but high up, as if searching for Japanese to challenge the raid. The sound of their whistling was far away, but the menacing note was there just the same.

A scrawny, half-starved Chinese feeding his chip-retort said, "*Ming yat-yat teng ng't.* Soon it will be hot for these East Island monkeys," to the tender of the firebox. Even if Davies had understood, he was too full of his own thoughts to have been listening.

The firebox Cantonese whispered, "First one sky-tiger comes, to look-see. Then come more. When the Americans finally arrive, I intend to run into the jungle."

"The hill-savages will kill you."

"At least it will be a quick death," was the calm reply.

Davies, chained to his log, knew that his days of carrying out the instructions given him at Manila must be over. But it wouldn't be so bad to die now, with the sound of American attack in his ears; and before long the result of the attack was changing the black sky into a wild blaze like no sunset any man had ever seen. The sight of it brought a smile to Davies' lips.

They must've hit Tamsui, he decided, thinking of the port at the river's mouth, *or maybe Keelung. Or Taihoku and the airfields. Or the field I heard about at Nineteen, the fancy new one at Toyen.*

THERE WAS double consternation in the morning, when the pariahs were being unchained and marched off for work. During the night, a link of the chain which had fastened an Ainu to a log had been filed away, and the pariah was gone. Davies was shuffling along in line with those pariahs who had already been released when the shout went up. His mouth was full of dry millet-cake, breakfast, when he heard, "*It-te shi-matta! Ai!* He has escaped! How?"

Davies wondered also. In the excitement of yells and running guards, it was an easy matter for Koropok to slip ahead in the line and reach the scene. He saw the log to which the vanished pariah had been chained, and also that portion of the chain which remained like a black snake on the ground. He was sure, instantly, that the Ainu could not have filed himself free; the filing had been done as close to the former prisoner's body as could be managed by whoever had done it, but much too close for the man himself to have worked the file. And Lew doubted that a pariah would have tried to escape, even if the Ainu had somehow been able to steal a file. Who could have done it?

Kudzumi had arrived, and was screaming the same question. The ex-gendarme stooped and picked up the length of chain which remained fastened to the log, and Koropok stared at the brightness where the link had been filed apart. For a moment all he thought was, *Who could have done it, and why?*—and then he became cold.

He was seeing now that the cut had been made squarely and at right angles; and he knew, from watching metal-pipe-menders, that Japanese began to file by drawing the tool toward them at a sharp and easy angle, just as all Orientals used their tools in exactly the opposite manner from Occidentals, And this meant that the cuts made on the metal stems, or any metal, were always on a slant. In true Asiatic fashion, following the custom of centuries, the cut would be made square later by additional filing. But whoever had filed this chain, Davies was sure, wouldn't wait around to square the cut.

As Kudzumi began to threaten and question and promise reward all at the same moment, Davies' skin was prickling. What had those Chinese been saying? Something about a sky-tiger coming over Formosa for a look-see? Wasn't that it? And the single plane had been followed by a few others, previous to the actual mass attack, according to the Chinese. Certainly no attack in force would have been made without careful reconnaissance.

Suppose one of the ships, on recon, had crashed? Suppose the crew lived? And suppose that, if the Taiyals found these men and didn't kill them, the savages saw the growing of the Americans' beards as time passed, and somehow made the Americans understand that there were bearded men in chains in the camphor camp? The Taiyals would know nothing about Ainu pariahs. To them, and to the crashed fliers, the bearded men would be Japan's enemies.

The severing of the chain must have been done by an Occidental. Tools in a crashed plane would certainly include a metal file.

The wire fence was searched inch by inch, and found intact. The earth beneath it was examined to find where the damnable Ainu dog had disappeared. Nothing was found.

"He did not fly off in an airplane," Kudzumi screeched finally, after the camp resembled a newly taken beachhead in appearance.

The workers were not sent to the jungle, but were chained up again. Koropok, at his own log, had time for consideration.

The Taiyals, the head-hunting savages, hated the Japanese,

and with cause. They had beheaded a little Korean; but they had not beheaded the Ainu in the jungle, nor the Ainu who had been chained in the camp. Those two had been carried off, instead of dying as the Korean had died. Why hadn't they been immediately beheaded? Had the gentle Korean been killed, as he stripped camphor leaves, because he was similar in appearance to Japanese? And had the two Ainu workers been abducted, unharmed, because they were so dissimilar? Because they might be Americans?

By the following morning, Lew had reasoned out what seemed a complete case. He had even explained to his own satisfaction how the Ainu had been removed from the camp after the chain was filed: some Taiyal had indicated to the Americans now in the jungle that the wire fence was something which brought death if touched, and any fellow who handled engines and wiring would know what could be done about that. With electrification gone, the fence could be climbed by the rescuer, and by the unthinking, docile Ainu after the chain had been filed. When this had been accomplished, the wires of the fence could be made live again.

CHAPTER III

THE HEAD-HUNTERS

THE JUNGLE seemed more alive, somehow, to Davies, as if the continuing glare in the sky, from whatever was burning so fiercely to the west, had made animals and birds uneasy. Rock-monkeys cried; once a spotted deer raced across the trail; deeper in the jungle a tiger cat screamed. The birds were restless, flashing back and forth.

The same uneasiness throbbed in Davies. Sooner or later, Kudzumi's memory was going to know Koropok the Ainu for one of the officers who had called for K-k-k-katy in the bar. The camp commander was coming closer in recollection. But it was more than this which was hammering in Davies' head.

When the men sent out to look for the Korean finally found him, his body had been gashed by a spear and his head was gone.

Not even the sunrise could vie with the flaming western sky… and when the work-gangs were lined up the men made strange shadows within the camp. Kudzumi himself stormed up and down the rows of sad Koreans and humble Ainu; if he kicked one, he slapped the next. When he saw Koropok, he stopped short, staring until Davies feared that the ex-gendarme was remembering.

"*Ichido o me k-k-k-katta k-k-k-koto g-g-g-g-ga'mam,*" Kudmuzi crackled. "Yes I have once met you. But where? *Where?* Oh I recall Nineteen, but it was not there. No. Before that. Shanghai? No. Osaka? No. Manila? Manila? Answer me, *inu!* Was it Manila? Speak, or—"

Koropok the Ainu said, "What is a Manila, O lord?"

"Fool," shouted Kudzumi "*Bak-k-k-k-k-*"

The *k* in the Japanese word for fool, *baka,* continued as if Kudzumi could not get it out of his mouth. Some Japanese, probably one of Kudzumi's subordinates who had hoped for promotion to camp commander, laughed. The former gendarme whirled, face suffused. Everything else was wiped out of his head. Laughed at, before pariahs and dogs and his own guards!

"Tonight," said Kudzumi, "there will be an accounting!"

The work-gangs shuffled off after that.

DAVIES HAD a look at the log and the severed chain as he walked with the others. He saw, near the log itself, what he had been unable to see when there had been guards about it; there was a round mark in the earth, made, Davies was positive, by the knee of the person who had filed the chain with a square cut. No Orientals kneeled at their work. They squatted. An American, an Occidental, would have worked on one knee. The circular indentation was so near the log that footsteps had not obliterated it. To Davies, it was final proof.

The work began. Davies' axe slashed off huge chips, delighting the guards, because this gang must outdo all others, lest Kudzumi's anger be aroused. One of the guards even patted Koropok's arm and smiled.

"*Okkai ticksha,*" said Koropok in Ainu, deliberately. "*Okkai!*"

"What does that mean?"

In Japanese, Koropok explained, like a patted dog, "I work like a man."

"Do not let the honorable commander hear you say '*ok-k-k-kai*'," the guard warned, giggling, "or he will turn you into something not recognizable as a man at all. Now cut more chips and do not waste time."

When Davies paused to wipe off sweat, he tried to listen to jungle-sounds. No men had been sent to strip leaves. The guards kept everyone as close as possible, as much in sight as possible. Morning became noon, and noon's time of no-shadows advanced swiftly for Davies this day. He had made his best guess at the time the Korean had been speared and beheaded; but it was a guess only.

At last he could wait no longer.

Standing with downcast head, and with one of the guards actually looking at him, Davies laughed, shortly, as the Ainu had laughed once in the northern province. He was acting as best he could; he lifted his head and looked at the guard, as one who concealed nothing and had nothing to conceal. Then he shouted, "O.K., fellows! O.K.! Come and get me! O.K."

The jungle threw the sound back: *Ohhhhhhhh kayyyyyyy!* That was all.

What did I expect? thought Davies, axe swinging again. *Did I think anything would happen right away?* Or would anything happen at all?

The Japanese guard grinned, but made no protest.

So Koropok chopped away, and the day wore on. It was an hour before Davies yelled again, and the jungle repeated his cry.

When the order came to stop, collect tools, and shoulder the sacked chips, all Davies' hope had gone. *You argued yourself into what you wanted to believe,* he told himself. *It was just something nice to think.*

"You dogs are slow as the *Amerika-jin* when their officers drive the cowards to attack," one of the guards complained. Then he gasped, "*Aita!*" and made a convulsive grasp at the hurled spear which had ripped through him, his rifle falling to earth, and he on top of it, with the spear's shaft pointing skyward.

His mate's finger squeezed the trigger of the gun which the other Japanese was holding. Bullets from the down-pointed gun thudded into the ground a fraction of time before the guard also fell, pierced.

Out of the jungle swarmed unearthly slim and naked figures, silent as shadows; to Davies, in that first instant, it was as if the demons of hell had come out of the jungle. The Taiyals' dark bodies glistened; their heads were covered with wicker baskets shaped like feudal helmets, some of which were topped with deer horns, and others with white, grinning Skulls,

The first swift, silent rush was so fast, so unexpected, even by Davies after he had given up hope, that the American did not see exactly what happened. Some of the Formosans ringed the trembling Ainu and Korean workers with spears. Others had hacked off the heads of the Japanese. Several of the noise-less attackers had, without other objective, seized the fallen rifles of the dead guards, and the revolvers at their belts, and the ammunition also. Not a word had been spoken.

A Taiyal held up the head of a guard.

Then one of the head-concealed figures said, "That way, it looks good." In English.

Davies began to shiver like the pariahs, but for a different reason. His throat was dry and tight. He was cold all over. He was unable to identify which of the men had spoken. Some of the attackers were taller than others; but some Formosans were tall, too. If he had really heard what he thought he'd heard, why hadn't the speaker demanded who it was that had shouted in English?

Davies said hoarsely, "I guessed right."

One of the men who had snatched up a rifle and ammunition belt said from behind the concealment of his head-basket, "And what did you guess right about, you damned bow-legged Nip rice-bag? Talk chop-chop!"

From the way the strange helmet was facing, the American within it believed a Korean, smooth of face, must have spoken. Davies didn't blame the caution shown by the man. Who would expect anyone except an English-speaking Japanese to have called out in the jungle? Even so, Lew wanted to say, "D'you know what it means to have this happen? D'you know how I feel?"

Instead, controlling himself, he said, "I guessed that a Korean worker was killed because the Formosans thought he was a Japanese. I guessed that the Ainu weren't killed because they might be white men. I guessed that the attack in force must've been preceded by reconnaissance, and—"

"And you *know,*" the other snapped, "that those shots were heard by your little playmates, so you are talking until they can get here, eh?"

Something deep within Davies snapped. He had to fight for control as he said, "Take me with you. Question me later, but—"

"The Marines aren't much on asking questions!"

Davies thought he saw the trap. "Nuts," he said sharply. "No go. If you were on reconnaissance, you're no Marine. Sea-going bellhops don't fly."

Someone called, "Run up Maggie's drawers on that one, Major. Maybe the guy has been asleep since the war began—"

"I've been in Japan since the war began," said Lew. His voice rose. "My name's Davies. Lieutenant in the Air Force. Detached from duty in Manila. I—oh, damn it to hell, Major, how can you expect proof?"

A DIFFERENT voice drawling pleasantly, asked, "And I suppose you'd like to be flying a bomber again, Lieutenant?"

"A P-40," said Davies.

"I think," the questioner drawled, "he's O.K., Major. Combat Intelligence was told by the Army's G-2 to look out for Santa Claus with a black beard, who might be anywhere." As the tall intelligence officer who had been assigned to the reconnaissance spoke, he walked nearer to Koropok the pariah. Still drawling, the concealed mouth must have been grinning. "Merry Christmas, fella!"

Davies, as hand gripped hand, tried to speak, but could not.

"We'd better shove off," the major said.

The Koreans and the Ainu had stood without interest. What would happen to them? Davies said, "These poor devils will be questioned and tortured as soon as the Nips from camp get here."

The Marine intelligence officer spoke to one of the Taiyals who was holding a Japanese head. He spoke in slow, precise Japanese, school-learned. "*Koto wa deki-masho ka?* Can they go with us? They are not Japanese, but only men who have been treated as you have. They might be useful."

The Taiyal chief's slim body rocked as he said, "They have submitted like dogs. No. They are useless."

"*Sayo demo gozaimasho ga,*" said Davies swiftly. "That is probably so, but some of them are hillmen such as you, in their own land which was stolen from them by the apes. Some of them," went on Lew, doubting it himself, "would kill Japanese if given half a chance."

"You talk too damn fast," Caldwell, the intelligence officer,

Out of the jungle swarmed unearthly, silent figures.
It was as if the demons of hell had appeared.

chuckled. He added, "If they could get by just a night or two back in camp—"

"One night of Japanese questioning," said Lew, "is more hell than a civilized man can imagine." He added quietly, "I know."

"We can't antagonize the natives," Caldwell explained to Davies. "We need them. Everything depends on them."

Davies turned to the Taiyal chief. Under the Formosan's horned wicker helmet, worn only when on head-hunting expeditions, was a chain of the teeth of animals and brilliant red berries. The head of the Japanese guard was under the Taiyal's arm, and Lew had to force himself to speak to the invisible face behind the helmet instead of to the grinning, close-cropped head.

"They," said Davies, pointing to the pariahs, "are hillmen. If they could kill a hairless ape, as you have done, they would no longer be dogs."

"I," said the Taiyal, "was a slave of the apes. The men of my father's tribe, to which I finally returned, believe the sun opened when the hairy men dropped from the sky. I do not. You are like the men who descended. You are a fighter. Those who stand together like frightened deer are not fighters." His basket-covered head came closer to Davies' bearded, gaunt face. "You, I see, have been their slave also." He paused, and Lew wondered what horrible memories moved the Formosan while he stared at the pariahs. "Let them come with us," he said slowly.

The Taiyal chief grunted a command. The unresisting pariahs and Koreans did as the Formosan leader ordered, shuffling wearily into the jungle, with Taiyal braves ahead and behind, and the chief walking with the Americans. And the Formosan night came down fast, but not until Davies knew that there were five airmen, three of whom had not spoken before; and not until he heard the weird, distant howling which meant that guards from the camp had found their decapitated comrades and nothing else where the camphor trees had been chipped....

The Taiyal village, of fifty men, with their women and solemn children, was high on the slope of the mountain. Outside of the little settlement, as if on guard, Formosans appeared magically out of the gloom. The village itself was almost invisible. The huts were only half as high as a man, being built over the excavations from which the walls of the tiny dwellings were built. The interior was paved with stone, as Davies learned when he followed the other Americans into one of the huts and went down the notched pole which served as a ladder. No sooner were they inside, and removing the wicker head-coverings, than women brought food—wild pig and sweet potatoes and taro, all boiled together, and seasoned with ginger root.

The twisted cloth wick in an earthenware bowl gave the most feeble and flickering of lights. Around it the men squatted on the floor, Davies with ease, since he had rested in this manner since being in Japan.

"Give," Major Smith said; and when Davies began to talk, the major ran his hand over his chin, which gave off a scratching sound, being long unshaven. It was a long time, and late, before the major said, "It couldn't happen."

"That's what the Nips think," grinned Lew. "That's why it works."

"Worked," said the major. "Past tense. No more. Now... you listen. You've got to know what we intend to do." He spoke quickly, incisively. At the end he said, "Tsunum, the chief, is all for it."

Davies felt his heart beginning to pound, and the pounding began to creep into his head. A chance to get back at the Nips! A chance to fight! *And I begin to crack up now?* thought Lew wildly, as the hammering sound pounded away, loud, throbbing. *I get my chance, and can't take it?*

Only then did he realize that the pounding was coming from outside the hut, and wasn't in his battered head at all; the growing yellow-red light slanting down into the hut told him that all was well with him. With the others, who grinned broadly, he went out into the hard-packed open space of the village.

The ferocious Taiyals were celebrating the victory over their enemy. Just beyond where a fire blazed was a post, similar to the Ainu god-posts Davies knew about; and at the top of the post was a skull, to the chin and cheeks of which hair had been glued. Like Indians in the firelight, the native Formosans danced proudly up to the village diety, and, to the accompaniment of stamped feet and fierce and savage prayers, offered to it the latest spoils, the heads of the enemy.

It was a long time before Davies slept.

THE NEXT day, and the next, passed swiftly. Men with whom to talk, and so much to talk about—how a 38 performed, and the fire-power of a 61, and what a B-29 was like. "Damned if I believe it," Lew would say again and again. Marines on the Marianas! What MacArthur was up to. And, from Lew, how the Nips were reacting, and what their pilot training was supposed to be like, from the boastings he'd overheard at Nineteen; and how they were depending more and more on substitutes and plastics, but without proper research men and facilities to do a good job. And about home. Always about home.

As the sun marked the passing of noon on the second day, Caldwell remarked to Davies, now completely one of them, "It ought to go well. Tsunum's scouts have the picture for us. He was sure that some smarty-pants in camp would lay a trap, which is exactly what happened. That's our meat."

The Japanese commander, Davies learned, had baited his trap carefully, according to the savages who had raced through the jungle and back to the village. No men had been sent to fell and chip camphor on the previous day, but now three parties had been hurried into the jungle. Not only were over half of the laborers now armed Japanese but a shrewd disposition of other guards, possibly men rushed up from the coast, were waiting to ambush any Taiyals who attempted to slip up on the workers. The savages by now knew the location of every Japanese.

"And," said Major Smith, "the notion that we'd attack the camp itself simply hasn't occurred to the rice-bags! They and their fool electrified fence!"

Davies, when the party started out, would have liked the feel of one of the rifles, but the butt of Caldwell's revolver felt pretty damned good. It was difficult to keep from whistling as he walked along single file with the others, led by one of the Taiyals. It was difficult to keep from whistling because he was part of a venture which meant more than the elimination of a few Nips in a Formosan camphor camp.

He wondered if K-k-k-katy would be in camp. He thought so; he hoped so. K-k-k-katy, who had been a gendarme, would never risk his head.

What the Americans wanted was a simple matter. They were uninterested in killing the guards, although this would be necessary. They were after weapons.

Jennings, who had been the navigator, walked beside Davies. He said, "How the natives get through this jungle is beyond me. You're sure you're stopped dead, by some cliff or by those damned thorns on the creepers, but you never are. How many times," he asked, "did you think you were stopped dead, Lew?"

"Plenty," Davies grinned. "Sometimes I was, too."

"Being alone is what'd get me."

"It got me plenty," admitted Davies.

He put his hand up to brush away a jungle-fly, but it was a bit of fuzzy loose wicker from the head-helmet which he, too, now wore. Even if the mission failed or was fouled up, the major had insisted, there was no reason to allow the Nips to realize who was attacking them, nor to let some rice-bag go scooting off and break the news to somebody down on the west Formosan coast.

"But it's funny," Lew said, "how you forget." He thought, *Home! I'll go home.*

By the time the camphor camp was in sight and the attackers were flat on their bellies, Davies could think of nothing else. Home!

Ahead was the electrified wire; one of the Americans was snaking his way toward it. Behind the wire a guard strutted. When his back was turned, the American slipped nearer, until a final dash would take him to the fence, where it would be simple for someone other than a savage to take the heat off the wires of the fence. Several times the Taiyal chief, Tsunum, whispered, "*Sho sho.* Wait." But waiting was not easy for the attackers, nor for Davies. He had waited a long time for something like this. Odds made no difference.

Since Japanese had been sent into the jungle disguised as workers, more than the usual number of Koreans and Ainu remained chained to their logs in daytime. *I have been chained for three years,* was in Davies' head. *Three years. Three years a pariah. But that's over. If I'm killed now, or later, I die with my people, fighting. I'm through with this masquerade at last.*

T H E J A PA N E S E guard was pacing his way nearer to the point where he and his fellow-guard would, with German-Japanese exactness, meet. Just as they came close, bringing their rifles across their chests, a long scream of agony, of horrible dying, set one guard to staring and the other to whirling around. Japanese-fashion, both discharged their weapons instantly, at nothing but the sound, then both ran toward it. Other Japanese, some armed with an imitation of the American Browning, rushed out of the guard-hut, firing out through the fence as they ran.

The heat was off the wire when the Americans reached it and, except for a few scratches, climbed safely over, Tsunum with them. No orders were needed now. The first shots dropped the men with the imitation BAR's. Davies, watching for Kudzumi and not seeing him, did the next best thing: he kept firing at the assistant camp commander until the *click-click-click* of his emptied weapon sent its message to his head. But the

Japanese was down, whether from Davies' shots or Caldwell's rifle couldn't be known. With a leader, the guards did exactly what could be expected: they came close together to fight.

"It is very wonderful," Tsunum's muffled voice exulted.

Here was the last thing which the Japanese had expected—uncivilized Taiyals attacking them, and with firearms. Faced with such an unheard-of thing, no Japanese soldier or guard was able to do anything more sensible than die; and dying they were. For over the fence behind the guards now poured the ferocious unsubdued Formosans, announced in advance only by their hurled spears. The Taiyals in their head-helmets leaped joyously to the attack, with a long, long score to avenge and a whiskered god waiting for bloody offerings.

A S   T H E Americans held fire while the Formosans were finishing up what remained of the guards left in the camphor camp, Davies thought, *I'll bet Kudzumi is drunk. He's in a mess, as the new commander. Since he's arrived, everything has gone wrong. He's losing more face every day, and this will finish him.*

A Taiyal screamed. Davies saw the dripping head which the savage had hacked off. Swiftly, Lew moved away. He wanted Kudzumi for himself. Kudzumi represented Japan to Davies, Kudzumi belonged to him.

Lew hurried to the one painted building within the camp. He didn't hear the cat-stepping Tsunum behind him.

There was a light in the commander's room. Davies' gun was empty, but this did not concern him. Kudzumi, if sober, would be fighting; Kudzumi, gendarme, or not would shout, "*Aaaaaaa! The Tenno!*" and die for His Imperial Highness, the little solemn figurehead of the war lords who believed he was the son of the sun. It was possible that the commander would be in the jungle with the guards, but this Davies doubted. He knew gendarmes too well.

Davies, with his shadow behind him, and Tsunum standing in the shadow, opened the door, gun up as if ready to fire.

Kudzumi was crouched on the floor, on a clean white mat.

To his left was a low stand, a fire-box for smoking, and a pipe, the ash from which had fallen to the floor. To his right, on a piece of faded black silk threaded with silver, was a dirk, the *wakizashi* employed in hara-kiri in *seppuku*. But before Kudzumi was that which did not belong in a ceremony of honorable suicide: a bottle of whiskey. Not much liquid remained in the bottle.

A Taiyal screamed. Davies saw the dripping head which the savage had hacked off.

The camp commander, the former gendarme, was in a white kimono, the color of death. The cotton fabric had been carefully drawn away from his belly, into which he must plunge the knife because of his disgraceful conduct in permitting what had happened at the camp even before this final attack upon it. Only death by his own hand would release his entire family from disgrace.

He was so drunk that he imagined he had an audience far different from the two men who watched him.

He swayed slightly, drooled, "*Mada hayo g-g-g-goz'masunu k-k-k-ka?* Oh is it not too soon? Oh, honorable sirs gathered to assist me in honorable death, how kind you are in according me this honor! I am greatly indebted to you. But I have a few words to say before I perform *seppuku.*"

He paused, as if wondering what the words might be; and then he whimpered, "Oh, I have not been helped by the *much-whissukee!* I do not wish to die! I—"

"Hello, K-k-k-katy," said Davies.

He watched the glaze slowly slip from Kudzumi's eyes. Perhaps nothing else in the world could have shocked the Japanese sufficiently to sober him to any understanding at all. Kudzumi did not move, neither his eyes nor his hands nor his mouth. He looked like a malevolent image of ancient ivory, stained and discolored to a sickly brown by interment in a tomb. He looked like Futsunushi, a deity produced from blood but who was painted as if with no blood in his face.

Davies wanted the Japanese to know. He said, "The next drink I have, K-k-k-katy, won't be served by a Japanese spy."

Kudzumi said, "*Aaaaaa!*"

That was enough. Davies, despite the cruelty and past reputation of the former gendarme, had no desire to play with him. But how the devil did you finish off a fellow who just sat and stared at you? Davies had sworn to get rid of the damnable Kudzumi. And Kudzumi knew now, beyond any doubting, that the face hidden by the helmet must be that of an American.

The Japanese's hand flashed to the dirk. At the same instant, as Davies tensed contentedly to release the force which had been bottled up during his years as Koropok the pariah, Tsunum stepped forward, silent as a shadow. There was a blue flash, like a piece of blue silk before Davies' eyes, as the Formosan swept a long blade in a semicircle; then blood spattered over Davies. A single blow had severed Kudzumi's head.

"Now," said Tsunum softly, from his own knowledge of the Japanese, "he has indeed lost face!"

Davies nodded. He stepped across the twitching body, almost slipped on the mat and then on the blood running to the bare floor. Kudzumi, if Davies knew anything of the Japanese, had left an explanatory note. It was on the desk; Lew's eyes ran over the zigzag characters swiftly.

Of course Kudzumi had performed *seppuku* because of disgrace; of course the camp commander had been ordered to kill himself by his superiors, who thus were able to wash their own hands of any blame because of the abductions and killings; of course Kudzumi had been forced to obey, even if he lacked the courage.

What interested Davies most in the note was this:

> Before cleansing myself of disgrace, I have personally marked certain camphor oils for certain factories. I pray that their use, which will astonish the uncivilized men of the United States, will also bring our victory the sooner.

Davies read this once, and then again, until Tsunum said, "We must go. I see from your clenched hands that the words do not make you happy."

"I just had a dream," said Davies slowly, and then left the room. Tsunum followed, carrying Kudzumi's grinning head.

THERE WAS no semblance of resistance; all of the Japanese were dead. Davies hurried over to the exultant group of victors, who had already gathered the imitation BAR's and rifles and ammunition.

"Been waiting," said Major Smith. He nodded at the head which Tsunum was carrying, "Something special?"

"The commander," said Davies.

"*Rip ho,*" Caldwell urged. "We've done our stuff."

Lew said, "Before you go, you've got to chain me up."

"No," said the major, "and that's an order."

Davies said, "With you, I'm just another rifleman, that's all. Much as I want it. Here, I might get away from this damned place. I've got to get away. I've got places to get to. The Nips are playing with plastics and camphor oil, I know where it's being done. So what the hell?"

"Knock it off," said the major. "I won't have it. Hell, man, you've been thinking about home! Even if you don't make it, or we don't, look at the fun we're going to have! I know what

I'm talking about. So does Caldwell. It isn't just talk. It's the real straight skinny." Major Smith was in deadly earnest. "And you'd prefer being with these damned stinking Nips—"

"They don't stink so bad when they're dead," drawled Caldwell. "It's a beautiful stink. I like it. And I think," he said, even more slowly, "that you, sir, would do what Davies is going to do. I think we all would."

The major said, "Hell." He said then, as Tsunum plucked at his arm, "Hell and damnation. We'll get some special ones for you, Davies."

One by one, the Americans gripped Davies' hand. Nothing

"Hello, K-k-k-katy," said Davies and watched the drunken glaze slowly slip from Kudzumi's eyes.

more was said, no word at all. But when they had gone, back into the jungle, and Davies was again chained to a log where, with Kudzumi dead, he would be only another pariah to the Japanese guards, his throat ached and ached.

To have gone with the others! Davies knew what was intended. Caldwell, the Marine intelligence officer, knew where the Formosan landings were to be made by American forces. So the crashed crew of the reconnaissance ship and the Taiyals, now armed with BAR's, would cross the island and prepare a surprise for the Japanese on the east coast, above the point of amphibious landing.

The Japanese would never come close to finding these jungle fighters who would be on flank and rear when the Marines stormed ashore. Even a few men, so led, would drive the Japanese wild and play the devil with their defense; and when men were sent against them, the Taiyal-guided Americans would be elsewhere, pouring it on again. The Nipponese would be thoroughly confused, and nothing was worse for them than confusion, doubt, the lack of something they could understand.

They'll go crazy, thought Lew. *Absolutely crazy.*

He eased himself as comfortably as he could against the log. He had to attempt to do something about this camphor-plastic. It was undoubtedly important. And it was better to think about it than about home, or about the tight handclasps of the Americans as they left him here in Formosa.

But what he actually thought was this: first there'd be an air attack, fighters and dive-bombers, with smudges of smoke far out at sea, although not from the skulking Japanese Navy. Then those smudges would turn into ships which would hammer and pound at the selected beachheads where the Nips had their caves in the rock between So-o and Dainano, down where the cliffs were six thousand feet high straight to the water, but where rivers formed beaches also....

Planes and ships and men. Men!

Chained, Davies, with eyes closed, saw the attack. It could have but one outcome, and that was because of *men*.

Koropok was one of them.

THE LAST BANZAI

THE PATH along which eight men, all stocky and bearded and in tattered jackets such as Ainu wore, were being taken by over-age Japanese infantrymen led through a thicket of blossoming camellias, striped like peppermint-stick candy. Only one of the bearded outcasts ever glanced back, when there was an opening, to the village in which they had spent the night, in chains. There he could see the shining roof of the temple, the jagged lightning-blue lake, the huddle of recently erected shacks already crowded with men and women too old to work, with children still too young to twist bomb-fuses. All had been evacuated from the cities. Tokyo was far behind.

While the stolid, beaten-down pariahs plodded silently ahead, each burdened to the breaking-point with a heavy pack, the infantrymen were cheerful. Only one of the bearded men, the one who had glanced back, listened to what was said, his swarthy face as blank and exhausted as any of the other seven. Unlike the others, his eyes were grim and bitter, as if all hope were gone.

Even from what the Japanese said, no hint was given as to where the Ainu were being escorted, nor for what purpose, although the way was always up, higher and higher into the central Japanese mountains. But it would be a remarkable loca-tion, Sergeant Tsumikawa shouted, as he kicked a stumbling pariah, in which human dogs could die miserably, and undoubtedly would. For loyal Japanese infantrymen, laughed the bow-legged sergeant, it would be a post of luxuries and comforts, to which they had been ordered instead of joining the ranks of those who killed thousands of *Amerika-jin* sea-fighting Marine devils; and although these orders were repugnant to soldiers who would delight in slaying Americans, one obeyed the commands issued in the name of the Tenno and never complained. For while the sea-devil Marines had learned to parry the honorable tricks of Japanese warfare, there were some clever and beautiful tricks which the *Amerika-jin* stinking-skins had not

"I would give the dog a taste of metal, but buckles are difficult to polish after being bloodied and I do not intend to receive a reprimand for the condition of our equipment."

found out about… and all of the Japanese laughed loudly when the sergeant said this, as if they knew what these tricks were.

None of the pariahs changed expression, not even the sturdiest of their number, who had glanced back so grimly and bitterly. He shambled along with the others, bent cringingly to his load, as if he were merely another of the hairy men instead

of an American, the one American not a prisoner in Japan but on duty. Lieutenant Llewelyn Davies, known to Ainu and Japanese alike as "Koropok."

He had been in Japan since the outbreak of war to do what he could to disrupt the Japanese war effort. Why he and the seven pariahs were being taken to the central Japan mountains he had no idea; he only knew that each footstep took him that much farther away from Tokyo, Osaka, Nagoya—where he could do something. As the son of a medical missionary who had lived for many years with the Ainu, he knew that whatever the Japanese had in store for the seven Ainu and himself would not be pleasant. He was half surprised that the infantrymen hadn't mentioned what this would be, on the Japanese theory that it was clever to frighten victims whenever possible.

Whatever it was, Davies decided, when the narrow trail began to twist down a dark ravine, it couldn't be much worse than the Formosan camphor camp where he had been last year. Everyone except the natives had been shipped out of Formosa now that American bombers were within range, and fighters from carriers. Japan, now as always, was terribly spy-conscious. What would happen to Koropok, if ever his disguise were penetrated, would make whatever lay ahead of the pariahs seem like a festival. Death would not come fast.

Davies did know this much: work assigned to the pariahs was always such work as the Japanese refused to do. Slaughtering of cattle. Mending of *geta*. Cleaning of latrines. Lew, as Koropok, had done all of these things; and while he had been doing them he had caused the Nipponese plenty of trouble, and had gone undetected. Where the Ainu were being taken meant degrading and possibly dangerous work. Davies had hopes that this might be related to the war, and that the isolated location might mean secret fabrication or experimentation, in which case he would have a chance to foul matters up for the Japanese. After what Sergeant Tsumikawa had said, this was very unlikely. Why would such a place be a hell-hole for the outcasts, and yet a luxurious spot for the Japanese?

The next long hour was spent in negotiating the ravine, so narrow and wooded no man could see ahead. At first the way led down in short zigzags, but after the descent the climb began again. Not until a little man-made broadening in the path was reached, with forward vision blocked by trees and the massive rock formation on the opposite side as well as where the path was cut, did Davies receive the first hint as to where he might be going.

In the flat spot there was a small shrine before which the soldiers bowed low. It was no more than a wooden platform covered with leafless branches. In front of a mirror on the platform, a mirror of steel edged with red lacquer, were offerings of gray, green, and black cloth horses, rice in both the grain and in the ear, scummy bowls of saki, squares of yellowing silk.

Davies knew that the mirror was the *shintai,* the symbol, of the sun-goddess; he had never seen one with the red-lacquered edge before, and if he had dared he would have turned it around

Middle-ages infantrymen muttered
prayers before the shintai, *the mirror that*
was the symbol of the sun-goddess.

to see what characters or design might be on the reverse side. He did finally understand, from the prayers which the middle-aged infantrymen were muttering, that the symbol was a true-fire-mirror, and represented the dreaded mountain fire-god, Kagu-tsuchi.

With this knowledge, it was easy for Davies to realize that the party was nearing the volcanic hot springs district of central Japan. The sergeant's remarks concerning luxuriousness was proof; for the Japanese, there is no greater luxury than soaking themselves in steaming mineral water until their faces became purple. But why should such a place, if the Ainu were going to it, mean misery for the outcasts? Because of what their tasks might be when they arrived? This didn't seem sufficient reason to Davies. There had to be something more.

He puzzled over this, because he didn't want to believe that his usefulness in Japan might well be at an end. If this should prove to be true, *I won't take one damn thing more from the yellow devils,* Lew decided.

AS the Japanese, devotions finished, kicked the pariahs to their feet to indicate that it was time to move ahead again, Davies made himself consider what could be in store for the outcasts, for himself. Suppose there was a hot spring resort, where Japanese bathed luxuriously, to which the Ainu were being taken. Suppose also that it was a place where generals and admirals went, according to Tokyo gossip, in order to rest and recover a proper valiant fighting spirit—at least those officers who hadn't ripped their bellies open after defeats. Wouldn't it be logical to conclude that nothing would be believed better for these samurai-descendants' war-courage than to have some pariah dogs to boot around?

Japanese farmers, clerks and schoolboys, turned soldier, were taught to bayonet Chinese civilians in order to develop a killer instinct and to build morale. Japanese noncoms were encouraged to slap white women around and thus develop a feeling of superiority. The treatment of prisoners at Bataan was largely for the purpose of showing common Japanese infantrymen that the once-feared Americans were weak and cowardly opponents. All of this was in line with what Davies was thinking.

But, if they start torturing me just so some Nips can get all pepped up and go back to fight, decided Davies, *and if I'm dead sure I can't do anything and have no chance to get away, nobody can blame me if I get me a Jap or two this time. There is a limit to what a fellow can stand.*

This notion grew and grew and took such complete possession of the man who had been so alone in Japan for so long that when Sergeant Tsumikawa began amusing himself by picking up rocks along the path and offering to bet his corporal as to the exact spot on a particular Ainu he could hit, and whether the rock would knock the pariah down or merely bring blood, Davies' hands clenched.

Tsumikawa saw this.

"*Jitsu ni negattari kanattari de gozarimasu,*" snarled the sergeant "This ugly dog Koropok is an enemy as well as a slave. He desires to prevent me from grenade-throwing practice. *Ho!* We will see about that!"

The sergeant jerked off Koropok's pack. For one infinitesimal fraction of time there was nothing of the Ainu pariah in Llewelyn Davies' haggard, bitter face, in his tensed body. Everything he had suffered, everything he knew American prisoners had suffered, was waiting to explode.

Then, swiftly, he looked exactly like a submissive outcast again. Like Koropok. Why take only a dumb sergeant with him when he went?

He was thrown to the path, face downward. One soldier held his wrists, another grabbed his ankles, getting in a quick, sly twist of muscles for his own enjoyment. The sergeant ordered a third soldier to unbuckle his belt and hand it over; Tsumikawa sighed gustily with pleasure as he gave the belt a few preliminary swishes in the air—and then brought it down on Koropok's bared back.

The leather was like a brand being applied. Searing. Expertly wielded. But even as Davies' teeth came together, to hold any sound of pain back in his throat, he wondered why he didn't feel the agonizing bite of the buckle.

As if in answer, Tsumikawa shrilled, "I would give the dog a taste of metal, but buckles are difficult to polish after being wetted with animal blood, and I do not intend to receive a reprimand for the condition of our equipment. Because I am unable to beat him properly," the sergeant growled, bringing down the belt in a savage crisscross slash, "I will add this incident to the account of this foul, whiskered dog. I will not forget him! No!"

The belt came down again.

"It was thus," boasted Tsumikawa, "that I beat an *America-jin* prisoner. Oh, how he screamed aloud and pleaded with me!" Up went the belt, and down. "And how clever are our superiors, who have enticed the Americans back to Bataan in order to seize more of them, thus ending the war gloriously for us." Slash, slash, slash. "Even a pariah dog," panted Sergeant Tsumikawa, taking a deep breath and a different grip, "has more courage than the *Amerika-jin*."

The taste of blood from his own gnawed lip was in Davies' mouth. *You idiot*, he was accusing himself, *this serves you right. You gave yourself away. If you'd been trying to accomplish something, you'd have failed. Maybe a damned good beating will knock some sense into your thick Welsh head.*

That same head was beginning to spin, and numbness was spreading down from it to his whole body. Davies knew he dared not lose consciousness; but could he prevent it from happening? If he passed out, Tsumikawa might decide that Koropok was not worth being carried by the already-burdened Ainu, and would merely tumble him down to the rocky bottom of the ravine; and that would be that.

Fighting to retain his senses, feeling little pain from the continued beating, Davies stared ahead, to where he could see the rock wall through the trunks of the trees. The rock itself was black. Lew's eyes fastened on the one variation in color, a greenish circular patch, an indentation, but a green unlike any grass that ever grew. It seemed to brighten to a more vivid green, and then to change to a coppery blue, which was suddenly shot through with yellow and silver.

I'm seeing things, Davies thought desperately. *I can't let go. I don't dare let go!* The silvery yellow was becoming a whitish mist before his eyes, like fog, like steam, like forgetfulness. *I've got to hang on,* he kept trying to tell himself; but he didn't see color at all now, but only the mist, and the slashes didn't really hurt at all, and he was getting sleepy... sleepy....

Tsumikawa, excited by the punishment and pain he was inflicting, and because a man was prone and he was standing, armed, above him, screamed, "I will beat him until he begs for mercy, or I will kill him," but Davies heard none of the words. "I will slash away his nose and ears until he resembles one of the very *raibyo-yami* we can soon mock and laugh at. And," the noncom said grimly, withholding the belt, "I intend to flay this Koropok, and then use a round piece of his Ainu hide in order to protect myself against contamination. If a man has such a charm, and purifies a different part of his body nightly with salt and water, and spits in the face of every *raibyo-yami* he sees, he will remain strong and healthy."

In Davies' head was only, *He talks too damn much.*

"We go where there are *raibyo-yami,* lepers?" asked Corporal Ashiuni, whispering because of the frightening information. "Oh! I thought we were to enjoy ourselves guarding prisoners. We all thought this. Lepers! Oh, terrible!"

"*Shiranu koto aro monka,*" cried Tsumikawa. "If you spent your money in Number One waiting-houses, you would know what goes on. I knew." Standing straddled over Koropok, delighted with such a position of dominance and with a wide-eyed audience, the sergeant continued, "And do not wail, 'Oh, terrible!' You should be shouting, 'What a magnificent secret weapon has been contrived by Japan!'"

The private who was holding Davies' ankles looked up. He said, "I do not understand. What weapon, please?"

"You are a cow-faced peasant," the sergeant yelled. "Listen! *Amerika-jin* prisoners have been taken to the hot springs where lepers are given treatments. There is an entire colony of *raibyo-yami* where we go. The enemy soldiers are to care for the lepers now. Is that plain, stupid one? The Americans will sicken, will become miserable *raibyo-yami* shortly. Then we will send them back to regular prison camps, so they will contaminate other Americans. When this is learned in America—the fate of white devils who dare to bomb Japan and to sink our ships with their fiendish underwater boats—then no cowardly American who hears of this will so much as fly over Japan again, nor go to sea in a submarine, and we will win the war. Do you understand our cleverness now, manure-brain?"

Davies' head had cleared just enough to tell him that this must be the boastful fool sergeant sounding off; but could there be any truth to what Tsumikawa shouted? Lew's back felt as if hot metal were pressed against it. Would there be more beating? And how much of the harangue had he missed?

"Now," said Tsumikawa, taking a fresh grip on the belt, "I will get on with the business of beating this hairy Koropok to death."

CORPORAL ASHIUNI, bold because Tsumikawa had borrowed a few coins from him when the sergeant had returned, without so much as a single *sen,* from the licensed quarter, said, "If you beat him too badly, how will you get a good piece of skin for your charm against uncleanliness? And I should like a bit of hide, also."

"I can cut off a piece before I cut him into red ribbons," chuckled Tsumikawa. "Give me your bayonet."

For a fraction of time, not much longer than it took for the corporal's bayonet to rasp from its sheath, Davies was witless. Would it do any good to put up a feeble fight which the Japanese would enjoy? Was he going to die here, uselessly?

Nothing in his life had ever been so difficult as to review, lightning-fast, a situation which demanded a head in good working order, and Davies', while Tsumikawa stropped the bayonet on the belt, was momentarily as dull as Koropok's own brain was supposed to be. Then....

A round piece of my skin, thought Lew. *As a charm against leprosy. What've I ever heard about* raibyo-yami? *And where?*

Through his head flashed something which Tsumikawa himself had mentioned. A waiting-house.

Koropok had worked at a famous one, Number Nineteen.

I remember, Davies thought. *That Jap doctor who came all the time. Tsumikawa got his dope from overhearing the same guy. How much do I remember of what the Nip M.D. said, and how much can I make up? Well, here goes....*

As the hands holding him down tightened, and as Tsumikawa plucked up Koropok's swarthy skin preparatory to making an incision, the American mumbled in clipped Ainu accent,

> *"Oni ha sot'*
> *Fu' ha uch',*
> Whoever becomes bloody
> And meets a leper,
> Himself will be unclean
> For a thousand years.
> He becomes unclean,
> His wife becomes unclean,
> His sons become—"

"Where did you hear such lies?" shouted Tsumikawa, bayonet poised. "How dare you repeat them? How dare you plead to live? Speak!"

"*Shinj' shinj'nai w' hito j'yu d'su,*" Koropok whined. "Oh, lord, it is what I heard at Nineteen—"

"Liar! What do you know of Number Nineteen?"

Koropok said, "I worked there, lord. It must be written in my papers. You have my papers, lord. I worked at Nineteen, lord. I—"

"You talk too much," said the sergeant; but he did not touch Koropok with the bayonet, and he did not kick him. Instead, he looked at the bloody belt. Then he looked at his hands. "Dry," he muttered. "No blood has touched me."

The soldier whose belt had been used had turned and was bobbing up and down as he prayed in the direction of the shrine they had passed. Tsumikawa had dropped the bayonet, and was staring at Koropok's papers which he had taken out. The corporal had retrieved his bayonet.

"He was at Nineteen," Tsumikawa grunted. "That much is true. He could have overheard what he repeated. It was at Nineteen that I myself overheard a few things, as I have told you." The sergeant began to grin. "I am a fortunate man," he remarked. "I am going to live, strong and clean, until I kill many Americans. What is it to kill a pariah dog? Nothing! Yes, I am a lucky man, and—"

"But what about me?" whimpered the soldier whose belt had been bloodied.

"Take the belt by the buckle," ordered Tsumikawa, "so that no blood touches you. Go to the bottom of the ravine and wash the belt. Make sure that the leather is well cleansed. And when you come back," commanded the sergeant, "see to it that you walk far behind us until the belt is dry. Then I will examine it—with my eyes, of course. Go! Why do you wait?"

"I could drop the belt into the ravine—"

Tsumikawa cried, "What? Do you want to waste material needed in the war? Do you want to have me reprimanded because you have no belt? Oh, what a selfish person you are! *Kataku ii-tsuketa zo!* Obey your orders!"

When the private climbed nervously down the rock side of the chasm, to where water ran at the bottom, he kept eyeing the belt as if it were a venomous snake. He was trembling so violently that he had difficulty in keeping his feet.

Tsumikawa looked down at Koropok. "I am a kind man," said the sergeant. "I allow you your life."

Koropok said, "Yes, lord," and squirmed on the ground just enough so that he could touch the talkative sergeant's dusty shoe with his forehead. "I am your dog," whimpered Lieutenant Davies, exactly as a pariah would have done.

"I will see to that," grinned Tsumikawa.

I'll bet you will, thought Lew. *You won't forget that fear, because of what I repeated about lepers, stopped you from the fun of killing me.*

As the private climbed down to the bottom of the chasm he kept eyeing the belt as if it were a venomous snake.

The path, before long, began to reveal what the hot spring country would be like; a thin coating of old volcanic ash rose, agitated by the feet of the party, and soon everyone was sneezing. As the trees thinned, Davies got his first real glimpse of a wild land. He could see stupendous red cliffs, scarred and lined, rising higher and higher; above the tops of the peaks were wispy cloud-mists. It took concentration to stare ahead, while seeming to be only a shambling pariah, because the pack on Koropok's back, rubbing up and down, felt as if it were pulling off the skin between the slashes made by the belt. But, even so, he was alive.

As a great boulder, seemingly poised on a shelf of the rock wall above the path, was passed, the scene ahead became visible, all at once. There was a deep and narrow valley, far down, with a village beside the lake which reached to the base of the surrounding cliffs, mirroring the hot spring town, the cliffs, and the clouds. From hundreds of steam-vents in the precipitous slopes issued torrents of steam and sulphurous vapors. From these, to Davies' ears, came the sound of a dull booming, like soft and distant thunder.

SOON THE path crossed the chasm on a narrow, swaying hand-bridge, reaching the volcanic side of the ravine. The odor of sulphur grew stronger with every footstep. It was not long before the Japanese and Ainu, and Koropok, were threading forward slowly between hissing vents, each having a patch of rotten-looking yellow ground about it. At times the openings in the rock were so close that jets of steam concealed portions of the party, and Tsumikawa would command a halt until all of the pariahs were accounted for. The roaring never ceased, and made the already-aching head of the American dizzy with pain. Now and again the earth underfoot squirmed and shook; now and again a fine ash, like a fog, sifted down from some erupting volcano deep in central Japan's uneasy mountains.

"*Jigoku,*" the soldier just behind Koropok kept repeating, between prayers to the fire-god. *Jigoku.* Hell. The Japanese word for the hot spring country.

And hell for the Americans who are there, thought Davies.

For a full half hour this continued; then the real descent to the village, the lake, began. Again and again the ravine had to be crossed, Once on a bridge strung on what looked to Davies like a piano wire, so hard was the granite to which the suspension had to be made; and it twanged like taut piano wire, too, when he flipped his finger against it. Finally the path became broader and showed signs of being well-traveled, as if used by the villagers to reach the charcoal-burners' huts niched where there was room enough. Then the party reached the flat of the valley, walked under a huge red *torii,* and Tsumikawa gave the order to halt at the guard house.

The acrid smell of sulphur was overpowering. Clouds of steam hung over the central portion of the village called Tatsuto-zo; it came, Davies guessed, from the baths. He glanced about carefully, knowing that the slightest sign of interest, even from a pariah, would arouse the suspicions of the Japanese. He had time only to mark the series of bamboo pipes to his right, through which water must reach some of the bathing places, when the shrill challenge of the guard brought a chubby and youthful lieutenant from the guard house.

Tsumikawa had drawn up his platoon on each side and to the rear of the pariahs. The guns of the men were pointed at the head-hanging Ainu. Tsumikawa saluted sloppily.

"Second Class Sergeant Tsumikawa, Decoration of the Sixth Order, reports with eight Ainu as ordered," he said.

The chubby lieutenant glanced at his watch; and Davies, seeing the insignia on the strap, knew that it was American. "You are late," the lieutenant announced. "I have been kept here waiting for you."

"Regrets," bowed the sergeant.

What he's thinking, Davies was too sure, *is that I'm responsible for the delay. I'll get the works before long.*

"*Thore tha ikamathen,*" Lieutenant Omuko lisped. "What is

your excuse? I suppose that you were enjoying yourself some-where?"

"No, lord." Tsumikawa jerked his head toward Koropok. "That dog caused me some slight trouble, which I rectified."

"Rectified! You talk like a teacher or a priest! And you probably lie. I—"

A deeper voice grated, "*Ara! mata hajimatta!* There you are, at it again! Omuko, will you never learn not to discipline a soldier in front of low persons such as Ainu? The next time this take place...."

With the major's warning in the air, the lieutenant bowed his head; but, as he did so, Davies caught the baleful look shot in his direction.

So he doesn't like me, either, thought Lew.

The major's slitted eyes slid from one soldier to another. Suddenly his voice rasped, "You, there! Number five, right rank! What is the matter with your belt? Have you been sleeping in the mud like a Filipino ox?"

The private's mouth popped open. He blinked as if he were facing a firing squad; but he was unable to say a word.

"Sergeant," the major said, "have you given your men the idea that they come to Tatsuto-zo to enjoy themselves at the baths? Do they believe there is no need to maintain their equipment in proper order, nor—"

"Major," a different Japanese voice broke in, coming from the side of where the lieutenant and major were standing, "this is not the place to conduct inspection. I would expect such action from a raw *shiganhei,* but not from a senior officer. What would you think," the gray-haired colonel snapped, "were I, the commandant here, to speak so improperly when there are inferior dogs standing around? Answer that! No! Do not answer. Send those pariahs in to me, one by one, and I myself will determine what shall be done with them. I will miss my dinner, but I cannot trust so simple a duty to anyone. *Ai!* It is annoying. I do not like it."

The major bowed deeply, smiling all over his face as if he had been complimented; and, as he allowed his eyes to flick toward Davies, the American knew that the major had heard how Koropok had been mentioned. That the major had no love for him, he was sure. *I'm going to get the works,* Lew realized, *unless I can do something about it. And if there is one single thing I might accomplish around here, I've got to be alive in order to do it.*

"Bring me the papers of these animals," Colonel Sakirumu ordered. "My food will cool while I do what others should be doing."

He's the only one who doesn't want my hide nailed up, Davies decided. *How can I do anything to keep him on my side?*

There was one possibility, Davies felt, remembering exactly what the colonel had complained about; but when the lieutenant touched Sergeant Tsumikawa secretly on the arm, and whispered in his ear, Davies guessed from the way in which Tsumikawa half-turned in his direction, that whatever Lieutenant Omuko was saying must involve Koropok the Ainu. And he was right.

There was fear in Tsumikawa's eyes as he forced himself to obey the lieutenant, as he saluted the colonel, bowed, and saluted again.

But Tsumikawa, as before, had plenty of words when once his mouth opened, in spite of his nervous fright in addressing such a high officer, even if the lieutenant had ordered him to do so. "Lord," said the talkative sergeant, almost bleating, "I apologize for speaking before you. But there is nothing in the papers of the pariah named Koropok to indicate that he is unpatriotic and dangerous, though he is an evil person. He caused trouble on the way to Tatsuto-zo, lord-colonel. He is responsible for everything which has happened—"

"What has happened," snapped Colonel Sakirumu, "is that my dinner is spoiling. Do you think, Sergeant, that I am afraid of a pariah? Oh, do not start to tell me again. You are as noisy as the radio. Koropok? Well, send him to me first, and I will take some of the dangerousness out of him."

And so Koropok, head hanging, stood before Sakirumu's desk.

Take it easy, he told himself. *The old boy has what passes in Japan for a sense of humor. That is, he'll joke when he sticks a knife into you.*

CHAPTER 11

THE SULPHUR BATHS

"**K**OROPOK," THE colonel said. He rubbed his hands together. "I am going to give you a choice. Would you prefer helping the *Amerxka-jin* bathe the lepers, or would you like to be used for bayonet practice?"

Davies mumbled, "Neither, lord."

"What? You refuse to name a choice?"

"I have never been in a Presence before," said Davies, and fell on hands and knees. *And does he love this fawning!* Lew was willing to bet, from the way he could hear the colonel's indrawn breath and the following gusty exhalation and Japanese-fashion spitting. "Lord," Koropok continued pleadingly, "is there no way in which I can serve a Greatest One?"

Colonel Sakirumu said, "*Nani?* What are you talking about? You are a pariah, a slaughterer of food-animals, a stinking less-than-nothing." The colonel paused, and then asked, "What service can you give?"

Monkey-curiosity got him, exulted Davies. He said, "Lord, I was a servant at a famous place. At Number Nineteen in Tokyo. I can clean, and I can scrub the back. I can also scratch the back for itching. I can accompany *geisha* and *ne-san* safely to your presence for your enjoyment. I can bring food so quickly that there is steam rising when I set down the rice. I can—"

"Bring it, then," shouted the colonel, "and we will see."

If he had expected that a foolish Ainu would goggle and ask where the kitchen might be, thus giving the colonel a delightful story to repeat, Sakirumu was mistaken. Davies, instinctively, because he had to be always aware of everything, had already examined the office, and figured out where the sleeping-room must be, and where the room in which food was prepared. He had leaped to his feet before the Japanese finished speaking, and, running as he had run at Number Nineteen, with bearlike but fast gait, he was on his way to the kitchen....

He was ladling rice from the pot before the old woman's rusty kimono hissed as she turned to see what was happening; he had a bowl filled with smoking horseflesh from Manchukuo as her mouth opened. When she squealed in terror, "The *Amerika-jin* have dropped down from the sky!" he had pickled plums heaped on a plate and the chopsticks beside them, and he could hear, as he picked up the tray, the howl of laughter from the colonel, because of what the cooking-woman had screamed.

Davies would have liked to have called, "Funny as hell, isn't it? The old cook thinks that whiskers only grow on Americans. She's probably never seen an Ainu." Then he thought to himself, *I wonder which of you is the dumb one. And can I put it to use?*

Sakirumu called out something to prevent the cooking-woman from rushing outside and giving an alarm; he examined the tray critically when Koropok placed it on the desk before him. Koropok squatted beside the desk, jumping up to pick up a plum-pit which the colonel spat out, racing to the kitchen to bring fresh, hotter water for tea, waiting until a blazing match almost burned his fingers so as to have a light ready for the colonel's cigarette.

It was as good as a play, the colonel decided. This Ainu, Koropok, coming from Nineteen, was well-trained; and while regulations forbade Japanese servants, nothing had been said about pariahs. *The dog has taken a liking to me, for one reason or another,* decided Sakirumu; and, being a Japanese, he couldn't wait to find out why. He approached the subject in truly Oriental fashion.

"Why do you wish to serve me instead of Major Sompuji?" he inquired. "Do you know what a major is, Koropok?"

Koropok bowed. "At Number Nineteen," he said, in clipped Ainu dialect, "there came colonels and generals and admirals, lord. That is how I knew."

"Yes, yes," Sakirumu said, " but why did you select me?"

Koropok lowered his head again. "I dare not answer," he said.

"Come! I am a kind man. You may reply. If you do not reply," said Sakirumu, "I may not be so kind."

"If I answer, I will be beaten," whined Koropok. *Play the game, boy,* Davies was telling himself. *He's hooked.* "I dare not speak against an officer of His Imperial Majesty, lord. If I do—"

"Answer!"

"Lord," said Koropok, making his voice shake, "I could hear how envious were the other officers, and the major-officer, and how they hastened to decide everything before you appeared, and so I knew you were a Greatest One, and—"

Colonel Sakirumu blinked. He said only, "*Naruhodo!* I see!" but Davies guessed what the colonel was thinking. Not until Sakirumu finished another fat Egyptian cigarette, from Singapore, did the Japanese speak again. Then he said, "I will take my bath in the evening, Koropok. See to it that you are there with fresh towels and a bran-bag and my bottle of whiskey."

He fell for it, Davies realized. *He's got himself a servant for free, making him a smart guy. And he's got somebody so dumb that he can safely ask him to do things, including checking on other officers.*

To Davies, this meant more than escaping death, or a horrible task in the leper colony. It meant a chance to get around.

While Koropok cleaned the colonel's sleeping-room, after finding the towels and bran-bag for scrubbing, and the bottles of excellent Scotch—the labels of which made Lew remember Manila, and home—he began the first preliminary to any planning as to what he might do: he began to figure on how he could contact the American prisoners. It was safe to assume that as long as he was the colonel's servant, and brought him

*Koropok ran to the colonel with a tray loaded
with smoking horseflesh from Manchukuo,
rice, and a bowl of pickled plums.*

food, Sakirumu wouldn't permit him to be exposed to either
the *raibyo-yami* or the Americans who were around them. Not
Sakirumu.

Davies slid over this latter. It was a barrier to be surmounted only after he decided, if decision were possible, what could
be done.

By the time Lew wrapped the towels in a clean piece of
cotton, and pinned the allow-to-pass badge on his tattered
jacket, he was beginning to wish that troop-carrying transports,
such as he had heard officers returned from Manila talk about,
might fly over Tatsuto-zo. Then after fighters and dive bombers
had leveled the village, the prisoners could be flown off. Such
a wish told Davies clearly that he was unable to figure out
anything to do. Suppose, for example, he were able to get the
prisoners away: where could they go? Or suppose he managed
to get guns to them, on the theory that it would be better to

die fighting than to suffer, as lepers, for the rest of their lives? This, also, meant the finality of death. *A fellow can kill himself, if it comes to that… although it'd be better to go out, as I thought of doing, by taking some Nips along with me.* The masquerader knew that to reveal himself, without being able to help, would bring a torturing let-down to the suddenly-hopeful prisoners. *It would be hell*, thought Davies.

Tatsuto-zo was built, on the narrow valley floor, with rock cliffs on the close sides, in terraces. Koropok, challenged often, sometimes held while a guard bleated for his corporal, passed the tea-house on the first terrace, seeing, inside, a few girls and many officers. Next came the series of wooden houses in which the Shinto priests lived; and why it was so near the tea-house Davies could guess. The Shintoists' vows of celibacy were never seriously carried out. Davies, as Koropok at Number Nineteen, knew plenty about that.

From the houses of the priests a flight of stone steps led up to a wooden gateway, on which were carved flowers and symbols of the fire-god and beards and animals impossibly mated. It was necessary to walk through the courtyard, so narrow was the village and so few the paths, and past the temple itself, with its gilded ascending and descending dragons on either side of the entrance. A pair of stone fire-breathing lions guarded the bronze-studded wooden doors. And priests, at this late hour of no-prayer, were beginning to amble in groups toward the baths, towels slung over their arms. They smoked and laughed and gossiped as they walked, all of them, now that the Buddhist priests had lost power, contented and fat and comfortable men. The war was good to them. Women made many offerings, in order that their husbands and sons might return victoriously and safely.

KOROPOK FELL in behind one of the groups, wisely not walking ahead of them. He listened closely, too. A fellow never knew when he might pick up some delectable bit of gossip which could be retold to the colonel, along with whatever variations might be helpful and suitable.

Davies thought, *But I mustn't kid myself, or the poor devils who are imprisoned here. On one hand, here's a military installation, damn well guarded, right in the heart of Japan. On the other hand, so what? Me. One guy. A pariah.*

What else was there? Lepers.

Davies' head was bowed low as he walked, but not because he was playing his part as an Ainu. His hopes were equally as low.

The only thing about which the priests grumbled was the lack of young acolytes; the war had taken them off, and it was necessary for the priests to ring their own bells, prepare their own food, pour their own liquor. Davies' ears pricked up when he overheard one paunched Shintoist say that surely some of the lazy *Amerika-jin* prisoners could be spared from standing around and doing nothing in order to serve religious men, which was pretty fair proof that the Japanese hadn't made up their minds as to what should be done with the Americans here. Better proof, Lew was sure, than what the talkative sergeant had said.

Soon Japanese officers, many of them old, joined the priests. Almost all of the officers walked with legs wide apart, and their faces twisted with pain as they advanced slowly and with curses.

"My blisters are so thick," one old captain complained, "that I would consider leading my company in a charge more pleasurable than getting into the water. But I keep telling myself that one must not question the orders of our superiors. I tell you," he muttered, "that the acid in the water bites into me like pincers! It is a good thing we are a race of heroes, or we could not cure ourselves so painfully. But it is worth while to suffer," he added, beginning to grin, "for the enjoyment of being patted dry by American officers. Yes!"

Davies was wondering if this statement of the captain, plus the presence of lepers, wasn't responsible for the story which the sergeant had heard at Nineteen. If so, the prisoners here weren't too badly off, not when compared to the fate of other prisoners. And, if so, he ought to have a chance to see the Americans closely. The thought of an American face was enough to make his heart beat faster. He had been in Japan for a long time… friendless.

He was passed by guards through a final gate, and came to the platform inside the bath-house where officers and priests undressed to nakedness. Beyond the raised place was the pool itself, sulphurous yellow and acid green, with greenish steam rising from it and hanging above, like fog. The fog was thickest at the hot-water inlet, thinnest where a bamboo pipe allowed just enough icy mountain water to drip down so that it was humanly possible for bodies to stand the heat of the curative baths. Standing against the walls, like recruits waiting for an order, were lines of bandy-legged Japanese, big-bellied Japanese, scrawny Japanese, and, Davies saw as he peered through the steam, Colonel Sakirumu.

Koropok edged carefully along the pool's edge until he reached his master, and then crouched down at his feet.

The bath-master shouted, "*Mo yoroshii ka?* Prepare!"

Each of the naked Japanese, as if mechanical men, turned, and took from the wall behind them an eight-foot-long board, a foot wide, and came again to attention at the edge of the pool. "Prepare the bath!" the bath-master ordered. Each Japanese dipped an end of his board into the pool, and began splashing the water from right to left, much as if they were digging with spades. They brought the board down with a smack after lifting it, and as they splashed the water they chanted in unison, directed by the bath-master:

> "*Sama wa tennin!*
> *Otome no sugata:*
> My maid is willing!
> I see her form
> In the baths…."

When the song became more obscene and ribald, the priests, instead, chanted:

"*Sama mo kokoro mo*
Kawaru kana!
Form changes until
Your tears fall!
You must enter the pool
Of the Divine Reflection of the sun!"

Slap, smack, splash. Bodies swayed in unison. The sound was deafening, as, according to the bathers' belief, air was being driven into the water of the pool. Soon the Japanese were glistening with sweat; soon the bath-songs were forgotten, and a wild chant came from both officers and priests, which concerned the victory of Japan over the rest of the world.

At the moment that the last bull voice hoarsened, the bathmaster gave the next order. The boards were replaced, and the seven Ainu who had been with the party came from the outside with a heavy beam, which was laid from one edge of the pool to the other. They shuffled off to return with another beam, and with more, until the pool was divided into lanes just wide enough to accommodate lines of bathers. While this was being done, the Japanese had knelt down, pouring dippersful of water over their heads, and gasping at the heat of the water. Envious eyes saw that Colonel Sakirumu's Ainu servant was performing this necessary duty for him.

"Enter!" commanded the bath-master, after the temperature of the water had been finally tested, and the drip of the cold water carefully checked.

Down into the pool went the Japanese. A long moan went up, an "*Aiiiiii!*" of torture rose with the thick steam. Koropok enjoyed the sound. *I hope you cook, the lot of you,* he thought, staring down at the rows of slowly purpling dark faces. *I hope you cook, and then I'd like to split you open, like lobsters.* The grim and tight lips of the officers marked them from the open-mouthed and gasping Shintoists as the hot acid water bit into their blistered, sore-covered bodies.

The lamentation died down after the first minute of the

three-minute immersion. At first Koropok heard only the ticking of a clock; then he could hear, from a pool beyond, a similar moan rising, and, from the orders of the bath-master there, knew that the next bathhouse must be for lepers.

H E H A D no time to think about this; into the bath-house here, in a single file, came men with towels and wads of soft cotton. White men. Thin. Soldiers guarded every four Americans. The latter were ranged around the pool, and stood waiting for the bathers to leave the pool and be dried off.

The second minute began to tick away. Davies, as if merely staring stupidly at the rising steam, glanced up.

There was a dreadful fascination for him in the mere presence of the men behind him; that they could grin at the spectacle of the Japanese in the near-boiling water was one of the swellest things Davies had ever thought about. Swell. None of these men was licked. Far from it. No wonder that the Japanese, aware at last of the caliber of the foe they fought, sought wildly for some means by which they could frighten America away from Japan—no wonder Japan was worrying about the belt of steel which was tightening about Nippon.

"Three-minute eggs," Davies heard one of the men say.

He waited for the blow which usually followed anything said by a prisoner, but the guards paid no attention to what was said. So Davies, as Koropok the Ainu, stood up slowly, towels hanging over his arm. He shambled a few steps to one side, so that he was between the near group of four men, and at the greatest distance from the guard on either side.

"Santa Claus," a prisoner said.

"Maybe a Russian," said another.

A third American argued, "Koreans wear beards, don't they?"

"He's pretty young to be a grandpa," grinned the man who had first spoken. "I wonder if his gal makes him shave on his birthdays?"

Davies said, voice low, "Nuts to the lot of you! Keep talking and don't stare at me."

From the temple a file of priests began to amble toward the baths.

The clock was ticking….

There was, as Davies feared, a fraction of time in which every one of the four near him was silent. He himself dared not glance at either of the guards to see if they had heard him speak. Then one of the prisoners said, "Hell," and there was utter disbelief in his voice. Whether this came because of what he heard, or thought, Davies didn't know.

"It's the heat," a prisoner said. "Or the humidity."

Davies was about to speak again when the bath-master shrieked, "Slowly! Up! Out! Three minutes!"

The bathers' bodies were purple-red, puffed. Up and out they came, parboiled in spite of the cold water which had slightly tempered the steaming pool. Koropok began to pat Colonel Sakirumu's body gently. He said, above the puffing of the officer, "I have not the bottle, lord. Someone saw me with it. Someone said, 'How can a dog of a pariah have a bottle?' and took it from me, lord. Oh, do not beat me!"

Sakirumu said, "I can believe it, with so many envious men here!" before thinking. Then he growled, "Of course I will beat you!" but Davies was reasonably sure that there would be no beating at all.

Dutifully, he waited until Sakirumu was ready to return to the platform and begin dressing; the colonel did not hurry, knowing that all of his subordinates must wait until he left. The priests, hungry and noisy, were held to no such custom, and were first out of the bathhouse. When Sakirumu finally departed, accepting salutes from everyone, the prisoners and their guards were already gone.

Outside, refreshingly cool after the steaming bath, a junior officer approached the colonel, halted, and saluted.

"Sir," he said, "it is reported that your servant spoke words with the *Amerika-jin* prisoners."

So they let the prisoners talk, and then try to pick up things, thought Davies, cold as ice. *The guards understand English.*

"What damned gabbling fool reported such a thing?" snapped Sakirumu. "Major Sompuji, doubtless?"

The intelligence officer said, "Sir, it was reported directly to me by a guard. Damning words were spoken. This Koropok spoke of machinery—"

"What?" bellowed the colonel. Into his head, as into all Japanese heads, suspicion buzzed; but when he looked at Koropok, standing with open mouth and attitude of complete Ainu ignorance, he began to snort. "Machinery? Lieutenant, have you lost your senses? What does this animal know of machinery? Nothing! What machinery did he mention? Tell me that!"

The intelligence officer stood his ground. "Sir," he said, apologetically but firmly, "he spoke of a piece of metal with a screw thread known as a nut—"

"You are a damned fool!" Colonel Sakirumu snorted. He began to laugh. "What a guard who lived in America must have heard," said the colonel, delighted to parade his own superior knowledge before an intelligence officer, "was the word 'nut'. Oh, I am not one to boast, but even I, in my few months in Washington, learned such a word. And it was not the pariah who said it. Certainly it was one of the prisoners. I am sure of that. Now go away and do not bother me any more. If," Colonel Sakirumu ended sharply, "you wish to perform your duty, go and find who stole my bottle of *Scotchu whisuki!*"

"Did this one drink it? " asked the intelligence officer un-wisely, glaring at Koropok. "And did he tell you a lie—"

The bathers' bodies were purple-red, puffed
and parboiled from the steaming pool.

Again Sakirumu's Japanese-fashion suspicion made him, also, look at Koropok. "I do not remember his telling me *what* the thief looked like," said Sakirumu. "*Ho!* You drank my *whisuki*, dog!"

"No, lord," whimpered Koropok. Solemnly, simulating a trembling, he described Sergeant Tsumikawa exactly, ending with, "Oh, lord, I am very afraid of him!"

"So long as you are my servant," said the colonel, remembering that the newly-arrived sergeant had been assigned to Major Sompuji, "nobody but a colonel dares to beat you. Bah! There is gossip and envy around this place until it is all like a priest's apartment! I am sick to death of it!"

Koropok followed him, thinking, *I've got to be careful. That's twice I've slipped. The third time I may not be so lucky.* Somehow, he must warn the prisoners about what he himself should have considered—that the Japanese would have guards who understood English, and would use whatever was overheard to Japan's advantage. Somehow, this had to be done, and soon.

His new kennel was in the open, behind the colonel's kitchen. As he lay there, that night, he was tortured by the odor of the colonel's cigarettes. It was midnight when the officer's snores sounded like the escaping steam of the baths; it was past midnight before Koropok the Ainu, at full length on the ground, smoked the first of Colonel Sakirumu's cigarettes.

A GAME began in the morning. First after the colonel departed on inspection duties, several American prisoners were escorted to the colonel's house on the pretext that Colonel Sakirumu would enjoy having his floors scrubbed by American officers. The guards saw to it that Koropok, the pariah, had many opportunities to speak to the prisoners; Koropok went on with his work as if the Americans were not there. Nor did the prisoners speak, except among themselves. Davies could not be sure if they had caught his warning signal of tightly compressed lips, not easily seen because of his black beard, or if they were on guard for some other reason. Not a word passed between pariah and prisoners….

But many words were spoken when Colonel Sakirumu returned. The Japanese was so furious that Davies was afraid the old boy would have apoplexy.

"Sompuji!" the colonel kept repeating, half aloud, half to himself. "Sompuji! There is a person who covets my position! One of these days he will overstep himself, and when I am finished with him the only recourse he will have will be to slit open his belly. Oh, how I distrust that man! How he gathers satellites! I am sick and tired of him! Some day I will cook his goose—"

Davies was perfectly willing to help in roasting Major Sompuji, provided it would serve his own purpose. And as the days passed, one much like another, he began to learn that Major Sompuji, victim of every losing-of-face that the colonel could manage for him, not only had no love for his commanding officer, but none for his colonel's servant, either, mainly because Koropok continued to serve Sakirumu exactly as a favorite guest at Number Nineteen in Tokyo would have been served; and the colonel liked his comforts. Once a word-of-mouth message was brought to Koropok, when the colonel was away on duties, brought by a sly-eyed noncom from Sompuji's command, ordering Koropok to go immediately to the leper's bath-house as an attendant. *And if I do,* thought Davies, *that's where I spend the rest of my life.* The honorable colonel, his master, Koropok told the noncom, had insisted that he, Koropok, was not to leave the house.

Once again, the abbot of the temple requested that the stocky Koropok be offered to the shrine, which would be proof of Colonel Sakirumu's devotion—proof to the enraged colonel that somehow Major Sompuji had wormed his way into the confidence of the oily priests.

"Perhaps with Scotch he stole from me," raged Sakirumu.

It was all amusing to Davies; but it was accomplishing

nothing. Yet, when a fellow stopped to think, what could be accomplished here? Free the prisoners? No use. Where could they go, except to death? Do something to stop the flow of propaganda about the terrible fate of flying officers and submarine officers when captured? Impossible. As a week, and another, went by, Lew felt that his first fears—that his usefulness had ended—were being borne out.

Colonel Sakirumu was his best, his only hope of getting away. If the comfort-loving colonel should be transferred, Koropok the Ainu intended to go along with him. Anywhere would be better than here. And so Koropok, more slyly and vastly more shrewdly than Sompuji, played the game....

The one thing which was happening was that Koropok, permitted to cook his own food in the kitchen, was in better shape than he had ever been since he had come to Japan. But what was the use of that, Davies asked himself, if he couldn't do anything?

The jealousies around him were typical military jealousies, the sort always taking place in a back-wash installation far from actual combat. Davies was careful not to do the things which, as Sakirumu's servant, he might have done. Undoubtedly he could have sought errands which would allow him to contact the prisoners; no good would result. No accomplishment.

He was stretched out behind the kitchen, half asleep, when a hand touched his shoulder. Instinctively, perfect in his masquerade after two slips, Koropok cringed, but with body tensed and ready.

"Hi, boy," he heard, so softly that it sounded like a waiting-maid at Nineteen awakening an honorable-guest from drunken sleep. "Lew!"

For a long moment the *sssssss* of steam somewhere in Tatsuto-zo came to Davies' ears loudly, and hissed into his head.

He rose to his elbow. Staring.

Then he said, "Charley. Charley Crane."

Hand gripped hand.

"Long time no see," said Crane. "This is the first chance I had to get out of the stockade. I can get back O.K. I—"

Davies whispered, "Lie flat. Two o'clock guard. There's a moon."

The two Americans were motionless as the ground on which they lay, until the guard had passed. Then Crane whispered, "I crash-landed at Iwo Jima. Remember when you left Manila, Lew? For Japan. And—"

The abbot of the temple had requested that
Koropok be offered to the shrine.

"How about the guys?" Davies whispered back, news-hungry. "How about—"

"Listen, boy. It's swell to talk. But I didn't come for that. Listen, and get it straight, because I don't dare try coming out again. If the Nips nab me, O.K. But they mustn't suspect you. You've got a job, fellow, a hell of a job, if you can get away from here. Can you?"

Davies said, "Yes."

"Roger. I—"

"Roger? What about him?"

Crane laughed in his throat. "I meant O.K., Lew. I forgot how long you've been away. Listen! We've got a G-2 fellow with us. You don't need details about what happened, but he had a job to do in Japan, and couldn't get away with it. So—we get chances to talk safely sometimes—I told him about you, when I knew who you were, and I've got all the dope from him, Lew, if you can get away to do it. It's really something...."

"Shoot," said Davies.

Then he listened. Once or twice he asked quick questions. At the very end he grinned. "Could be," he said.

"We'll kick up a fuss when word gets out that a pariah has escaped," said Crane. "That should keep too many rice-bags from being sent after you, and—"

"No," Lew said shortly. As he said, grinning again, "You'll know when I'm gone," he was thinking, *I must've had getting away in mind all the time. I can manage it. And pay off some scores at the same time.* "Now," he said quietly, soberly, "I'll repeat what you've told me."

Once more the men gripped hands.

When he was alone, Davies thought, *No time to waste. The sooner I get going the better.* He began to grin. *Yes, the gang'll know when I leave.*

He was glad that he had never taken advantage of his position as the colonel's servant, and glad also that the other seven Ainu, true beaten-down pariahs, had not caused the slightest trouble at Tatsuto-zo, something which would have reacted on him. And he was delighted that the feud between Sakirumu and Sompuji still continued. Lastly, his own physical condition would make possible a real try at what the G-2 officer wanted done…. And so, the rest of the night, Davies slept happily, like a log, like a stupid and unthinking, unworrying Ainu.

CHAPTER III

TRIAL BY FIRE

HE KNELT beside Colonel Sakirumu's *zabuton* in the morning, with tea. The colonel's uniform was freshly pressed, the colonel's shoes shone. The colonel's first cigarette of the morning was waiting for the colonel's fingers.

"Lord," said Koropok, as Sakirumu sucked down tea and smoke at the same moment, "A little something has entered my stupid ears—"

"So?" said Sakirumu, recalling other bits of information which had come from the pariah. "You have my permission to speak."

Koropok bowed.

"Lord, it has come to my ears that the priests have made a writing. The honorable second-to-you lord Sompuji asked them to make the writing. I heard that it concerns you, my master. I—"

Sakirumu's face began to purple, as if he were being parboiled in the baths. "I wondered how long it would be before he tried something like that!"

"If it is the desire of your lordship," said Koropok, "I can steal this paper. It is in the abbot's sleeping-room, and—"

"Ah! Get it for me, Koropok, and you will be rewarded! Yes! Perhaps I can buy a wife for you. Perhaps I—Get it, dog, or I will beat you until you cannot stand. Koropok, I have always treated you well, and…."

*par-boiledKoropok stretched out on the
ground before his kennel and smoked one
of Colonel Sakirumu's cigarettes.*

"I will get it," promised Koropok. "Have I permission to
absent myself from the baths this evening, lord?"

"You will steal it when the priests bathe! Excellent!" Sakirumu almost said, in his mixed anger and pleasure, "You have
more sense than the Imperial Intelligence Office," but refrained
with difficulty. He did say, "It was a fortunate day when I selected you as my servant," which made Davies hide a grin in
his beard.

That's step Number One, thought Lew. *Now for Number Two*

He waited for the colonel to leave before taking an unfre-
quented path to the rear door of Major Sompuji's house.
Sompuji goggled at him, but said only, "Have you brought a
message from your master?" as he decided that here, indeed,
was something to report! A pariah dog, an Ainu, entrusted with
Imperial orders from the commandant!

Koropok said, whiningly, "Lord, I am to tell a lie about you—"

"What?" Out of Sompuji's mouth popped what he thought:
"He stops at nothing, that old hog." Then, suspiciously, he asked,
"What is this lie you are to tell about me? If you do not speak
instantly, I will turn you into less-than-a-man."

"I am to say," said Koropok, "that you often have words with
the prisoners. I am to say that when the war is over you have

arranged to go to America. I am to say that you will receive, there, a large sum of money."

Sompuji's face turned a dirty gray ash. "How do you know this?" he muttered. "And why do you tell me, since you are the colonel's dog?"

"I know because I heard," Koropok whined. "The colonel drank much *whisuki*, and talked much. I tell you because… you will laugh at me, lord."

The major had never been so far from laughing in his life. He knew too well what even a false accusation from his commanding officer would mean for T. Sompuji. In a chattering voice he insisted, "Speak!"

"I am a pariah, lord. But Japan is my land. The Tenno is my god. What my master demands of me is not—not… I cannot say large words, lord."

"Not patriotic," said Sompuji mechanically.

Koropok bowed in assent.

"*Sa mo nakereba,*" the major said, thinking aloud. "It is not so, but… oh, how damaging! Oh, who will believe my only proof, which is the unbelievable word of an Ainu pariah? Oh, how he has me!"

"Lord," said Koropok softly, "I could help you."

"You will say that the colonel has ordered you to tell this lie? *Ho!* How can you match wits with him? How can you answer the questions of Intelligence? You will be trapped, and when you are tortured you will confess that you talked with me, and I will be more deeply involved than ever. I—"

"Tonight," said Koropok, "this very evening, before bathing, I am to be at the well-guarded spot from which water comes to the pool, lord. Before the colonel, my master, trusts me to speak to the Personage about you, I must repeat my story to my master at the last moment, so I will make no mistakes in what I say about you. I go to the large rock near the thick bamboo, lord, at the place of water-emerging-from-mountain. You, and some Great One whose words would be believed, could hide and listen. What the Great One hears would be your proof."

"The abbot Gonzozumo," said Sompuji. He began to smile broadly. "The word of a hero-priest who refused to listen to the pleas of the *Amerika-jin* priests at Bataan will be believed in Tokyo. *Aaaaa!*"

The major patted Koropok's shaggy head.

"Give me your writing-permission to go to the guarded-spot from which the water comes to the pools, lord."

"Why? You go on orders from your master."

Koropok said, "My master says, 'Go here,' and 'Go there.' Suppose, this time, I am stopped before I reach the spot? Suppose my master finds out about this, and, after a delay, I do not repeat the story for you and the Great One to hear? Suppose my master becomes suspicious and arranges a different meeting-place at the last moment, of which I cannot inform you? Suppose—"

"Your father must have been Japanese," grinned Sompuji, clicking his teeth. "I see what you mean." He pulled paper toward him, and began to write the pass for Koropok the Aniu. "And I intend to reward you," he promised.

Sure, thought Lew. *By killing me, after you've heard what you think you'll hear, so I can't do any talking about it in the future.*

Koropok took the pass; and that was step Number Two.

Number Three was easy. He would need food, enough so that he could avoid every village on his way back to Tokyo. This came from the kitchen, and to it Davies added a package of the colonel's fat cigarettes. He thought about putting some Scotch in a small bottle, because he would probably need it later, but finally decided against this. The smell on him, if he were picked up after the job was done, *if* it could be done, would be incriminating.

He needed a few other things. Being able to amble around, he was able to secure what he wanted. Where he got them didn't interest the Japanese. He was the colonel's servant.

When afternoon came, and the sun left the gorge and Tat-suto-zo, Davies was ready. *Before,* he was thinking, *I could plan things in advance. Now, it's whatever comes up. That's because we're closing in on the Nips. What I'd like,* thought Lew, *is to live long enough to see a landing. But what's going to happen, if the G–2 boy is right, will be something!* As Davies half-closed his eyes, he was almost seeing what might result if he accomplished his job. And so he was smiling as he left the colonel's house, slowly, always shuffling like a pariah....

The exodus toward the evening-bath had already started. Colonel Sakirumu would be there early, Lew was sure, so that the old boy could have the pleasure of looking at Major Sompuji and thinking how the major was getting the works at the hands of a pariah who, probably at this very moment, was stealing the papers at the temple. But Major Sompuji wouldn't be at the baths—and Sakirumu was going to worry about the absence. Sakirumu would send a messenger to find the major, but the messenger would first go to the temple, providing Sompuji left word where he was going; and, after that, nobody would know where abbot and officer had gone.

Except me, thought Lew. *I know where they're going.*

H E   B E G A N walking toward the great rock and clump of bamboo, behind which water was piped, hot and cold alike, to the pools, always watchful to see if Sompuji had anyone following him. But when he came almost to the post where a guard challenged anyone advancing further, Koropok left the path swiftly and, body low, darted toward the patch of bamboo leading away from the village. When he reached the clump, he dropped to his knees and snaked his way along, cursing under his breath each time the bamboo leaves rustled, because there was no wind.

He had something wrapped in cloth in his hand, and when he could see, through bamboo, the darkness of the rock, he removed the covering. The metal of the wrench felt good in his hand. Hard. Cold. His fingers were metal about the handle, and his eyes, now that he saw the two crouched Japanese hiding by the rock, turned as metallic and cold as the steel.

The more of a mess there is in Tatsuto-zo, Davies thought again, *and the greater the puzzle seems to the Japs, the surer I am that they won't bother about what happened to Koropok, except what appears to be obvious. Not,* he told himself, *that I need any excuse for what I'm going to do now.*

He crept forward. Beside Sompuji's khaki, the abbot's black robes seemed even darker. The black robe looked like a perched vulture.

The two Japanese were silent. So was Koropok's approach. Six feet away, Davies rose to his feet. His mouth formed, "*Bataan!*" as, wrench swinging, he leaped ahead. He struck once. Struck twice. Into the blow went everything he had seen, ev-

*Koropok began to pat Colonel Sakirumu's
body lightly with the towel.*

erything he intended to accomplish. Swiftly, coldly, he pulled
first one and then the other of the bodies under the thicket.

Wrench in hand again, he circled the thicket until he came
to the big wooden pipes, side by side, which carried hot and
cold water to the pools. No need to wonder which was which,
Steam escaped where the bamboo pipes were mechanically
jointed; below the man-made joints, on the ground, were dis-
colorations, vitriolic blues and coppers and thick incrustations
of yellow flowers of sulphur.

Listening, Davies waited. Soon he heard the shouts and
singing, and the splashing cadence of the boards beating on the
water; and then, grinning, he uncoupled a joint of the cold-
water pipe. Water like frost, icy, instantly spattered to earth, so
cold that the touch of it, which tempered what was almost
liquid steam in the other pipe, seemed actually to burn Davies'
hand.

Fellows, thought Lew, as a slow grin parted his beard, *all
you've got to do is watch what happens, and you'll get the first hint
that I'm on my way. Watch how they cook, fellows! Not one Jap
officer'll dare scream or get out as the water grows hotter and hotter…
and if old Sakirumu pulls out first, he'll lose plenty of face, or so he's
thinking right now… The whole damn lot'll be hospitalized, if they
don't boil to death.* Although the Japanese might wonder who
had killed Major Sompuji, the colonel would swear, if he lived,
that the jealous major had engineered the performance in order
to remove his hated commanding officer. *And Tokyo's apt to
believe it, too,* Lew decided.

Keep looking, fellows, Davies kept thinking. *Maybe they'll beat
you later, to prove they're Japs, but what you're seeing should make
it worth it. See 'em cook!* It made Koropok a little sorry that he
himself couldn't see it, that all prisoners couldn't see it, that
Chinese and Koreans couldn't see it. *And they don't dare get out,
because they're all heroes, all Japs!*

Next, it was time to take care of Koropok.

In this, even as the shouts of the guards inside the bath-house rose, indicating that some of the officers in the pool must be actually dying, Davies was fortunate. He raced back to Saki-rumu's quarters, unseen as he avoided all guard-posts; outside of the colonel's he saw a stocky figure. He identified it as Tsumi-kawa's, the sergeant who had been assigned to Major Sompuji after arriving at the village, and now here, Davies reasoned, at Sompuji's orders, to nab and dispose of Koropok as soon as the pariah returned from the supposed meeting.

At the exact moment the sergeant realized that the yells from the bath-house were no longer the impassioned pre-bathing choruses, Davies smashed him over the head, and carried him into the empty house.

The dishes in which Koropok would have served the cold mushroom soup, custard-topped, the pickled eggplant and sliced raw fish from the lake, were all ready, taken from cupboards by the old woman who did the cooking. She was long gone; Koropok, after serving the colonel, washed the plates and bowls—and Koropok, now, went swiftly to work. The place would burn beautifully. The wood was dry and old. A good dash of cooking-oil here, a pouring of oil on the sergeant's body, a lighted match—and Davies grabbed up his already made-up bundle....

It was not difficult to reach the high wire fence on the Tokyo-side of Tatsuto-zo undetected. It was less easy to wait, hidden, until a guard cried, "*Kwaji! Kwaji!* Fire!" and all guards' eyes turned toward the village. Then Davies was over the wire and, making use of all concealment, on his way.

Gone was the shambling Ainu gait. He walked easily and swiftly, his pack light on his shoulder. He tingled, at what was past, at how he felt now, and at what was ahead. When he turned back, flames from the colonel's house rose straight and high, hot yellow and hot scarlet, in the windless valley; and there was a rush of black, oily smoke shooting through the fierce color of the fire.

You'll hear that an Ainu burned to death, fellows, thought Davies, *and you'll hope it isn't so. Keep on hoping.*

When Davies came to the wire-supported bridge, he wondered if he should destroy it. It would be easy to send it crashing down... but, although this would slow a pursuit, if anyone suspected that it was not the pariah's charred body which remained in the gutted house, yet it would be damnable evidence of an escape.

Davies had made his plan. He had to stick to it.

Once he was forced to hide, off the path, while charcoal-burners, with their big sacks, staggered on to their huts for the night. Once he had to tighten his body against the rock wall, thinking he saw in the darkness a movement which might be someone approaching; but a moment later a long hooting told him that it was only the shadow of a *ho-to-to-gi-su* bird swooping down the chasm after food.

The gorge was dark; soon it became black. When Davies came to the diabolical plateau where the earth shook, only starlight on the jets of steam from the yellow vents told him what to avoid. Death was all around him, the deadlier because of night; but it was at night that he must travel, and he knew it. During the day he had to keep out of sight. He was Koropok the Ainu, and the only paper he had was a pass from Major Sompuji, and it, if discovered, would be more than enough to kill him. But he wanted to keep the pass. He might need it.

On the fourth evening, as he ate food from his dwindling store in the pack and prepared to move on again, toward Tokyo, he saw the sky turning bright, eastward, at an hour when no sun rose, and in a direction where no sun set. How great, how damaging, was the raid which caused the fires Davies had no way of knowing; but after he was striding along a tree-bordered road, always ready to hide in one of the fields should a Japanese appear, the flaming heaven seemed as if a volcanic eruption must be under it. Destruction.

Nobody'll worry about one pariah now, thought Davies with

satisfaction. The G-2 boy had known what he was talking about. Things were happening. One of these days, Lew was beginning to believe at last, Americans would be storming ashore on Japan's mainland, and to hell with Formosa or landings in China. Hit the Nips where they really lived! *And if I use ordinary care,* Davies told himself, *maybe I'll be alive to see how we bust the Japanese myth of impregnability.*

He did not enter Tokyo at all, when at last he neared it. Instead, he kept far to the southwest of the belt line, through country and past Shinjuku and Yoyogi, past Meguro, always heading toward Yokohama. He was worried about crossing the bridges over the canals, but did it unchallenged. What kept him moving rapidly, always at night, was billowing smoke from the city's outskirts. Not factory smoke, but factories burning. And behind him was the tremendous column of smoke, from another attack, where portions of Tokyo still smouldered.

Davies wondered what would be docked in Tokyo Bay, and beyond the Yokohama breakwater, as he neared the end of his journey. The G-2 man was right again; Japan had too much to think about to worry over one person now, not when there was daily reconnaissance and nobody knew when bombers would sweep over the cities to start Tokyo blossoms, fire, to blooming again.

IF an American, as badly disguised as the G-2 fellow would have been after he was set ashore, could get away with this, Davies felt, *it ought to be a cinch for me.* The American Intelligence officer's disguise wasn't dumb; he was prepared to be caught on what was a wild gamble for high stakes, and had been, but had appeared to his captors as a crashed flyer. The G-2 man had planned to hide in the marshy, deserted stretch on lower Tokyo Bay, where Davies was now, and just about opposite the town of Futtsu, above the channel, until the time for action. Davies, however, saw no reason for doing this himself and so Koropok shuffled into a small village called Sasamosa, also opposite Futtsu on the channel into the bay, and presented the permit

*The abbot, in his black robes, looked like
a perched vulture beside Sompuji.*

from Major Sompuji. Although the permit would have been a death warrant if Koropok had been apprehended near the hot springs, it was far different now. To the police officer in Sasamosa, it was something to bow before.

Koropok had to eat. But the village had plenty of need for a pariah to curse as the Ainu dog humbly begged for *geta* to repair—and the Ainu dog found plenty of time to shamble along the sea road, too, in his search for customers.

On the sea road, at the narrows, the channel into the bay, Davies saw what he had come to see. On the far shore, near

Futtsu, a sand spit, exposed at low tide, reached out into the dirty water. Only small boats could pass over the spit. Along it was a heavy wire fence, strung along poles driven into the sand and down to the mud beneath. Where the sand spit ended, and the channel began, was the anti-submarine net, of which Davies could see the row of buoys, metal canister buoys, by means of which the net stretched out to a small, anchored tug. A second, and larger tug was some five hundred feet nearer to the shore where Davies stood. Between the two craft, fastened to the bottom by many hawsers, was the opening to the net. From the near tug, the net continued toward Davies, to shallow water, where another wire obstruction had been built.

Davies, always moving in case he was observed from either shore or tugs, studied the operations there, and found them exactly as the G-2 officer had said they would be. Reconnaissance certainly had been damned good.

Signals flashed in code from a control tower told of the approach of identified Japanese ships. For them, the net was opened, and then quickly closed again. Prying submarines were not wanted in Tokyo Bay; and now that the undersea craft were slipping along the very coast, with Japanese convoys forced to seek the shelter of the rugged shores of Japan itself, the net had assumed greater and greater importance. Should it be destroyed by a bombing attack, all bay shipping would be alerted, and all defenses readied. But....

There were shore patrols, when convoys moved. Davies had been told about that. When there were American planes overhead, the patrols rushed out in force. Koropok kept away from the shore at such times.

As days passed, Davies wondered if the carefully-conceived plan of G-2 had been abandoned. And yet the G-2 officer had said that sooner or later it was going to be carried out, and that he himself had been warned not to become impatient. Koropok, already years in Japan, needed no such warning. He waited, and he learned; and more and more often Tokyo was bombed, and Yokohama, and that was wonderful. It was worth waiting for.

On the afternoon that the two village policemen began running around informing everyone that on this night no one would be permitted to walk on the streets, Davies wondered whether the time had come. Obviously, a huge convoy was going to pass the net gate. Coming in? Going out? Either way, it would be destroyer-guarded, and well protected from American subs. Obviously also, what G-2 had planned was the sort of thing which would work only once, and so must be worth while; and, even then, there had to be complete coordination and luck.

When the police officer saw Koropok in his usual place, huddled over a pair of worn-out *geta* as he crouched against the side of an abandoned hut in the center of the village, the Japanese did not so much as stop to give any orders to the fool of a pariah. What use was it?

Davies worked away on the clogs. Afternoon became evening. Was this the night? No lights burned in the village; but that was as always. Someone sang a long-winded fisher-song:

> "*Ichiban bune e tsumi-kondi,*
> *Kawaguchi oshikomu o-yagodoo....*"

Then the *oooooo* grew and grew and became a low engine roar and, clearly, Davies heard the *tat-tat-tat* of a fighter plane's guns. While it might be some Nip plane being tested over the marshes beyond the village, it could also be the first signal....

It was. From a second plane, high up, a starry spatter of light appeared, and, as Davies counted to ten, a second. That was the second signal.

I wonder what the Nips make of it? thought Lew, quietly putting down the *geta* and standing up. *I'll bet they're getting ready for another raid.*

He had no difficulty in leaving the village at all. When he came to the marsh, he ran. He fell headlong once; ran all the faster once he regained his feet. When he reached the shore, he waded into the ooze, looked swiftly from side to side, saw no sign of the shore patrol yet, and then began to swim toward the anchored net vessels. The current was strong even before he neared the channel. The G-2 fellow was right again; a man, to do this, had to be a good swimmer.

A light flashed directions to the net-gate ships; acknowledgment blinked back. Then darkness settled down....

Davies swam to the last buoy supporting the immovable portion of the net, between near ship and shore, and, clinging to it, took a deep, lung-filling breath. Then, looking toward Tokyo and Yokohama, he waited again. He was ready to go completely under water in case searchlights swept along the water, the net supported by his buoy....

Minutes past before faintly, and very high, Davies thought he heard the sound of engines, with the peculiar high, whistling note which marked American fighters; but he wasn't sure. Perhaps it was only the water lapping against the buoys and the ship. But it could have been aircraft.

What he heard next was the net-gate being opened. Almost before it was wide, a destroyer boiled through it, with its wash banging Davies against the buoy. A second sliced through the opened net. Davies hadn't marked their approach, having been looking up the bay, and not oceanward; and the vessels were entering, not leaving. The G-2 man's word to Lew had said nothing of the direction from which ships might come, or why.

Davies saw now the bulk of great ships. Troop-carriers. Transports. Luxury liners of peacetime days. In line they came, beam-directed in the black night, behind the destroyers. They were flanked by more destroyers and by a horde of escort craft, each on edge to drop depth bombs, and forming a perfect screen against any undersea attack. As Davies saw the number of the transports, as well as their size, it came to him that Japan was at last moving troops to the mainland. It came to him that Japan was now preparing for an attack directly on Japan!

G-2, Davies saw, had certainly spotted Japanese procedure during convoying. As soon as the escort craft passed through the net-gate, each dashed away from the big ships, darting toward the docks. The transports were believed safe—and the escort craft needed to refuel hastily in order to return to patrol duty along the American-infested coastline, where there was danger to Japanese shipping....

The boys on our side who're in this, Davies thought, *have guts.* Wash from the enormous transports swept over him. *Damned if I'd try it,* Lew told himself. *Compared to what they're going to try, my job's a cinch. All I've got to do is give 'em a few minutes—and there never was a Jap yet who could do anything when taken by surprise. He's got to be set.*

T H E L A S T of the troopships ploughed through the net-gate. The control blinker began to wink its yellow eye again as the escort craft behind the transports hurried through the gate. Davies slowly relaxed his grip on the buoy, took a quick look at the near gate-vessel, and began to swim under water. He rose once, and twice; then he reached the dozen hawsers at the gate-ship's stern, and waited.

Can the boys see me? he wondered. *Are they watching?* It was too dark to see anything as small as a man's head, and Davies knew it. He knew, also, that listening devices would tell when the winches clanked and the net was being drawn together—and when, and if, the action ceased....

The last escort craft passed through the gate. The convoy was safe in the great bay, with its thousands and thousands of combat units. Someone on the gate-vessel above Davis shouted, "*Banzai!*" and then Lew began to pull himself up on the hawser. Slowly. Carefully. Reconnaissance had to be right about everything, or this was the finish of Llewelyn Davies. The absolute finish.

Aerial recon was right. A Japanese sailor, a winchman, stood beside the winch as it began to draw the net shut. A Japanese sailor. One sailor.

Davies' hands closed around the Japanese' throat with such force that there was a little crackling sound, as if bones broke.

*Lew didn't wait for
the Japanese. Axe
swining, he met them.*

The clank of the winch covered the tiny noise. Instantly, Davies
held the Jap's body as in a vise, keeping the dying sailor between
him and the wheelhouse....

Clank... clank... clank....

Davies, reaching down, did exactly as the G-2 officer had
said he should do. The winch clanked away, but no longer was

it drawing in the cable to close the net. The cable slipped constantly instead.

Clank... clank....

It was nice of the Japanese to copy American machinery, Davies was thinking. It made things easier. It made this possible.

Were American subs passing through? The black water, still moving from the wash of the ships ahead, and slapping against the side of the gate-vessel, told Lew nothing. But no orders were being yelled from the wheelhouse, proof that Japanese listening devices must be useless with so many screws turning in the bay. A minute or two was all the sub boys had asked for. Just a few scant minutes!

The blinker on the far gate-ship began to blink. Here was danger; Davies knew it. The man stationed at the winch there, which was allowing the cable to rim out—or where it should be running out—must have reported to his officer that this was not happening. In moments, someone on the ship where Davies was concealed behind the dead sailor would come running to see what was wrong.

But certainly two or three minutes had already passed. Had the subs gone through the net-opening? And if they had, how would they get out?

G-2 said they'd get away in the excitement. That was good enough understanding of the Japanese. G-2 said also that if they didn't get away, a good bag would make it a worthwhile sacrifice. G-2 said—

There was a great flash in the harbor. A sudden roar. In the blinding light, a transport, loaded with troops, seemed to be blown into the sky; and almost before Davies' eyes could tell him how the ship had exploded, there was a second wild brilliance, brighter than the first, as torpedoes struck home, as more torpedoes streaked to their target.

Tokyo Bay was illuminated as it had never been before; and as if the white fire rocketing toward the black heaven were a signal, bombers began to roar in from the sea. Coordination! The bombers were high, fighter-preceded; some separated themselves from the huge ones and began to scream down.

Dive-bombers, guessed Davies. *The sort of ship I've never seen.*

And they were after the net-vessels, so that the subs, *Pike, Sturgeon, Shark,* would have a chance to escape. The deadly

avenging fish, with deadlier fish inside their slim steel hulls. The avengers.

"Get away as soon as you can," had been the G-2 officer's advice. "That is, if you can."

Bombs missed. Bullets sprayed the wheel-house.

Hell, thought Lew, as those Japanese not hit scrambled out, *I'll give you a few seconds more, gang.* He dropped the dead sailor and grabbed up the fire axe fastened to the cabin. He didn't wait for the Japanese. Axe swinging, he met them.

What the Japanese saw nobody could know. Certainly not a docile, beaten-down pariah. A bearded American, perhaps. Perhaps one of those deadly Americans who didn't shave throughout a voyage. Or perhaps something demoniacal. A devil out of the ocean. A devil whose body became a ruddy color in the light as it charged from white to the hue of flame, and at whose instigation the sea and the ship rocked with explosions in the bay.

One of the Japanese turned and ran. Another leaped ahead, shrieking. "*Banzai!*" but only half the word was uttered, because Davies' axe took him across the mouth. A third, the ship's junior officer, stood like an ox awaiting slaughter—and the Ainu were the slaughterers-of-animals....

Davies took one final look at the magnificent sight he was seeing. Sheets of fierce fire. Black smoke billowing up and up and up. He couldn't see the thousands of heads bobbing in the water, any more than he could see the thousands trapped on the ships. All he could see was flame, and smoke; and it came to him then that the fire had actually started in central Japan, when he himself had ignited Colonel Sakirumu's quarters. That was where it had started.

One final look. Then Davies, although he knew he ought to slip into the water, in case anyone from the other gate-vessel might be looking, dove in squarely. He was laughing as he swam, because he was already wondering just how Radio Tokyo was going to tell the world how Japan had won the first battle of Tokyo Bay.

ABOUT THE AUTHOR

M Y P E O P L E came across the plains just behind the ill-fated Donner party, which makes me a Native Son, although I've never practiced the profession. Born in San Francisco, in 1893. As a youngster the family business was in the Orient; two years there, a year in the States. The Philippines in the days when garters were worn without stockings, and shoes carried in the hand by the natives; when the pariahs in Japan did not show their faces along respectable streets; when the Chinese believed foreigners originated from the hairs of curly white dogs.

University of Wisconsin, ex-1914; ex-salesman, ex-advertising manager, ex-reporter. For the first, saw no reason for waiting a few months merely to get a degree; the second, promised everything the sales-manager told me was true about his wares; the third, didn't and don't play golf; the fourth, quit after seeing 42 executions and refused to cover any more.

In fact, I seem to be ex-everything except husband; have the same wife I started out with thirteen years ago, plus two potential Badger halfbacks.

Started writing in 1923; and consequently have to my credit many short stories and five novels. Once won a tennis cup. Voted for LaFollette for President. Have seen Clara Bow at close range and wasn't even singed. Like trout fishing immensely, especially in the high Sierras.

For the rest, we live on the top of a hill in a small sleepy

California town just north of
San Francisco; there are iris and
columbine and poppies and
mission-bells not a hundred feet
from the house. And the birds
come within a yard of the house
to get bread in the rainy season
(I'm Native Son enough not to
say Winter) and right how we're
trying to get a gray squirrel to
eat almonds out of our hands;
he'll come a foot away, but that's
his limit.

*Sidney Herschel
Small*

That's about all, except that I
insist it was the fire and not the
earthquake that did the damage; maybe I'm a worse and more
rabid Native Son than I thought I was.

www.ingramcontent.com/pod-product-compliance
Lightning Source LLC
Chambersburg PA
CBHW051638050726
47502CB00011B/1175